Desert
Death-Song

Desert
Death-Song

A Collection of Western Stories

By

Louis L'Amour

Skyhorse Publishing

Skyhorse Publishing books may be purchased in bulk at special discounts for sales promotion, corporate gifts, fund-raising, or educational purposes. Special editions can also be created to specifications. For details, contact the Special Sales Department, Skyhorse Publishing, 307 West 36th Street, 11th Floor, New York, NY 10018 or info@skyhorsepublishing.com.

Skyhorse® and Skyhorse Publishing® are registered trademarks of Skyhorse Publishing, Inc.®, a Delaware corporation.

www.skyhorsepublishing.com

10 9 8

Library of Congress Cataloging-in-Publication Data is available on file.
ISBN: 978-1-62636-010-5

Printed in the United States of America

TABLE OF CONTENTS

KEEP TRAVELIN', RIDER

CHAPTER ONE: Guns of Change

When Tack Gentry sighted the weather beaten buildings of the G Bar, he touched spurs to the buckskin and the horse broke into a fast canter that carried the cowhand down the trail and around into the ranch yard. He swung down.

"Hey!" he yelled happily, grinning. "Is that all the welcome I get?"

The door pushed open and a man stepped out on the worn porch. The man had a stubble of a beard and a drooping mustache. His blue eyes were small and narrow.

"Who are yuh?" he demanded. "And what do yuh want?"

"I'm Tack Gentry!" Tack said. "Where's Uncle John?"

"I don't know yuh," the man said, "and I never heard of no Uncle John. I reckon yuh got onto the wrong spread, youngster."

"Wrong spread?" Tack laughed. "Quit your funnin'! I helped build that house there, and built the corrals by my lonesome, while Uncle John was sick. Where is everybody?"

1

The man looked at him carefully, then lifted his eyes to a point beyond Tack. A voice spoke from behind the cowhand. "Reckon yuh been gone awhile, ain't yuh?"

Gentry turned. The man behind him was short, stocky and blond. He had a wide, flat face, a small broken nose and cruel eyes.

"Gone? I reckon yes! I've been gone most of a year! Went north with a trail herd to Ellsworth, then took me a job as a segundo on a herd movin' to Wyoming."

Tack stared around, his eyes alert and curious. There was something wrong here, something very wrong. The neatness that had been typical of Uncle John Gentry was gone. The place looked run down, the porch was untidy, the door hung loose on its hinges, even the horses in the corral were different.

"Where's Uncle John?" Tack demanded again. "Quit stallin'!"

The blond man smiled, his lips parting over broken teeth and a hard, cynical light coming into his eyes. "If yuh mean John Gentry, who used to live on this place, he's gone. He drawed on the wrong man and got himself killed."

"What?" Tack's stomach felt like he had been kicked. He stood there, staring. "He drew on somebody? Uncle John?"

Tack shook his head. "That's impossible! John Gentry was a Quaker. He never lifted a hand in violence against anybody or anything in his life! He never even wore a gun, never owned one!"

"I only know what they tell me," the blond man said, "but we got work to do, and I reckon yuh better slope out of here. And," he added grimly, "if yuh're smart yuh'll keep right on goin', clean out of this country!"

"What do yuh mean?" Tack's thoughts were in a turmoil trying to accustom himself to this change, wondering what could have happened, what was behind it.

"I mean yuh'll find things considerably changed around here. If yuh decide not to leave," he added, "yuh might ride into Sunbonnet and look up Van Hardin or Dick Olney and tell him I said to give yuh all yuh had comin', tell 'em Soderman sent yuh."

"Who's Van Hardin?" Tack asked. The name was unfamiliar.

"Yuh been away all right!" Soderman acknowledged. "Or yuh'd know who Van Hardin is. He runs this country. He's the ramrod, Hardin is. Olney's sheriff."

Tack Gentry rode away from his home ranch with his thoughts in confusion. Uncle John! Killed in a gunfight! Why, that was out of reason! The old man wouldn't fight. He never had, and never would. And this Dick Olney was sheriff! What had beome of Pete Liscomb? No election was due for another year, and Pete had been a good sheriff.

There was only one way to solve the problem and get the whole story, and that was to circle around and ride by the London ranch. Bill could give him the whole story, and besides, he wanted to see Betty. It had been a long time.

The six miles to the headquarters of the London ranch went by swiftly, yet as Tack rode, he scanned the grassy levels along the Maravillas. There were cattle enough, more than he had ever seen on the old G Bar, and all of them wearing the G Bar brand.

He reined in sharply. What the? . . . Why, if Uncle John was dead, the ranch belonged to him! But if that was so, who was Soderman? And what were they doing on his ranch?

Three men were loafing on the wide veranda of the London ranch house when Tack rode up. All their faces were unfamiliar. He glanced warily from one to the other.

"Where's Bill London?" he asked.

"London?" The man in the wide brown hat shrugged. "Reckon he's to home, over in Sunbonnet Pass. He ain't never over here."

"This is his ranch, isn't it?" Tack demanded.

All three men seemed to tense. "His ranch?" The man in the brown hat shook his head. "Reckon yuh're a stranger around here. This ranch belongs to Van Hardin. London ain't got a

ranch. Nothin' but a few acres back against the creek over to Sunbonnet Pass. He and that girl of his live there. I reckon though,"
he grinned suddenly, "she won't be there much longer. Hear tell
she's goin' to work in the Longhorn Dance Hall."

"Betty London? In the Longhorn?" Tack exclaimed. "Don't
make me laugh, partner! Betty's too nice a girl for that! She
wouldn't . . ."

"They got it advertised," the brown hatted man said calmly.

An hour later a very thoughtful Tack Gentry rode up the
dusty street of Sunbonnet. In that hour of riding he had been
doing a lot of thinking, and he was remembering what Soderman
had said. He was to tell Hardin or Olney that Soderman had sent
him to get all that was coming to him. Suddenly, that remark
took on a new significance.

Tack swung down in front of the Longhorn. Emblazoned on
the front of the saloon was a hugh poster announcing that Betty
London was the coming attraction, that she would sing and
entertain at the Longhorn. Compressing his lips, Tack walked
into the saloon.

Nothing was familiar except the bar and the tables. The man
behind the bar was squat and fat, his eyes peered at Tack from
folds of flesh. "What's it for yuh?" he demanded.

"Rye," Tack said. He let his eyes swing slowly around the
room. Not a familiar face greeted him. Shorty Davis was gone.
Nick Farmer was not around. These men were strangers, a tight
mouthed, hard eyed crew.

Gentry glanced at the bartender. "Any ridin' jobs around
here? Driftin' through, and thought I might like to tie in with
one of the outfits around here."

"Keep driftin'," the bartender said, not glancing at him. "Everybody's got a full crew."

One door swung open and a tall, clean cut man walked into
the room, glancing around. He wore a neat gray suit and a dark hat.
Tack saw the bartender's eyes harden, and glanced thoughtfully at

the newcomer. The man's face was very thin, and when he removed his hat his ash blond hair was neatly combed.

He glanced around, and his eyes lighted on Tack. "Stranger?" he asked pleasantly. "Then may I buy you a drink? I don't like to drink alone, but haven't sunk so low as to drink with these coyotes."

Tack stiffened, expecting a reaction from some of the seated men, but there was none. Puzzled, he glanced at the blond man, and seeing the cynical good humor in the man's eyes, nodded.

"Sure, I'll drink with you."

"My name," the tall man added, "is Anson Childe, by profession, a lawyer, by dint of circumstances, a gambler, and by choice, a student.

"You perhaps wonder," he added, "why these men do not resent my reference to them as coyotes. There are three reasons, I expect. The first is that some subconscious sense of truth makes them appreciate the justice of the term. Second, they know I am gifted with considerable dexterity in expounding the gospel of Judge Colt. Third, they know that I am dying of tuberculosis and as a result have no fear of bullets.

"It is not exactly fear that keeps them from drawing on me. Let us say it is a matter of mathematics, and a problem none of them has succeeded in solving with any degree of comfort in the result. It is: how many of them would die before I did?

"You can appreciate, my friend, the quandary in which this places them, and also the disagreeable realization that bullets are no respecters of persons, nor am I. The several out there who might draw know that I know who they are. The result is that they know they would be first to die."

Childe looked at Tack thoughtfully. "I heard you ask about a riding job as I came in. You look like an honest man, and there is no place here for such."

Gentry hunted for the right words, then he said, "This country looks like it was settled by honest men."

Anson Childe studied his glass. "Yes," he said, "but at the right moment they lacked a leader. One was too opposed to violence, another was too law abiding, and the rest lacked resolution."

If there was a friend in the community, this man was it. Tack finished his drink and strode to the door. The bartender met his eyes as he glanced back.

"Keep on driftin'," the bartender said.

Tack Gentry smiled. "I like it here," he said, "and I'm stayin'!"

He swung to the saddle and turned his buckskin toward Sunbonnet Pass. He still had no idea exactly what had happened during the year of his absence, yet Childe's remark coupled with what the others had said told him a little. Apparently, some strong, resolute men had moved in and taken over, and there had been no concerted fight against them, no organization and no leadership.

Childe had said that one was opposed to violence. That would have been his Uncle John. The one who was too law abiding would be Bill London. London had always been strong for law and order, and settling things in a legal way. The others had been honest men, but small ranchers, and individually unable to oppose whatever was done to them. Yet whatever had happened, the incoming elements had apparently moved with speed and finesse.

Had it been one ranch, it would have been different. But the ranches and the town seemed completely subjugated.

The buckskin took the trail at an easy canter, skirting the long red cliff of Horse Thief Mesa and wading the creek at Gunsight. Sunbonnet Pass opened before him like a gate in the mountains. To the left, in a grove of trees, was a small adobe house and a corral.

Two horses were standing at the corral as he rode up. His eyes narrowed as he saw them. Button and Blackie! Two of his uncle's favorites and two horses he had raised from colts. He swung down and started toward them, when he saw the three people on the steps.

He turned to face them, and his heart jumped. Betty London had not changed.

Her eyes widened, and her face went dead white. "Tack!" she gasped. "Tack Gentry!"

Even as she spoke, Tack saw the sudden shock with which the two men turned to stare. "That's right, Betty," he said quietly, "I just got home."

"But—but—we heard you were dead!"

"I'm not." His eyes shifted to the two men. A thick shouldered, deep chested man with a square, swarthy face, and the lean rawboned man wearing a star. The one with the star would be Dick Olney. The other must be Van Hardin.

Tack's eyes swung to Olney. "I heard my Uncle John Gentry was killed. Did yuh investigate his death?"

Olney's eyes were careful. "Yeah," he said, "he was killed in a fair fight. Gun in his hand."

"My uncle," Tack replied, "was a Quaker. He never lifted a hand in violence in his life!"

"He was a might slow, I reckon," Olney said coolly, "but he had the gun in his hand when I found him."

"Who shot him?"

"Hombre name of Soderman. But like I say, it was a fair fight."

"Like blazes!" Tack flashed. "Yuh'll never make me believe Uncle John wore a gun! That gun was planted on him!"

"Yuh're jumpin' to conclusions," Van Hardin said smoothly. "I saw the gun myself. There were a dozen witnesses."

"Who saw the fight?" Gentry demanded.

"They saw the gun in his hand. In his right hand," Hardin said.

Tack laughed suddenly, harshly. "That does it! Uncle John's right hand has been useless ever since Shiloh when it was shot to pieces tryin' to get to a wounded soldier. He couldn't hold a feather in those fingers, let alone a gun!"

Hardin's face tightened, and Dick Olney's eyes shifted to Hardin's face.

"You'd be better off," Hardin said quietly, "to let sleepin' dogs lie. We ain't goin' to have yuh comin' in here stirrin' up a peaceful community."

"My Uncle John was murdered," Gentry said quietly, "I mean to see his murderer punished. That ranch belongs to me. I intend to get it back!"

Van Hardin smiled. "Evidently, yuh aren't aware of what happened here," he said quietly. "Your Uncle John was in a non-combatant outfit durin' the War, was he not? Well, while he was gone, the ranch he had claimed was abandoned. Soderman and I started to run cattle on that range and the land that was claimed by Bill London. No claim to the range was asserted by anyone. We made improvements, then durin' our temporary absence with a trail herd, John Gentry and Bill London returned and moved in. Naturally, when we returned the case was taken to court. The court ruled the ranches belonged to Soderman and myself."

"And the cattle?" Tack asked. "What of the cattle my uncle owned?"

Hardin shrugged. "The brand had been taken over by the new owners and registered in their name. As I understand it, yuh left on a trail herd immediately after yuh came back to Texas. My claim was originally asserted during yore Uncle's absence. I could," he smiled, "lay claim to the money yuh got from that trail herd. Where is it?"

"Suppose yuh find out?" Tex replied. "I'm goin' to tell yuh one thing: I'm goin' to find who murdered my uncle, if it was Soderman or not. I'm also goin' to fight yuh in court. Now, if yuh'll excuse me," he turned his eyes to Betty who had stood wide-eyed and silent, "I'd like to talk to Bill London."

"He can't see yuh," Hardin said. "He's asleep."

Gentry's eyes hardened. "You runnin' this place too?"

"Betty London is going to work for me," Hardin replied. "We may be married later, so in a sense, I'm speaking for her."

"Is that right?" Tack demanded, his eyes meeting Betty's.

Her face was miserable. "I'm afraid it is, Tack."

"You've forgotten your promise then?" he demanded.

"Things—things changed, Tack," she faltered. "I—I can't talk about it."

"I reckon, Gentry," Olney interrupted, "it's time yuh rode on. There's nothin' in this neck of the woods for yuh. Yuh've played out yore hand here. Ride on, and you'll save yourself a lot of trouble. They're hirin' hands over on the Pecos."

"I'm stayin'," Gentry said flatly.

"Remember," Olney warned, "I'm the sheriff. At the first sign of trouble, I'll come lookin' for yuh."

CHAPTER TWO: The Fight Begins

Gentry swung into the saddle, his eyes shifted to Betty's face and for an instant, she seemed about to speak, then he turned and rode away. He did not look back. It was not until after he was gone that he remembered Button and Blackie.

To think they were in the possession of Hardin and Olney! The twin blacks he had reared and worked with, training them to do tricks, teaching them all the lore of the cow-country horses and much more.

The picture was clear now. In the year in which he had been gone these men had come in, asserted their claims, taken them to carpetbag courts, and made them stick. Backing their legal claims with guns, they had taken over the country with speed and finesse. At every turn, he was blocked. Betty had turned against him. Bill London was either a prisoner in his own house, or something was wrong. Olney was sheriff, and probably they had their own judge.

He could quit. He could pull out and go on to the Pecos. It would be the easiest way. It was even what Uncle John might have wished him to do, for John Gentry was a peace loving man. Tack Gentry was of another breed. His father had been killed fighting Comanches, and Tack had gone to war when a mere boy. Uncle John had found a place for himself in a non-combatant outfit, but Tack had fought long and well.

His ride north with the trail herd had been rought and bloody. Twice they had fought off Indians, once they had mixed it with rustlers. In Ellsworth, a gunman named Paris had made trouble that ended with Paris dead on the floor.

Tack had left town in a hurry, ridden to the new camp at Dodge, and then joined a trail herd headed for Wyoming. Indian fighting had been the order of the day, and once, rounding up a bunch of steers lost from the herd in a stampede, Tack had run into three rustlers after the same steers.

Tack downed two of them in the subsequent battle, and then shot it out with the other in a day-long rifle battle that covered a cedar and boulder strewn hillside. Finally, just before sundown, they met in hand-to-hand combat with bowie knives.

Tack remained long enough to see his old friend Major Powell with whom he had participated in the Wagon Box Fight, and then had wandered back to Kansas. On the Platte he joined a bunch of buffalo hunters, stayed with them a couple of months, and then trailed back to Dodge.

Sunbonnet's Longhorn Saloon was ablaze with lights when he drifted into town that night. He stopped at the livery stable and put up his horse. He had taken a roundabout route, scouting the country, so he decided that Hardin and Olney were probably already in town. By now they would know of his call at the ranch, and his meeting with Anson Childe.

He was laboring under no delusions about his future. Van Hardin would not hesitate to see him put out of the way if he attempted to regain his property. Hardin had brains, and Olney was no fool. There were things Gentry must know before anything could be done, and the one man in town who could and would know was Childe.

Leaving the livery stable he started up the street. Turning, he glanced back to see the livery man standing in the stable door. He dropped his hand quickly, but Gentry believed he had signaled someone across the street. Yet there was no one in sight, and the row of buildings seemed blank and empty.

Only three buildings were lighted. The Longhorn, a smaller, cheaper saloon, and the old general store. There was a light upstairs over the small saloon, and several lights in the annex to the Longhorn which passed as a hotel, the only one in Sunbonnet.

Tack walked along the street, his boot heels sounding loud in the still night air. Ahead of him was a space between the buildings, and when he drew abreast of it he did a quick sidestep off the street, flattening against the building.

He heard footsteps, hesitation, and then lightly running steps and suddenly a man dove around the corner, grated to a stop on the gravel, staring down the alleyway between the buildings. He did not see Tack, who was flattened in the dense shadow against the building and behind a rain barrel.

The man started forward suddenly, and Tack reached out and grabbed his ankle. Caught in midstride, the fellow plunged over on his head, then lay still. For an instant, Gentry hesitated, then struck and shielded a match with his left hand. It was the brown hatted man he had talked to on the porch of London's ranch. His head had hit a stone, and he was out cold.

Swiftly, Tack shucked the fellow's gun and emptied the shells from it, then pushed it back in his holster. A folded paper had fallen from the unconscious man's pocket, and Tack picked it up. Then moving fast, he went down the alley until he was in back of the small saloon. By the light from a back window, he read the note.

"This," he muttered, "may help!"

> Come to town quick. Trouble's brewing. We can't have anything happen now. V. H.

Van Hardin. They didn't want trouble now. Why, now? Folding the note, he slipped it into his pocket and flattened against the side of the saloon, studied the interior. Only two men sat in the dim interior. Two men who played cards at a small table. The bartender leaned on the bar and read a newspaper. When the man turned his head, Tack recognized him.

"Red" Furness had worked for his father. He had soldiered with him. He might still be friendly. Tack lifted his knuckles and tapped lightly on the window.

At the second tap, Red looked up. Tack lighted a match and moved it past the window. Neither of the card players seemed to have noticed. Red straightened, folded his paper, then picking up a cup walked back toward the window. When he got there, he dipped the cup into the water bucket with one hand, and with the other, lifted the window a few inches.

"This is Tack Gentry. Where does Childe hang out?"

Red's whisper was low. "Got him an office and sleepin' room upstairs. There's a back stairway. Yuh watch yoreself."

Tack stepped away from his window and made his way to the stairway he had already glimpsed. It might be a trap, but he believed Red was loyal. Also, he was not sure the word was out to kill him. They probably merely wanted him out of the way, and hoped he could be warned to move on. The position of the Hardin group seemed secure enough.

Reaching the top of the stairs he walked along the narrow catwalk to the door. He tapped softly. After an instant, there was a voice. "What do you want?"

"This is Tack Gentry. Yuh talked to me in the saloon!" The door opened to darkness, and he stepped in. When it closed, he felt a pistol barrel against his spine.

"Hold still!" Childe warned.

Behind him a match struck, then a candle was lighted. The light still glowed in the other room, seen only by the crack under the door. Childe grinned at him. "Got to be careful," he said. "They have tried twice to drygulch me!

"I put flowers on their graves every Monday!" he smiled. "And keep an extra one dug. Ever since I had that new grave dug,

I've been left alone. Somehow it seems to have a very sobering influence on the local roughs."

He sat down. "I tire quicker than I once did. So you're Gentry! Betty London told me about you. She thought you were dead. There was a rumor that you'd been killed by the Indians in Wyoming."

"No, I came out all right. What I want to know, rememberin' yuh said yuh were a lawyer, is what kind of a claim they have on my ranch?"

"A good one, unfortunately. While you and your uncle were gone, and most of the other men in the locality, several of these men came in and began to brand cattle. After branding a good many, they left. They returned and began working around, about the time you left, and then they ordered your uncle off.

"He wouldn't go, and they took the case to court. There were no lawyers then, and your uncle tried to handle it himself. The judge was their man, and suddenly half a dozen witnesses appeared and were sworn in. They testified that the land had been taken and held by Soderman, Olney and Hardin.

"They claimed their brands on the cattle asserted their claim to the land, to the home ranches of both London and Gentry. The free range was something else, but with the two big ranches in their hands, and the bulk of the free range lying beyond their holdings, they were in a position to freeze out the smaller ranchers. They established a squatter's right to each of the big ranches."

"Can they do that?" Tack demanded. "It doesn't seem fair!"

"The usual thing is to allow no claim unless they have occupied the land for twenty years without hindrance, but with a carpetbag court, they go about as they please. Judge Weaver is completely in Van Hardin's hands, and your Uncle John was on the losing side of this war."

"How did Uncle John get killed?" Tack asked.

Childe shrugged. "They said he called Soderman a liar and Soderman went for his gun. Your uncle had a gun on him when

14

they found him. It was probably a cold-blooded killing because Gentry planned on a trip to Austin and was going to appeal the case."

"Have yuh seen Bill London lately?"

"Only once since the accident."

"Accident?"

"Yes, London was headed for home, dozing along in the buckboard as he always did, when his team ran away with him. The buckboard overturned and London's back was injured. He can't ride any more, and can't sit up very long at a time."

"Was it really an accident?" Tack wanted to know.

Childe shrugged. "I doubt it. We couldn't prove a thing. One of the horses had a bad cut on the hip. It looked as if someone with a steel tipped bull whip had hit the animal from beside the road."

"Thorough," Tack said. "They don't miss a bet."

Childe nodded. Leaning back in his chair he put his feet on the desk. He studied Tack Gentry thoughtfully. "You know, you'll be next. They won't stand for you messing around. I think you already have them worried."

Tack explained about the man following him, then handed the note to Childe. The lawyer's eyes narrowed. "Hmm, sounds like they had some reason to soft pedal the whole thing for awhile. Maybe it's an idea for us. Maybe somebody is coming down here to look around, or maybe somebody has grown suspicious."

Tack looked at Childe thoughtfully. "What's your position in all this?"

The tall man shrugged, then laughed lightly. "I've no stake at all, Gentry. I didn't know London or your Uncle John, either. But I heard rumors, and I didn't like the attitude of the local bosses, Hardin and Olney. I'm just a burr under the saddle with which they ride this community, no more. It amuses me to needle them, and they are afraid of me."

"Got any clients?"

"Clients?" Anson Childe chuckled. "Not a one! Not likely to have any, either! In a country so throttled by one man as this is, there isn't any litigation. Nobody can win against him, and they are too busy hating Hardin to want to have trouble with each other."

"Well, then," Tack said, "yuh've got a client now. Go down to Austin, demand an investigation. Lay the facts on the table for them. Maybe yuh can't do any good, but at least yuh can stir up a lot of trouble. The main thing will be to get people talking. They evidently want quiet, so we'll give them noise.

"Find out all you can. Get some detectives started on Hardin's trail. Find out who they are, who they were, and where they came from."

Childe sat up. "I'd like it," he said ruefully, "but I don't have that kind of money." He gestured at the room. "I'm behind on my rent here. Red owns the building, so he lets me stay."

Tack grinned and unbuttoned his shirt, drawing out a money belt. "I sold some cattle up north." He counted out one thousand dollars. "Take that. Spend all or any part of it, but create a smell down there. Tell everybody about the situation here."

Childe got up, his face flushed with enthusiasm. "Man! Nothing could please me more! I'll make it hot for them! I'll—" He went into a fit of coughing, and Tack watched him gravely.

Finally Childe straightened. "You're putting your trust in a sick man, Gentry!"

"I'm putting my trust in a fighter," Tack said drily. "Yuh'll do!" He hesitated briefly. "Also, check the title on this land."

They shook hands silently, and Tack went to the door. Softly, he opened it and stepped out into the cool night. Well, for better or worse the battle was opened. Now for the next step. He came down off the wooden stair, then walked to the street. There was no one in sight. Tack Gentry crossed the street and pushed through the swinging doors of the Longhorn.

The saloon and dance hall was crowded. A few were familiar faces, but they were sullen faces, lined and hard. The faces of bitter

16

men, defeated, but not whipped. The others were new faces, the hard, tough faces of gun hands, the weather beaten punchers who had come in to take the new jobs. He pushed his way to the bar.

There were three bartenders now, and it wasn't until he ordered that the squat, fat man glanced down the bar and saw him. His jaw hardened and he spoke to the bartender who was getting a bottle to pour Gentry's rye.

The bartender, a lean, sallow faced man, strolled back to him. "We're not servin' you," he said, "I got my orders!"

Tack reached across the bar, his hand shooting out so fast the bartender had no chance to withdraw. Catching the man by his stiff collar, two fingers inside the collar and their knuckles jammed hard into the man's Adam's apple, he jerked him to the bar.

"Pour!" he said.

The man tried to speak, but Tack gripped harder and shoved back on the knuckles. Weakly, desperately, his face turning blue, the man poured. He slopped out twice what he got in the glass, but he poured. Then Tack shoved hard and the man brought up violently against the backbar.

Tack lifted his glass with his left hand, his eyes sweeping the crowd, all of whom had drawn back slightly. "To honest ranchers!" he said loudly and clearly and downed his drink.

A big, hard-faced man shoved through the crowd. "Maybe yuh're meaning some of us ain't honest?" he suggested.

"That's right!" Tack Gentry let his voice ring out in the room, and he heard the rattle of chips cease, and the shuffling of feet died away. The crowd was listening. "That's exactly right! There were honest men here, but they were murdered or crippled. My Uncle John Gentry was murdered. They tried to make it look like a fair and square killin', they stuck a gun in his hand!"

"That's right!" A man broke in. "He had a gun! I seen it!"

Tack's eyes shifted. "What hand was it in?"

"His right hand!" the man stated positively, belligerently. "I seen it!"

"Thank you, pardner!" Tack said politely. "The gun was in John Gentry's right hand—and John Gentry's right hand had been paralyzed ever since Shiloh!"

"Huh!" The man who had seen the gun stepped back, his face whitening a little.

Somebody back in the crowd shouted out, "That's right! You're durn tootin' that's right! Never could use a rope, 'count of it!"

Tack looked around at the crowd and his eyes halted on the big man. He was going to break the power of Hardin, Olney and Soderman, and he was going to start right here.

"There's goin' to be an investigation," he said loudly, "and it'll begin down in Austin. Any of you fellers bought property from Hardin or Olney better get your money back."

"Yuh're talkin' a lot!" The big man thrust toward him, his wide, heavy shoulders looking broad enough for two men. "Yuh said some of us were thieves!"

"Thieves and murderers," Tack added. "If yuh're one of the worms that crawl in Hardin's tracks, that goes for you!"

The big man lunged. "Get him, Starr!" somebody shouted loudly.

CHAPTER THREE: Flood to Freedom

Jack Gentry suddenly felt a fierce surge of pure animal joy. He stepped back and then stepped in suddenly, and his right hand swung low and hard. It caught Starr as he was coming in, and caught him in the pit of the stomach. He grunted and stopped dead in his tracks, but Tack set himself and swung wickedly with both hands. His left smashed into Starr's mouth, his right split a cut over his cheekbone. Starr staggered and fell back into the crowd. He came out of the crowd, shook his head and charged like a bull.

Tack weaved inside of the swinging fists and impaled the bigger man on a straight, hard left hand, then he crossed a wicked right to the cut cheek and gore cascaded down the man's face. Tack stepped in, smashing both hands to the man's body, then as Starr jabbed a thumb at his eye, Tack jerked his head aside and butted Starr in the face.

His nose broken, his cheek laid open to the bone, Starr staggered back, and Tack Gentry walked in, swinging with both hands. This was the beginning. This man worked for Hardin and he was going to be an example. When he left this room Starr's face was going to be a sample of the crashing of Van Hardin's power. With left and right he cut and slashed at the big man's face, and Starr, overwhelmed by the attack, helpless after that first wicked body blow, crumpled under those smashing fists. He hit the floor suddenly and lay there, moaning softly.

19

A man shoved through the crowd, then stopped. It was Van Hardin. He looked down at the man on the floor, then his eyes dark with hate, lifted to meet Tack Gentry's eyes.

"Lookin' for trouble, are yuh?" he said.

"Only catchin' up with some that started while I was gone, Van!" Tack said. He felt good. He was on the balls of his feet and ready. He had liked the jarring of blows, liked the feeling of combat. He was ready. "Yuh should have made sure I was dead, Hardin, before yuh tried to steal property from a kindly old man!"

"Nothing was stolen," Van Hardin said evenly, calmly. "We took only what was ours, and in a strictly legal manner."

"There will be an investigation," Gentry replied bluntly, "from Austin. Then we'll thrash the whole thing out."

Hardin's eyes sharpened and he was suddenly wary. "An investigation? What makes you think so?"

Tack was aware that Hardin was worried. "Because I'm startin' it. I'm askin' for it, and I'll get it. There was a lot you didn't know about that land yuh stole, Hardin. Yuh were like most crooks. Yuh could only see yore side of the question and it looked very simple and easy, but there's always the thing yuh overlook, and you overlooked something"

The doors swung wide and Olney pushed into the room. He stopped, glancing from Hardin to Gentry. "What goes on here?" he demanded.

"Gentry is accusin' us of bein' thieves," Hardin said carelessly.

Olney turned and faced Tack. "He's in no position to accuse anybody of anything!" he said. "I'm arrestin' him for murder!"

There was a stir in the room, and Tack Gentry felt the sudden sickness of fear. "Murder? Are yuh crazy?" he demanded.

"I'm not, but you may be," the sheriff said. "I've just come from the office of Anson Childe. He's been murdered. Yuh were his last visitor. Yuh were observed sneaking into his place by the back stairs. I'm arresting yuh for murder."

The room was suddenly still, and Tack Gentry felt the rise of hostility toward him. Many men had admired the courage of Anson Childe, many men had been helped by him. Frightened themselves, they had enjoyed his flouting of Hardin and Olney. Now he was dead, murdered.

"Childe was my friend!" Tack protested. "He was goin' to Austin for me!"

Hardin laughed sarcastically. "Yuh mean he knew yuh had no case and refused to go, and in a fit of rage, yuh killed him. Yuh shot him."

"Yuh'll have to come with me," Olney said grimly. "Yuh'll get a fair trial."

Silently, Tack looked at him. Swiftly, thoughts raced through his mind. There was no chance for escape. The crowd was too thick, he had no idea if there was a horse out front, although there no doubt was, and his own horse was in the livery stable. Olney relieved him of his gun belt and they started toward the door. Starr, leaning against the door post, his face raw as chewed beef, glared at him evilly.

"I'll be seein' yuh!" he said softly. "Soon!"

Solderman and Hardin had fallen in around him, and behind them two of Hardin's roughs.

The jail was small, just four cells and an outer office. The door of one of the cells was opened and he was shoved inside. Hardin grinned at him. "This should settle the matter for Austin," he said. "Childe had friends down there!"

Anson Childe murdered! Tack Gentry, numbed by the blow, stared at the stone wall. He had counted on Childe, counted on his stirring up an investigation. Once started, he possessed two aces in the hole he could use to defeat Hardin in court, but it demanded a court uncontrolled by Hardin.

With Childe's death he had no friends on the outside. Betty had barely spoken to him when they met, and if she was going to work for Hardin in his dance hall, she must have changed much.

Bill London was a cripple and unable to get around. Red Furness, for all his friendship, wouldn't come out in the open. Tack had no illusions about the murder. By the time the case came to trial, they would have found ample evidence. They had his guns and they could fire two or three shots from them, whatever had been used on Childe. It would be a simple thing to frame him. Hardin would have no trouble in finding witnesses.

He was standing, staring out the small window, its lower sill just on the level of his eyes, when he heard a distant rumble of thunder and a jagged streak of lightning brightened the sky, then more thunder. The rains came slowly, softly, then in steadily increasing volume. The jail was still and empty. Sounds of music and occasional shouts sounded from the Longhorn, then the roar of rain drowned them out. He threw himself down on the cot in the corner of the room, and lulled by the falling rain, was soon asleep.

A long time later, he awakened. The rain was still falling, but above it was another sound. Listening, he suddenly realized what it was. The dry wash behind the town was running, probably bank full. Lying there in the darkness, he became aware of still another sound, of the nearer rushing of water. Lifting his head, he listened. Then he got to his feet and crossed the small cell.

Water was running under the corner of the jail. There had been a good deal of rain lately, and he had noted that the barrel at the corner of the jail had been full. It was overflowing and the water had evidently washed under the corner of the building.

He walked back and sat down on the bed, and as he listened to the water, an idea came to him suddenly. Tack got up and went to the corner of the cell, and striking a match, studied the wall and floor. Both were damp. He stamped on the stone flags of the door, but they were solid. He kicked the wall. It was also solid.

How thick were those walls? Judging by what he remembered of the door, the walls were all of eight inches thick, but how about the floor? Kneeling on the floor, he struck another match, studying the mortar around the corner flagstone.

Then he felt in his pockets. There was nothing there he could use to dig that mortar. His pocket knife, his bowie knife, his keys, all were gone. Suddenly, he had an inspiration. Slipping off his wide leather belt, he began to dig at the mortar with the edge of his heavy brass belt buckle.

The mortar was damp, but he worked steadily. His hands slipped on the sweaty buckle and he skinned his fingers and knuckles on the rough stone floor, yet he persevered, scraping, scratching, digging out tiny fragments of mortar. From time to time he straightened up and stamped on the stone. It was solid as Gibraltar.

Five hours he scraped and scratched, digging until his belt buckle was no longer of use. He had scraped out almost two inches of mortar. Sweeping up the scattered grains of mortar, and digging some of the mud off his boots, he filled in the cracks as best he could. Then he walked to his bunk and sprawled out and was instantly asleep.

Early in the morning, he heard someone stirring around outside. Then Olney walked back to his cell and looked in at him. Starr followed in a few minutes carrying a plate of food and a pot of coffee. His face was badly bruised and swollen, his eyes were hot with hate. He put the food down, then walked away. Olney loitered.

"Gentry," he said suddenly, "I hate to see a good hand in this spot."

Tack looked up. "I'll bet yuh do!" he said sarcastically.

"No use talkin' that attitude," Olney protested, "after all, yuh made trouble for us. Why couldn't yuh leave well enough alone? Yuh were in the clear, yuh had a few dollars apparently, and yuh could do all right. Hardin took possession of those ranches legally. He can hold 'em, too."

"We'll see."

"No, I mean it. He can. Why don't yuh drop the whole thing?"

"Drop it?" Tack laughed. "How can I drop it? I'm in jail for murder now, and yuh know as well as I do I never killed Anson Childe. This trial will smoke the whole story out of its hole. I mean to see that it does."

Olney winced, and Tack could see he had touched a tender spot. That was what they were afraid of. They had him now, but they didn't want him, they wanted nothing so much as to be completely rid of him.

"Only make trouble for folks," Olney protested, "yuh won't get nowhere. Yuh can bet that if yuh go to trial we'll have all the evidence we need."

"Sure. I know I'll be framed."

"What can yuh expect?" Olney shrugged. "Yuh're askin' for it. Why don't yuh play smart? If yuh'd leave the country we could sort of arrange maybe to turn yuh loose."

Tack looked up at him. "Yuh mean that?" Like blazes, he told himself. I can see yuh turnin' me loose! And when I walked out yuh'd have somebody there to smoke me down, shot escaping jail. Yeah, I know. "If I thought yuh'd let me go—" He hesitated, angling to get Olney's reaction.

The sheriff put his head close to the bars. "Yuh know me, Tack," he whispered, "I don't want to see you stick yore head in a noose! Sure, yuh spoke out of turn, and yuh tried to scare up trouble for us, but if yuh'd leave, I think I could arrange it."

"Just give me the chance," Tack assured him. "Once I get out of here I'll really start movin'!" And that's no lie, he added to himself.

Olney went away, and the morning dragged slowly. They would let him go. He was praying now they would wait until the next day. Yet, even if they did permit him to escape, even if they did not have him shot as he was leaving, what could he do? Childe, his best means of assistance, was dead. At every turn he was stopped. They had the law, and they had the guns.

His talk the night before would have implanted doubts. His whipping of Starr would have pleased many, and some of them would realize that his arrest for the murder of Childe was a frame. Yet none of these people would do anything about it without leadership. None of them wanted his neck in a noose.

Olney dropped in later, and leaned close to the bars. "I'll have something arranged by tomorrow," he said.

Tack lay back on the bunk and fell asleep. All day the rain had continued without interruption except for a few minutes at a time. The hills would be soggy now, the trails bad. He could hear the wash running strongly, running like a river not thirty yards behind the jail.

Darkness fell, he ate again, and then returned to his bunk. With a good lawyer and a fair judge he could beat them in court. He had an ace in the hole that would help, and another that might do the job.

He waited until the jail was silent and he could hear the usual sounds from the Longhorn. Then he got up and walked over to the corner. All day water had been running under the corner of the jail and must have excavated a fair sized hole by now. Tack knelt down and took from his pocket the fork he had secreted after his meal.

Olney, preoccupied with plans to allow Tack Gentry to escape, and sure that Tack was accepting the plan, had paid little attention to the returned plate.

On his knees, Tack dug out the loosely filled in dust and dirt, then began digging frantically at the hole. He worked steadily for an hour, then crossed to the bucket for a drink of water and to stretch, and then he returned to work.

Another hour passed. He got up and stamped on the stone. It seemed to sink under his feet. He bent his knees and jumped, coming down hard on his heels. The stone gave way so suddenly he almost went through. He caught himself, withdrew his feet from the hole, and bent over, striking a match. It was no more than six inches to the surface of the water, and even a glance told him it must be much deeper than he had believed.

He took another look, waited an instant, then lowered his feet into the water. The current jerked at them, and then he lowered his body through the hole and let go. Instantly, he was jerked away and literally thrown downstream. He caught a quick glimpse of a light from a window, and then he was whirling over and over. He grabbed frantically, hoping to get his hands on something, but they clutched only empty air. Frantically, he fought toward where there must be a bank, realizing he was in a roaring stream all of six feet deep. He struck nothing, and was thrown, almost hurtled down stream with what seemed to be overwhelming speed. Something black loomed near him and at the same instant the water caught at him, rushing with even greater power. He grabed again at the blob of blackness and his hand caught a root.

Yet it was nothing secure, merely a huge cottonwood log rushing downstream. Working his way along it, he managed to get a leg over and crawled atop it. Fortunately, the log did not roll over.

Lying there in the blackness, he realized what must have happened. Behind the row of buildings that fronted on the street, of which the jail was one, was a shallow, sandy ditch. At one end of it the bluff reared up. The dry wash skirted one side of the triangle formed by the bluff, and the ditch formed the other. Water flowing off the bluff and off the roofs of the buildings and from the street of the town and the rise beyond it had flooded into the ditch, washing it deeper, yet now he knew he was in the current of the wash itself, now running bank full, a raging torrent.

A brief flash of lightning revealed the stream down which he was shooting like a chip in a mill race. Below, he knew, was Cathedral Gorge, a narrow, boulder-strewn gash in the mountain down which this wash would thunder like an express train. Tack had seen such logs go down it, smashing into boulders, hurled against the rocky walls, then shooting at last out into the open flat below the gorge. And he knew instantly that no living thing could hope to ride a charging log through the black, roaring depths of the gorge and come out anything but a mangled, lifeless pulp.

The log he was bestriding hit a wave and water drenched him, then the log whirled dizzily around a bend in the wash. Before him and around another bend he could hear the roar of the gorge. The log swung, then the driving roots ripped into a heap of debris at the bend of the wash, and the log swung wickedly across the current. Scrambling like a madman, Tack fought his way toward the roots, and then even as the log ripped loose, he hurled himself at the heap of debris.

He landed in a heap of broken boughs, felt something gouge him, and then scrambling, he made the rocks and clambered up into their shelter, lying there on a flat rock, gasping for breath.

CHAPTER FOUR: Return with Death

A long time later he got up. Something was wrong with his right leg. It felt numb and sore. He crawled over the rocks and stumbled over the muddy earth toward the partial shelter of a clump of trees.

He needed shelter, and he needed a gun. Tack Gentry knew now that he was free they would scour the country for him. They might believe him dead, but they would want to be certain. What he needed now was shelter, rest, and food. He needed to examine himself to see how badly he was injured, yet where could he turn?

Betty? She was too far away and he had no horse. Red Furness? Possibly, but how much the man would or would not help he did not know. Yet thinking of Red made him think of Childe. There was a place for him. If he could only get to Childe's quarters over the saloon!

Luckily, he had landed on the same side of the wash as the town. He was stiff and sore, and his leg was paining him grievously. Yet there was no time to be lost. What the hour was he had no idea, but he knew his progress would be slow, and he must be careful. The rain was pounding down, but he was so wet now that it made no difference.

How long it took him he never knew. He could have been no more than a mile from town, perhaps less, yet he walked, crawled, and pulled himself to the edge of town, then behind the buildings until he reached the dark back stairway to Anson Childe's room. Step by step he crawled up. Luckily, the door was unlocked.

Once inside, he stood there in the darkness, listening. There was no sound. This room was windowless but for one very small and tightly curtained window at the top of the wall. Tack felt for the candle, found it, and fumbled for a match. When he had the candle alight, he started pulling off his clothes.

Naked, he dried himself with a towel, avoiding the injured leg. Then he found a bottle, and poured himself a drink. He tossed it off, then sat down on the edge of the bed and looked at his leg.

It almost made him sick to look at it. Hurled against a root or something in the dark, it had torn a great, mangled wound in the calf of his leg. No artery appeared to have been injured but in places his shinbone was visible through the ripped flesh. The wound in the calf was deeper. Cleansing it as best he could, he found a white shirt belonging to Childe, and bandaged his leg.

Exhausted, he fell asleep. When, he never recalled. Only hours later he awakened suddenly to find sunlight streaming through the door into the front room. His leg was stiff and sore, and when he moved it throbbed with pain. Using a cane he found hanging in the room, he pulled himself up and staggered to the door.

The curtains in the front room were up and sunlight streamed in. The rain seemed to be gone. From where he stood he could see into the street, and almost the first person he saw was Van Hardin. He was standing in front of the Longhorn talking to Soderman and the mustached man Tack had first seen at his own ranch.

The sight reminded him, and Tack hunted around for a gun. He found a pair of beautifully matched Colts, silver plated and ivory handled. He strapped them on with their ornate belt and holsters. Then, standing in a corner, he found a riot gun and a Henry rifle. He checked the loads in all the guns, found several boxes of ammunition for each of them, and emptied a box of .45s into the pockets of a pair of Childe's pants he pulled on. Then he put a double handful of shotgun shells into the pockets of a leather jacket he found.

He sat down then, for he was weak and trembling.

His time was short. Sooner or later someone would come to this room. Someone would either think of it or someone would come to claim the room for himself. Red Furness had no idea he was there, so would probably not hesitate to let anyone come up.

He locked the door, then dug around and found a stale loaf of bread, some cheese, then lay down to rest. His leg was throbbing with pain, and he knew it needed care, and badly.

When he awakened, he studied the street from a vantage point well inside the room and to one side of the window. Several knots of men were standing around talking, more men than should have been in town at that hour. He recognized one or two of them as being old timers around. Twice he saw Olney ride by, and the sheriff was carrying a riot gun.

Starr and the mustached man were loafing in front of the Longhorn, and two other men Tack recognized as coming from the old London ranch were there.

He ate some more bread and cheese. He was just finishing his sandwich when a buckboard turned into the street, and his heart jumped when he saw Betty London was driving. Beside her in the seat was her father, Bill, worn and old, his hair white now, but he was wearing a gun!

Something was stirring down below. It began to look as if the lid was about to blow off. Yet Tack had no idea of his own status. He was an escaped prisoner, and as such could be shot on sight legally by Olney or Starr, who seemed to be a deputy. From the wary attitude of the Van Hardin men he knew that they were disturbed by their lack of knowledge of him.

Yet the day passed without incident, and finally he returned to the bunk and lay down after checking his guns once more. The time for the payoff was near, he knew that. It could come at any moment. He was lying there thinking about that and looking up at the rough plank ceiling when he heard the steps on the stairs.

He arose so suddenly that a twinge of pain shot through the weight that had become his leg. The steps were on the front stairs, not the back. A quick glance from the window told him it was Betty London.

What did she want here?

Her hand fell on the knob and it turned. He eased off the bed and turned the key in the lock. She hesitated just an instant, and then stepped in. When their eyes met hers went wide and her face went white to the lips.

"You!" she gasped. "Oh, Tack! What have you been doing! Where have you been!"

She started toward him, but he backed up and sat down on the bed. "Wait. Do they know I'm up here?" he demanded harshly.

"No, Tack. I came up to see if some papers were here, some papers I gave to Anson Childe before he was—murdered."

"Yuh think I did that?" he demanded.

"No, of course not!" Her eyes held a question. "Tack, what's the matter? Don't you like me any more?"

"Don't I like yuh?" His lips twisted with bitterness. "Lady, yuh've got a nerve to ask that! I come back and find my girl about to go dancin' in a cheap saloon dance hall, and—"

"I needed money, Tack," Betty said quietly. "Dad needed care. We didn't have any money. Everything we had was lost when we lost the ranch. Hardin offered me the job. He said he wouldn't let anybody molest me."

"What about him?"

"I could take care of him." She looked at him, puzzled. "Tack, what's the matter? Why are you sitting down? Are you hurt?"

"My leg." He shook his head as she started forward. "Don't bother about it, there's no time. What are they saying down there? What's all the crowd in town? Give it to me, quick!"

"Some of them think you were drowned in escaping from jail. I don't think Van Hardin thinks that, nor Olney. They seem very disturbed. The crowd is in town for Childe's funeral, and because some of them think you were murdered once Olney got you in jail. Some of our friends."

"Betty!" The call came from the street below. It was Van Hardin's voice.

"Don't answer!" Tack Gentry got up. His dark green eyes were hard. "I want him to come up."

Betty waited, her eyes wide, listening. Footsteps sounded on the stairway, then the door shoved open. "Bet—" Van Hardin's voice died out and he stood there, one hand on the door knob, starring at Tack.

"Howdy, Hardin," Tack said, "I was hopin' yuh'd come."

Van Hardin said nothing. His powerful shoulders filled the open door, his eyes were set, and the shock was fading from them now.

"Got a few things to tell yuh, Hardin," Tack continued gently, "before yuh go out of this feet first I want yuh to know what a sucker yuh've been."

"A sucker I've been?" Hardin laughed. "What chance have yuh got? The street down there is full of my men. Yuh've friends there, too, but they lack leadership, they don't know what to do. My men have their orders. And then, I won't have any trouble with yuh, Gentry. Yore old friends around here told me all about yuh. Soft, like that uncle of yores."

"Ever hear of Black Jack Paris, Hardin?"

"The gunman? Of course, but what's he got to do with yuh?"

"Nothin', now. He did once, up in Ellsworth, Kansas. They dug a bed for him next mornin', Hardin. He was too slow. Yuh said I was soft? Well, maybe I was once. Maybe in spots I still am, but yuh see, since the folks around here have seen me I've been over the cattle trails, been doin' some Injun fightin' and rustler killin'. It makes a sight of change in a man, Hardin.

"That ain't what I wanted yuh to know. I wanted yuh to know what a fool yuh were, tryin' to steal this ranch. Yuh see, the land in our home ranch wasn't like the rest of this land, Hardin."

"What do you mean?" Hardin demanded suspiciously.

"Why, yuh're the smart boy," Tack drawled easily, "yuh should have checked before takin' so much for granted. Yuh see, the Gentry ranch was a land grant. My grandmother, she was a Basque, see? The land came to us through her family, and the will she left was that it would belong to us as long as any of us lived, that it couldn't be sold or traded, and in case we all died, it was to go to the State of Texas!"

Van Hardin stared. "What?" he gasped. "What kind of fool deal is this yuh're givin' me?"

"Fool deal is right," Tack said quietly. "Yuh see, the State of Texas knows no Gentry would sell or trade, knowin' we couldn't, so if somebody else showed up with the land, they were bound to ask a sight of questions. Sooner or later they'd have got around to askin' yuh how come."

Hardin seemed stunned. From the street below there was a sound of horses' hooves.

Then a voice said from Tack's left, "Yuh better get out, Van. There's talkin' to be done in the street. I want Tack Gentry!"

Tack's head jerked around. It was Soderman. The short squinty eyed man was staring at him, gun in hand. He heard Hardin turn and bolt out of the room; saw resolution in Soderman's eyes. Hurling himself toward the wall, Gentry's hand flashed for his pistol.

A gun blasted in the room with a roar like a cannon and Gentry felt the angry whip of the bullet, and then he fired twice, low down.

Soderman fell back against the door jamb, both hands grabbing at his stomach, just below his belt buckle. "Yuh shot me!" he gasped, round eyed. "Yuh shot—me!"

"Like you did my uncle," Tack said coolly. "Only yuh had better than an even break, and he had no break at all."

Gentry could feel blood from the opened wound trickling down his leg. He glanced at Betty. "I've got to get down there," he said, "he's a slick talker."

Van Hardin was standing down in the street. Beside him was Olney and nearby was Starr. Other men, a half dozen of them, loitered nearby.

Slowly, Tack Gentry began stumping down the stair. All eyes looked up. Red Furness saw him and spoke out, "Tack, these three men are Rangers come down from Austin to make some inquiries."

Hardin pointed at Gentry. "He's wanted for murdering Anson Childe! Also, for jail breaking, and unless I'm much mistaken he has killed another man up there in Childe's office!"

The Ranger looked at him curiously, then one of them glanced at Hardin, "Yuh all the hombre what lays claim to the Gentry place?"

Hardin swallowed quickly, then his eyes shifted. "No, that was Soderman. The man who was upstairs."

Hardin looked at Tack Gentry. With the Rangers here he knew his game was played out. He smiled suddenly. "Yuh've nothin' on me at all, gents," he said coolly. "Soderman killed John Gentry and laid claim to his ranch. I don't know nothin' about it."

"Yuh engineered it!" Bill London burst out. "Same as yuh did the stealin' of my ranch!"

"Yuh've no proof," Hardin sneered. "Not a particle! My name is on no papers, and yuh have no evidence."

Coolly, he strode across to his black horse and swung into the saddle. He was smiling gently, but there was sneering triumph behind the smile. "Yuh've nothin' on me, not a thing!"

"Don't let him get away!" Bill London shouted. "He's the wust one of the whole kit and kaboodle of 'em!"

"But he's right!" the Ranger protested. "In all the papers we've found, there's not a single item to tie him up. If he's in it, he's been almighty smart."

"Then arrest him for horse stealin'!" Tack Gentry said. "That's my black horse he's on!"

Hardin's face went cold, then he smiled. "Why, that's crazy! That's foolish," he said, "this is my horse. I reared him from a colt. Anybody could be mistaken, 'cause one black horse is like another. My brand's on him, and yuh can all see it's an old brand."

Tack Gentry stepped out in front of the black horse. "Button!" he said sharply. "Button!"

At the familiar voice, the black horse's head jerked up. "Button!" Tack called. "Hut! Hut!"

As the name and the sharp command rolled out, Button reacted like an explosion of dynamite. He jumped straight up in the air and came down hard, then he sunfished wildly, and Van Hardin hit the dirt in a heap.

"Button!" Tack commanded. "Go get Blackie!"

Instantly, the horse wheeled and trotted to the hitching rail where Blackie stood ground hitched as Olney had left him. Button caught the reins in his teeth and led the other black horse back.

The Rangers grinned. "Reckon, Mister," he said, "yuh done proved yore case. This man's a horse thief."

Hardin climbed to his feet, his face dark with fury. "Yuh think yuh'll get away with that?" His hand flashed for his gun.

Tack Gentry had been watching him, and now his own hand moved down, then up. The two guns barked as one. A chip flew from the stair post beside Tack, but Van Hardin turned slowly and went to his knees in the dust.

At almost the same instant, a sharp voice rang out. "Olney! Starr!"

Olney's face went white and he wheeled, hand flashing for his gun. "Anson Childe!" he gasped.

Childe stood on the platform in front of his room and fired once, twice, three times. Sheriff Olney went down, coughing and muttering. Starr backed through the swinging doors of the saloon and sat down hard in the sawdust.

Tack stared at him. "What the—"

The tall young lawyer came down the steps. "Fooled them, didn't I? They tried to get me once too often. I got their man with a shotgun in the face. Then I changed clothes with him and then lit out for Austin. I came in with the Rangers, then left them on the edge of town. They told me they'd let us have it our way unless they were needed."

"Saves the State of Texas a sight of money," one of the Rangers drawled, "anyway, we been checkin' on this here Hardin. On Olney, too. That's why they wanted to keep things quiet around here. They knowed we was checkin' on 'em."

The Rangers moved in and with the help of a few of the townspeople rounded up Hardin's other followers.

Tack grinned at the lawyer. "Lived up to your name, Pardner," he said. "Yuh sure did! All yore sheep in the fold, now!"

"What do you mean! Lived up to my name?" Anson Childe looked around.

Gentry grinned. "And a little Childe shall lead them!" he said.

HIS BROTHER'S DEBT

"You're yellow, Casady!" Ben Kerr shouted. "Yellow as saffron! You ain't got the guts of a coyote! Draw, curse you, fill your hand so I can kill you! You ain't fit to live!" Kerr stepped forward, his big hands spread over his gun butts. "Go ahead, reach!"

Rock Casady, numb with fear, stepped slowly back, his face gray. To right and left were the amazed and incredulous faces of his friends, the men he had ridden with on the O Bar, staring unbelieving.

Sweat broke out on his face. He felt his stomach retch and twist within him. Turning suddenly, he plunged blindly through the door and fled.

Behind him, one by one, his shame-faced, unbelieving friends from the O Bar slowly sifted from the crowd. Heads hanging, they headed homeward. Rock Casady was yellow. The man they had worked with, sweated with, laughed with. The last man they would have suspected. Yellow.

Westward, with the wind in his face and tears burning his eyes, his horse's hoofs beating out a mad tattoo upon the hard trail, fled Rock Casady, alone in the darkness.

Nor did he stop. Avoiding towns and holding to the hills, he rode steadily westward. There were days when he starved, and days when he found game, a quail or two, killed with unerring shots from a six-gun that never seemed to miss. Once he shot a deer. He rode wide of towns and deliberately erased his trail, although he knew no one was following him, or cared where he went.

Four months later, leaner, unshaven and saddle weary, he rode into the yard of the Three Spoke Wheel. Foreman Tom Bell saw him coming and glanced around at his boss, big Frank Stockman.

"Look what's comin'. Looks like he's lived in the hills. On the dodge, maybe."

"Huntin' grub, most likely. He's a strappin' big man, though, an' looks like a hand. Better ask him if he wants a job. With Pete Vorys around, we'll have to be huntin' strangers or we'll be out of help!"

The mirror on the wall of the bunkhouse was neither cracked nor marred, but Rock Casady could almost wish that it was. Bathed and shaved, he looked into tortured eyes of a dark, attractive young man with wavy hair and a strong jaw.

People had told him many times that he was a handsome man, but when he looked into his eyes he knew he looked into the eys of a coward.

He had a yellow streak.

The first time—well, the first time but one—that he had faced a man with a gun he had backed down cold. He had run like a baby. He had shown the white feather.

Tall, strongly built, skillful with rope or horse, knowing with stock, he was a top hand in any outfit. An outright genius with guns, men had often said they would hate to face him in a shootout. He had worked hard and played rough, getting the most out of life until that day in the saloon in El Paso when Ben Kerr, gunman and cattle rustler, gambler and bully, had called him, and he had backed down.

Tom Bell was a knowing and kindly man. Aware that something was riding Casady, he told him his job and left him alone. Stockman watched him top off a bad bronc on the first morning and glanced at Bell.

"If he does everything like he rides, we've got us a hand!"

And Casady did everything as well. A week after he had hired out he was doing as much work as any two men. And the jobs they avoided, the lonely jobs, he accepted eagerly.

"Notice something else?" Stockman asked the ranch owner one morning. "That new hand sure likes jobs that keep him away from the ranch."

Stockman nodded. "Away from people. It ain't natural, Tom. He ain't been to Three Lakes once since he's been here."

Sue Landon looked up at her uncle. "Maybe he's broke!" she exclaimed. "No cowhand could have fun in town when he's broke!"

Bell shook head. "It ain't that, Sue. He had money when he first came in here. I saw it. He had anyway two hundred dollars and for a forty-a-month cowpoke, that's a lot of money!"

"Notice something else?" Stockman asked. "He never packs a gun. Only man on the ranch who doesn't. You'd better warn him about Pete Vorys."

"I did," Bell frowned. "I can't figure this hombre, boss. I did warn him, and that was the very day he began askin' for all the bad jobs. Why, he's the only man on the place who'll fetch grub to Cat McLeod without bein' bullied into it!"

"Over in that Rock Canyon country?" Stockman smiled. "That's a rough ride for any man. I don't blame the boys, but you've got to hand it to old Cat. He's killed nine lions and forty-two coyotes in the past ninety days! If he keeps that up we won't have so much stock lost!"

"Two bad he ain't just as good on rustlers. Maybe," Bell grinned, "we ought to turn him loose on Pete Vorys!"

Rock Casady kept his palouse gelding moving steadily. The two pack horses ambled placidly behind, seemingly content to be away from the ranch. The old restlessness was coming back to Casady, and he had been on the Three Spoke only a few weeks. He knew they liked him, knew that despite his taciturn manner and desire to be alone, the hands liked him as well as did Stockman or Bell.

He did his work and more and he was a hand. He avoided poker games that might lead to trouble and stayed away from town. He was anxiously figuring some way to be absent from the ranch on the following Saturday, for he knew the whole crowd was going to a dance and shindig in Three Lakes.

While he talked little, he heard much. He was aware of impending trouble between the Three Spoke Wheel outfit and the gang of Pete Vorys. The latter, who seemed to ride the country as he pleased, owned a small ranch north of Three Lakes, near town. He had a dozen tough hands and usually spent money freely. All his hands had money, and while no one dared say it, all knew he was rustling.

Yet he was not the ringleader. Behind him there was someone else, someone who had only recently become involved, for recently there had been a change. Larger bunches of cattle were being stolen, and more care was taken to leave no trail. The carelessness of Vorys had given way to more shrewd operation, and Casady overheard enough talk to know that Stockman believed a new brain was directing operations.

He heard much of Pete Vorys. He was a big man, bigger than Rock. He was a killer with at least seven notches on his gun. He was pugnacious and quarrelsome, itching for a fight with gun or fists. He had, only a few weeks ago, whipped Sandy Kane, a Three Spoke hand, within an inch of his life. He was bold, domineering, and tough.

The hands on the Three Spoke were good men. They were hard workers, willing to fight, but not one of them was good enough to tackle Vorys with either fists or gun.

Cat McLeod was scraping a hide when Rock rode into his camp in Blue Spring Valley. He got up, wiping his hands on his jeans and grinning.

"Howdy, son! You sure are a sight for sore eyes! It ain't no use quibblin', I sure get my grub on time when you're on that ranch! Hope you stay!"

Rock swung down. He liked the valley and liked Cat.

"Maybe I'll pull out, Cat." He looked around. "I might even come up here to stay. I like it."

McLeod glanced at him out of the corners of his eyes. "Glad to have you, son. This sure ain't no country for a young feller, though. It's a huntin' an' fishin' country, but no women here, an' no likker. Nothin' much to do, all said an' done."

Casady unsaddled in silence. It was better, though, than a run-in with Vorys, he thought. At least nobody here knew he was yellow. They liked him and he was one of them, but he was careful.

"Ain't more trouble down below, is there? That Vorys cuttin' up much?" The old man noted the gun Rock was wearing for the trip.

"Some. I hear the boys talkin' about him."

"Never seen him yourself?" Cat asked quizzically. "I been thinkin' ever since you come up here, son. Might be a good thing for this country if you did have trouble with Vorys. You're nigh as big as him, an' you move like a catamount. An' me, I know 'em! Never seen a man lighter on his feet than you."

"Not me," Rock spoke stiffly. "I'm a peace-lovin' man, Cat. I want no trouble with anybody."

McLeod studied the matter as he worked over his hide. For a long time now he had known something was bothering Rock Casady. Perhaps this last remark, that he wanted no trouble with anybody, was the answer?

Cat McLeod was a student of mankind as well as the animals upon whom he practiced his trade. In a lifetime of living along the frontier and in the world's far places, he had learned a lot about men who liked to live alone, and about men who sought the wilderness. If it was true that Rock wanted no trouble, it certainly was not from lack of ability to handle it.

There had been that time when Cat had fallen, stumbling to hands and knees. Right before him, not three feet from his face and much nearer his outstretched hands lay one of the biggest rattlers Cat had ever seen. The snake's head jerked back above its coil, and then, with a gun's roar blasting in his ears, that head was gone and the snake was a writhing mass of coils, showing only a bloody stumb where the head had been!

Cat had gotten to his feet gray faced and turned. Rock Casady was thumbing a shell into his gun. The young man grinned.

"That was a close one!" he had said cheerfully.

McLeod had dusted off his hands, staring at Casady. "I've heard of men drawin' faster'n a snake could strike, but that's the first time I ever seen it!"

Since then he had seen that .44 shoot the heads off quail and he had seen a quick hip shot with the rifle break a deer's neck.

Now his mind reverted to their former topic. "If that Vorys is tied in with some smart hombre, there'll be hell to pay! Pete was never no great shakes for brains, but he's tough, tough as all get out! With somebody to think for him, he'll make this country unfit to live in!"

Later that night, McLeod looked over his shoulder from the fire. "You know," he said, "if I was wantin' a spread of my own, an' didn't care much for folks, like you, I'd go down into the Pleasant Valley Outlet, south of here. Lonely, but she's sure grand country!"

Two days later Rock was mending a bridle when Sue Landon walked over to him. She wore jeans and a boy's shirt, and her eyes were bright and lovely.

"Hi!" she said brightly. "You're the new hand? You certainly keep out of the way. All this time on the ranch and I never met you before!"

He grinned shyly. "Just a quiet hombre, I reckon," he said. "If I had it my way I'd be over there with Cat all the time."

"Then you won't like the job I have for you!" she said. "To ride into Three Lakes with me, riding herd on a couple of pack horses."

"Three Lakes?" He looked up so sharply it startled her. "Into town? I never go into town, ma'am. I don't like the place. Not any town."

"Why, that's silly! Anyway, there's no one else, and Uncle Frank won't let me go alone with Pete Vorys around."

"He wouldn't bother a girl, would he?"

"You sure don't know Pete Vorys!" Sue returned grimly. "He does pretty much what he feels like and everybody's afraid to say anything about it. Although," she added, "with this new partner he's got he's toned down some. But come on—you'll go?"

Reluctantly, he got to his feet. She looked at him curiously, not a little piqued. Any other hand on the ranch would have jumped at the chance, and here she had deliberately made sure there were no others available before going to him. Her few distant glimpses of Rock Casady had excited her interest, and she wanted to know him better.

Yet as the trail fell behind them, she had to admit she was getting no place. For shyness there was some excuse, although usually even the most bashful hand lost it when alone with her. Rock Casady was almost sullen and all she could get out of him were monosyllables.

The truth was that the nearer they drew to Three Lakes the more worried Rock grew. It had been six months since he had been in a town, and while it was improbable he would see anyone he knew, there was always a chance. Cowhands were notoriously footloose and fancy free. Once the story of his backing out of a gunfight got around, he would be through in this country, and he was tired of running.

Yet Three Lakes looked quiet enough as they ambled placidly down the street and tied up in front of the general store. He glanced at Sue tentatively.

"Ma'am," he said, "I'd sure appreciate it if you didn't stay too long. Towns make me nervous."

She looked at him, more than slightly irritated. Her trip with him, so carefully planned, had thus far come to nothing, although she had to admit he was the finest-looking man she had ever seen, and his smile was quick and attractive.

"I won't be long. Why don't you go have a drink? It might do you good!" She said the last sentence a little sharply, and he looked quickly at her, but she was already flouncing into the store, as well as any girl could flounce in jeans.

Slowly he built a cigarette, studying the Hackamore Saloon over the way. He had to admit he was tempted, and probably he was foolish to think that he would get into trouble or that anyone would know him. Nevertheless, he sat down suddenly on the edge of the board walk and lighted his smoke.

He was still sitting there when he heard the sound of booted heels on the boardwalk, and then he heard a raucous voice.

"Ha! Lookit here! One of them no 'count Three Spokers in town! I didn't think any of them had the sand!"

In spite of himself, he looked up, knowing instantly that this man was Pete Vorys.

He was broad in the shoulder, with narrow hips. He had a swarthy face with dark, brilliant eyes. That he had been drinking was obvious but he was far from drunk. With him were two tough-looking hands, both grinning cynically at him.

Vorys was spoiling for a fight. He had never been whipped and doubted there lived a man who could whip him in a tooth-and-nail knock-down and drag-out battle. This Three Spoker looked big enough to be fun.

"That's a rawhide outfit, anyway," Vorys sneered. "I've a mind to ride out there sometime, just for laughs. Wonder where they hooked this ranny?"

Despite himself, Rock was growing angry. He was not wearing a gun, and Vorys was. He took the cigarette out of his mouth and looked at it. Expecting trouble, a crowd was gathering. He felt his neck growing red.

"Hey, you!" Vorys booted him solidly in the spine, and the kick hurt. At the same time he slapped Casady with his sombrero. Few things are more calculated to enrage a man.

Rock came to his feet with a lunge. As he turned, with his right palm he grabbed the ankle of Vorys's boot, and with his left fist he smashed him in the stomach, jerking up on the leg. The move was so sudden, so totally unexpected that there was no chance to spring back. Pete Vorys hit the boardwalk flat on his shoulder blades!

A whoop of delight went up from the crowd and for an instant, Pete Vorys lay stunned. Then with an oath he came off the walk, lunging to his feet.

Rock sprang back, his hands wide. "I'm not packin' a gun!" he yelled.

"I don't need a gun!" Vorys yelled. It was the first time he had ever hit the ground in a fight and he was furious.

He stepped in, driving a left to the head. Rock was no boxer. Indeed, he had rarely fought except in fun. He took that blow now, a stunning wallop on the cheekbone. At the same moment, he let go with a wicked right swing. The punch caught Vorys on the chin and rocked him to his heels.

More astonished than hurt, he sprang in and threw two swings for Rock's chin, and Casady took them both coming in. A tremendous light seemed to burst in his brain, but the next instant he had Pete Vorys in his hands. Grabbing him by the collar and the belt, he heaved him to arm's length overhead and hurled him into the street. Still dazed from the punches he had taken, he sprang after the bigger man, and seizing him before he could strike more than an ineffectual punch, swung him to arm's length overhead again, and slammed him into the dust!

Four times he grabbed the hapless bully and hurled him to the ground while the crowd whooped and cheered. The last time, his head clearing, he grabbed Vorys' shirt front with his left hand and swung three times into his face, smashing his nose and lips. Then he lifted the man and heaved him into the water tank with such force that water showered around him.

Beside himself, Rock wheeled on the two startled men who had walked with Vorys. Before either could make a move, he grabbed them by their belts. One swung on Rock's face, but he merely ducked his head and heaved. The man's feet flew up and he hit the ground on his back. Promptly, Rock stacked the other atop him.

The man started to get up, and Rock swung on his face, knocking him into a sitting position. Then grabbing him, he heaved him into the water tank with Vorys who was scrambling to get out. Then he dropped the third man into the pool and putting a hand in Vorys's face, shoved him back.

For an instant then, while the street rocked with cheers and yells of delight, he stood, panting and staring. Suddenly, he was horrified. In his rage he had not thought of what this would mean, but suddenly he knew that they would be hunting him now with guns. He must face a shoot-out, or skip the country!

Wheeling, he shoved through the crowd, aware that someone was clinging to his arm. Looking down, he saw Sue beside him. Her eyes were bright with laughter and pride.

"Oh, Rock! That was wonderful. Just wonderful!"

"Let's get out of town!" he said quickly. "Now!"

So pleased was she by the discomfiture of Pete Vorys and his hands by a Three Spoker that she thought nothing of his haste. His eye swelling and his nose still dripping occasional drops of blood, they hit the trail for the home ranch. All the way, Sue babbled happily over his standing up for the Three Spoke, and what it meant, and all the while all he could think of was the fact that on the morrow Vorys would be looking for him with a gun.

He could not face him. It was far better to avoid a fight than to prove himself yellow, and if he fled the country now, they would never forget what he had done, and always make excuses for him. If he stayed behind and showed his yellow streak, he would be ruined.

Frank Stockman was standing on the steps when they rode in, and he took one look at Rock's battered face and torn shirt and come off the steps.

"What happened?" he demanded. "Was it that Pete Vorys again?"

Tom Bell and two other hands were walking up from the bunkhouse, staring at Rock. But already, while he stripped the saddles from the horses, Sue Landon was telling the story, and it lost nothing in the telling. Rock Casady of the Three Spoke had not only whipped Pete Vorys soundly, but he had ducked Pete and two of his tough hands in the Three Lakes' water tank!

The hands crowded around him, crowing and happy, slapping him on the back and grinning. Sandy Kane gripped his hand.

"Thanks, pardner," he said grimly, "I don't feel so bad now!"

Rock smiled weakly, but inside he was sick. It was going to look bad, but he was pulling out. He said nothing, but after supper he got his own horse and threw the saddle aboard, then rustled his gear. When he was all packed, he drew a deep breath and walked toward the ranchhouse.

Stockman was sitting on the wide veranda with Bell and Sue. She got up when he drew near, her eyes bright. He avoided her glance, suddenly aware of how much her praise and happiness meant to him. In his weeks on the Three Spoke, while he had never talked to her before today, his eyes had followed her every move.

"How are you, son?" Stockman asked jovially. "You've made this a red letter day on the Three Spoke! Come up an' sit down! Bell was just talking here, he says he needs a segundo, an' I reckon he's right. How'd you like the job? Eighty a month?"

He swallowed. "Sorry, boss. I got to be movin'. I want my time."

"You what?" Bell took the pipe from his mouth and stared.

"I got to roll my hoop," he said stiffly. "I don't want trouble."

Frank Stockman came quickly to his feet. "But listen, man!" he protested. "You've just whipped the best man around this country! You've made a place for yourself here! The boys think you're great! So do I! So does Tom! As for Sue here, all she's done is talk about how wonderful you are! Why, son, you came in here a drifter, an' now you've made a place for yourself! Stick around! We need men like you!"

Despite himself, Casady was wavering. This was what he had always wanted, and wanted now, since the bleak months of his lonely riding, more than ever. A place where he was at home, men who liked him, and a girl. . . .

"Stay on," Stockman said more quietly. "You can handle any trouble that comes, and I promise you, the Three Spoke will back any play you make! Why, with you to head 'em we can run Pete Vorys and that slick partner of his, that Ben Kerr, clean out of the country!"

Casady's face blanched. "Who? Did you say, Ben Kerr?"

"Why, sure!" Stockman stared at him curiously, aware of the shocked expression on Rock's face. "Ben Kerr's the hombre who come in here to side Vorys! He's the smart one who's puttin' all those fancy ideas on Pete's head! He's a brother-in-law of Vorys, or something!"

Ben Kerr—here!

That settled it. He could not stay now. There was no time to stay. His mind leaped ahead. Vorys would tell his story, of course. His name would be mentioned, and if not his name, his description. Kerr would know, and he wouldn't waste time. Why, even now. . . !

"Give me my money!" Casady said sharply. "I'm movin' out right now! Thanks for all you've offered, but I'm ridin'! I want no trouble!"

Stockman's face stiffened. "Why, sure," he said, "if you feel that way about it!" He took a roll of bills from his pocket and coolly paid over the money, then abruptly he turned his back and walked inside.

Casady wheeled, his heart sick within him, and started for the corral. He heard running steps behind him, then a light touch on his arm. He looked down, his eyes miserable, into Sue's face.

"Don't go, Rock!" she pleaded gently. "Please don't go! We all want you to stay!"

He shook his head. "I can't, Sue! I can't stay here. I want no gun trouble!"

There—it was out.

She stepped back and slowly her face changed. Girl that she was, she still had grown up in the tradition of the West. A man fought his battles with gun or fist, he did not run away.

"Oh?" Her amazed contempt cut him like a whip. "So that's it? You're afraid to face a gun? Afraid of your life?" She stared at him. "Why, Rock Casady," her voice lifted as realization broke over her, "you're yellow!"

Hours later, far back in the darkness of night in the mountains, her words rang in his ears. She had called him yellow! She had called him a coward!

Rock Casady, sick at heart, rode slowly into the darkness. At first he rode with no thought but to escape, and then as his awareness began to return, he studied the situation. Lee's Ferry was northeast, and to the south he was bottled by the Colorado Canyon. North it was mostly Vorys's range and west lay Three Lakes and the trails leading to it. East the Canyons fenced him off also, but east lay a lonely, little-known country, ridden only by Cat McLeod in his wanderings after varmints that preyed upon Three Spoke cattle. In that wilderness he might find someplace to hole up. Cat still had plenty of supplies, and he could borrow some from him. . . . Suddenly he remembered the canyon Cat had mentioned, the Pleasant Valley Outlet.

He would not go near Cat. There was game enough, and he had packed away a few things in the grub line when he had rolled his soogan. He found an intermittant stream that trailed down a ravine toward Kane Canyon, and followed it. Pleasant Valley Outlet was not far south of Kane. It would be a good hideout. After a few weeks, when the excitement was over, he could slip out of the country.

In a lonely canyon that opened from the south wall into Pleasant Valley Canyon, he found a green and lovely spot. There was plenty of driftwood and a cave hollowed from the Kaibab sandstone by wind and water. There he settled down. Days passed into weeks, and he lived on wild game, berries, and fish. Yet his mind kept turning northwestward toward the Three Spoke, and his thoughts gave him no rest.

On an evening almost three weeks after his escape from the Three Spoke, he was putting his coffee on when he heard a slight sound. Looking up he saw old Cat McLeod grinning at him.

"Howdy, son!" he chuckled. "When you head for the tall timber you sure do a job of it! My land! I thought I'd never find you! No more trail'n trout swimmin' upstream!"

Rock rose stiffly. "Howdy, Cat. Just put the coffee on." He averted his eyes, and went about the business of preparing a meal.

Cat seated himself, seemingly unhurried and undisturbed by his scant welcome. He got out his pipe and stuffed it full of tobacco. He talked calmly and quietly about game and fish, and the mountain trails.

"Old Mormon crossin' not far from here," he said, "I could show you where it is."

After they had eaten, McLeod leaned back against a rock. "Lots of trouble back at the Three Spoke. I reckon you was the smart one, pullin' out when you did."

Casady made no response, so McLeod continued. "Pete Vorys was some beat up. Two busted ribs, busted nose, some teeth gone. Feller name of Ben Kerr came out to the Three Spoke huntin' you. Said you was a yella dog an' he knowed you of old. He laughed when he said that, an' said the whole Three Spoke outfit was yella.

Stockman, he wouldn't take that, so he went for his gun. Kerr shot him."

Rock's head came up with a jerk. "Shot Stockman? He killed him?" There was horror in his voice. This was his fault—his!

"No, he ain't dead. He's sure bad off, though. Kerr added injury to insult by runnin' off a couple of hundred head of Three Spoke stock. Shot one hand doin' it."

A long silence followed in which the two men smoked moodily. Finally, Cat looked across the fire at Rock.

"Son, there's more'n one kind of courage, I say. I seen many a dog stand up to a grizzly that would high-tail it from a skunk. Back yonder they say you're yella. Me, I don't figure it so."

"Thanks, Cat," Rock replied simply, miserably. "Thanks a lot, but you're wrong. I am yellow."

"Reckon it takes pretty much of a man to say that, son. But from what I hear you sure didn't act it against Pete an' his riders. You walloped the tar out of them!"

"With my hands it's different. It's—it's—guns."

McLeod was silent. He poked a twig in the fire and relighted his pipe.

"Ever kill a man, son?" His eyes probed Rock's, and he saw the young rider's head nod slowly. "Who was it? How'd it happen?"

"It was—" he looked up, his face drawn and pale. "I killed my brother, Cat."

McLeod was shocked. His old eyes went wide. "You killed your brother? Your own brother?"

Rock Casady nodded. "Yeah," he said bitterly, "my own brother. The one person in this world that really mattered to me!"

Cat stared, then slowly his brow puckered. "Son," he said, "why don't you tell me about it? Get it out of your system, like."

For a long while Rock was silent, then he started to speak.

"It was down in Texas. We had a little spread down there, Jack and me. He was a shade older, but alway protectin' me, although I sure didn't need it. The finest man who ever walked, he was.

"Well, we had us a mite of trouble, an' this here Ben Kerr was the ringleader. I had trouble with Ben, and he swore to shoot me on sight. I was a hand with a gun, like you know, an' I was ready enough to fight, them days. One of the hands told me, an' without a word to Jack, I lit into the saddle an' headed for town.

"Kerr was gun-slick, but I wasn't worried. I knew that I didn't have scarcely a friend in town, an' that his whole outfit would be there. It was me against them, an' I went into town with two guns, an' sure enough on the prod.

"It was gettin' late when I hit town. A man I knowed told me Ben was around with his outfit and that nobody was goin' to back me one bit, them all bein' scared of Ben's boys. He told me, too, that Ben Kerr would shoot me in the back as soon as not he bein' that kind.

"I went huntin' him. Kidlike, an' never in no fight before, I was jumpy, mighty jumpy. The light was bad. All of a sudden, I saw one of Ben's boys step out of a door ahead of me. He called out, 'Here he is, Ben! Take him!' Then I heard runnin' feet behind me, heard 'em slide to a halt, an' I wheeled, drawin' as I turned, an' fired." His voice sank to a whisper.

Cat, leaning forward, said, "You shot? An' then . . . ?"

"It was Jack. It was my own brother. He'd heard I was in town alone an' he come runnin' to back me up. I drilled him dead center!"

Cat McLeod stared up at the young man, utterly appalled. In his kindly old heart he could only guess at the horror that must have filled Casady, then scarcely more than a boy, when he had looked down into that still, dead face and seen his brother.

"Gosh, son." He shook his head in amazed sympathy. "It ain't no wonder you hate gun fights! It sure ain't! But . . . ?" He scowled. "I still don't see . . ." His voice trailed away.

Rock drew a deep breath. "I sold out then, and left the country. Went to ridin' for an outfit near El Paso. One night I come into town with the other hands, an' who do I run into but

Ben Kerr. He thought I ran because I was afraid of him, an' he got tough. He called me—right in front of the outfit. I was goin' to draw, but all I could see there in front of me was Jack, with that blue hole between his eyes! I turned and ran."

Cat McLeod stared at Rock, then into the fire. It was no wonder, he reflected. He probably would have run too. If he had drawn he would have been firing on the image of his brother. It would have been like killing him over again.

"Son," he said slowly, "I know how you feel, but stop a minute an' think about Jack, this brother of yours. He always protected you, you say. He always stood up for you. Now don't you suppose he'd understand? You thought you was all alone in that town. You'd every right to think that was Ben Kerr behind you. I would have thought so, an' I wouldn't have wasted no time shootin', neither.

"You can't run away from yourself. You can't run no further. Someday you got to stand an' face it, an' it might as well be now. Look at it like this: Would your brother want you livin' like this? Hunted and scared? He sure wouldn't! Son, ever' man has to pay his own debt, an' live his own life. Nobody can do it for you, but if I was you, I'd sort of figure my brother was dead because of Ben Kerr, and I'd stop runnin'!"

Rock looked up slowly. "Yeah," he agreed, "I see that plain. But what if when I stepped out to meet him, I look up an' see Jack's face again?"

His eyes dark with horror, Rock Casady turned and plunged downstream, stumbling, swearing in his fear and loneliness and sorrow.

At daylight, old Cat McLeod opened his eyes. For an instant, he lay still. Then he realized where he was, and what he had come for, and he turned his head. Rock Casady, his gear and horse, were gone. Stumbling to his feet, McLeod slipped on his boots and walked out in his red flannels to look at the trail.

It headed south, away from Three Lakes, and away from Ben Kerr. Rock Casady was running again.

The trail south to the canyon was rough and rugged. The palouse was sure-footed and had a liking for the mountains, yet seemed undecided, as though the feeling persisted that he was going the wrong way.

Casady stared bleakly ahead, but he saw little of the orange and red of the sandstone cliffs. He was seeing again Frank Stockman's strong, kindly face, and remembering his welcome at the Three Spoke. He was remembering Sue's hand on his sleeve and her quick smile, and old Tom Bell, gnarled and worn with handling cattle and men. He drew up suddenly and turned the horse on the narrow trail. He was going back.

"Jack," he said suddenly aloud, "stick with me, boy. I'm sure goin' to need you now!"

*   *   *

Sandy Kane, grim-lipped and white of face, dismounted behind the store. Beside him was Sue Landon.

"Miss Sue," he said, "you get that buyin' done fast. Don't let none of that Vorys crowd see you. They've sure taken this town over since they shot the boss."

"All right, Sandy." She looked at him bravely, then squeezed the older man's hand. "We'll make it all right." Her blue eyes darkened. "I wish I'd been a man, Sandy. Then the boys would come in and clean up this outfit!"

"Miss Sue," he said gently, "don't fret none. Our boys are just honest cowhands. We don't have a gunfighter in the lot, nobody who could stand up to Kerr or Vorys. No man minds a scrap, but it would be plain suicide!"

The girl started to enter the store, then caught the cowboy's hand.

"Sandy," she said faintly, "look!"

A tall man with broad shoulders had swung down before the store. He tied his horse with a slip knot, and hitched his guns into place. Rock Cassady, his hard young face bleak and desperate, stared carefully along the street.

It was only three blocks long, this street. It was dusty and warm with the noon-day sun. The gray-fronted buildings looked upon the dusty canal that separated them, and a few saddled horses stamped lazily, flicking their tails at casual flies. It was like that other street, so long ago.

Casady pulled the flat brim of his black hat a little lower over his eyes. Inside he felt sick and faint. His mouth was dry. His tongue trembled when it touched his lips. Up the street a man saw him and got slowly to his feet, staring as if hypnotized. The man backed away, then dove into the Hackamore Saloon.

Rock Casady took a deep breath, drew his shoulders back, and started slowly down the walk. He seemed in a trance where only the sun was warm and the air was still. Voices murmured. He heard a gasp of astonishment, for these people remembered that he had whipped Pete Vorys, and they knew what he had come for.

He wore two guns now, having dug the other gun and belt from his saddlebags to join the one he had only worn in the mountains. A door slammed somewhere.

Ben Kerr stared at the face of the man in the door of the saloon.

"Ben, here comes that yellow-backed Casady! And he's wearin' a gun!"

"He is, is he?" Kerr tossed off his drink. "Fill that up, Jim! I'll be right back. This will only take a minute!"

He stepped out into the street. "Come to get it this time?" he shouted tauntingly, "or are you runnin' again?"

Rock Casady made no reply. His footsteps echoed hollowly on the board walk, and he strode slowly, finishing his walk at the intersecting alley, stepping into the dust, then up on the walk again.

Ben Kerr's eyes narrowed slightly. Some sixth sense warned him that the man who faced him had subtly changed. He lifted his head a little, and stared, then he shrugged off the feeling and stepped out from the building.

"All right, Yella-Belly! If you want it!" His hand swept down in a flashing arc and his gun came up.

Rock Casady stared down the street at the face of Ben Kerr, and it was only the face of Kerr. In his ear was Jack's voice: "Go ahead, kid! Have at it!"

Kerr's gun roared and he felt the hot breath of it bite at his face. And then suddenly, Rock Casady laughed! Within him all was light and easy, and it was almost carelessly that he stepped forward. Suddenly the .44 began to roar and buck in his hand, leaping like a live thing within his grasp. Kerr's gun flew high in the air, his knees buckled, and he fell forward on his face in the dust.

Rock Casady turned quickly toward the Hackamore. Pete Vorys stood in the door, shocked to stillness.

"All right, Pete! Do you want it or are you leavin' town?"

Vorys stared from Kerr's riddled body to the man holding the gun.

"Why, I'm leavin' town!" Vorys said. "That's my roan, right there. I'll just . . ." As though stunned, he started to mount, and Rock's voice arrested him.

"No, Pete. You walk. You hoof it. And start now!"

The bully of Three Lakes wet his lips and stared, then his eyes shifted to the body in the street.

"Sure, Rock," he said, taking a step back. "I'll hoof it." Turning, stumbling a little, he started to walk. As he moved, his walk grew swifter and swifter as though something followed in his tracks.

Rock turned and looked up, and Sue Landon was standing on the boardwalk.

"Oh, Rock! You came back!"

"Don't reckon I ever really left, Sue," he said slowly.

"My heart's been right here, all the time!"

She caught his arm, and the smile in her eyes and on her lips was bright. He looked down at her.

Then he said aloud, "Thanks, Jack!"

She looked up quickly. "What did you say?"

He grinned at her. "Sue," he said, "did I ever tell you about my brother? He was one grand hombre! Someday, I'll tell you." They walked back toward the horses, her hand on his arm.

DUTCHMAN'S FLAT

The dust of Dutchman's Flat had settled in a gray film upon their faces, and Neill could see the streaks made by the sweat on their cheeks and brows and knew his own must be the same. No man of them was smiling and they rode with their rifles in their hands, six grim and purposeful men upon the trail of a single rider.

They were men shaped and tempered to the harsh ways of a harsh land, strong in their sense of justice, ruthless in their demand for punishment, relentless in pursuit. From the desert they had carved their homes, and from the desert they drew their courage and their code, and the desert knows no mercy.

"Where's he headin', you reckon?"

"Home, mostly likely. He'll need grub an' a rifle. He's been livin' on the old Sorenson place."

Kimmel spat. "He's welcome to it. That place starved out four men I know of." He stared at the hoof tracks ahead. "He's got a good horse."

"Big buckskin. Reckon we'll catch him, Hardin?"

"Sure. Not this side of his place, though. There ain't no short cuts we can take to head him off and he's pointin' for home straight as a horse can travel."

"Ain't tryin' to cover his trail none."

"No use tryin'." Hardin squinted his eyes against the glare of the sun. "He knows we figure he'll head for his ranch."

"He's no tenderfoot." Kesney expressed the thought that had been dawning upon them all in the last two hours. "He knows how to save a horse, an' he knows a trail."

They rode on in near silence. Hardin scratched his unshaven jaw. The dust lifted from the hoofs of the horses as they weaved their way through the cat-claw and mesquite. It was a parched and sunbaked land, with only dancing heat waves and the blue distance of the mountains to draw them on. The trail they followed led straight as a man could ride across the country. Only at draws or nests of rocks did it swerve, where they noticed the rider always gave his horse the best of it.

No rider of the desert must see a man to know him, for it is enough to follow his trail. In these things are the ways of a man made plain, his kindness or cruelty, his ignorance or cunning, his strength and his weakness. There are indications that cannot escape a man who has followed trails, and in the two hours since they had ridden out of Freedom the six had already learned much of the man they followed. And they would learn more.

"What started it?"

The words sounded empty and alone in the vast stillness of the basin.

Hardin turned his head slightly so the words could drift back. It was the manner of a man who rides much in the wind or rain. He shifted the rifle to his left hand and wiped his sweaty right palm on his coarse pants leg.

"Some loose talk. He was in the Bon Ton buyin' grub an' such. Johnny said somethin' at which he took offense and they had some words. Johnny was wearin' a gun, but this Lock wasn't, so he gets him a gun an' goes over to the Longhorn.

"He pushed open the door an' shoots Johnny twice through the body. In the back." Hardin spat. "He fired a third shot but that missed Johnny and busted a bottle of whisky."

There was a moment's silence while they digested this, and then Neill looked up.

"We lynchin' him for the killin' or bustin' the whisky?"

It was a good question, but drew no reply. The dignity of the five other riders was not to be touched by humor. They were riders on a mission. Neill let his eyes drift over the dusty copper of the desert. He had no liking for the idea of lynching any man, and he did not know the squatter from the Sorenson place. Living there should be punishment enough for any man. Besides—

"Who saw the shooting?" he asked.

"Nobody seen it, actually. Only he never gave Johnny a fair shake. Sam was behind the bar, but he was down to the other end and it happened too fast."

"What's his name? Somebody call him Lock?" Neill asked. There was something incongruous in lynching a man whose name you did not know. He shifted in the saddle, squinting his eyes toward the distant lakes dancing in the mirage of heat waves.

"What's it matter? Lock, his name is. Chat Lock."

"Funny name."

The comment drew no response. The dust was thicker now and Neill pulled his bandanna over his nose and mouth. His eyes were drawn back to the distant blue of the lakes. They were enticingly cool and beautiful, lying across the way ahead and in the basin off to the right. This was the mirage that lured many a man from his trail to pursue the always retreating shoreline of the lake. It looked like water, it really did.

Maybe there was water in the heat waves. Maybe if a man knew how he could extract it and drink. The thought drew his hand to his canteen, but he took it away without drinking. The slosh water in the canteen was no longer enticing, for it was warm, brackish, and unsatisfying.

"You know him, Kimmel?" Kesney asked. He was a wiry little man, hard as a whipstock, with bits of sharp steel for eyes and brown muscle-corded hands. "I wouldn't know him if I saw him."

"Sure, I know him. Big feller, strong made, rusty-like hair an' maybe forty year old. Looks plumb salty, too, an' from what I hear he's no friendly sort of man. Squattin' on that Sorenson place looks plumb suspicious, for no man came make him a livin' on that dry-as-a-bone place. No fit place for man nor beast. Ever'body figures no honest man would squat on such a place."

It seemed a strange thing, to be searching out a man whom none of them knew. Of course, they had all known Johnny Webb. He was a handsome, popular young man, a daredevil and a hellion, but a very attractive one, and a top hand to boot. They had all known him and had all liked him. Then, one of the things that made them so sure that this had been a wrong killing, even aside from the shots in the back, was the fact that Johnny Webb had been the fastest man in the Spring Valley country. Fast, and a dead shot.

Johnny had worked with all these men, and they were good men, hard men, but good. Kimmel, Hardin and Kesney had all made something of their ranches, as had the others, only somewhat less so. They had come West when the going was rough, fought Indians and rustlers, then battled drought, dust and hot, hard winds. It took a strong man to survive in this country, and they had survived. He, Neill, was the youngest of them all, and the newest in the country. He was still looked upon with some reserve. He had been here only five years.

Neill could see the tracks of the buckskin and it gave him a strange feeling to realize that the man who rode that horse would soon be dead, hanging from a noose in one of those ropes attached to a saddle horn of Hardin or Kimmel. Neill had never killed a man, nor seen one killed by another man, and the thought made him uncomfortable.

Yet Johnny was gone, and his laughter and his jokes were a thing passed. They had brightened more than one roundup, more than one bitter day of heart-breaking labor on the range.

Not that he had been an angel. He had been a proper hand with a gun, and could throw one. And in his time he had had his troubles.

"He's walkin' his horse," Kesney said, "leadin' him."

"He's a heavy man," Hardin agreed, "an' he figures to give us a long chase."

"Gone lame on him maybe," Kimmel suggested.

"No, that horse isn't limpin'. This Lock is a smart one."

They had walked out of the ankledeep dust now and were crossing a parched, dry plain of crusted earth. Hardin reined in suddenly and pointed.

"Look there." He indicated a couple of flecks on the face of the earth crust where something had spilled. "Water splashed."

"Careless," Neill said. "He'll need that water."

"No," Kesney said. "He was pourin' water in a cloth to wipe out his horse's nostrils. Bet you a dollar."

"Sure," Hardin agreed, "that's it. Horse breathes a lot better. A man runnin' could kill a good horse on this Flat. He knows that."

They rode on, and for almost a half hour, no one spoke. Neill frowned at the sun. It had been on his left a few minutes ago, and now they rode straight into it.

"What's he doin'?" Kesney said wonderingly. "This ain't the way to his place!" The trail had turned again, and now the sun was on their right. Then it turned again, and was at their backs. Hardin was in the lead and he drew up and swore wickedly.

They ranged alongside him, and stared down into a draw that cracked the face of the desert alongside the trail they had followed. Below them was a place where a horse had stood, and across the bank something white fluttered from the parched clump of greasewood.

Kesney slid from the saddle and crossed the wash. When he had the slip of white, he stared at it, and then they heard him swear. He walked back and handed it to Hardin. They crowded near.

Neill took the slip from Hardin's fingers after he had read it. It was torn from some sort of book and the words were plain enough, scrawled with a flat rock for a rest.

That was a fair shutin anyways six aint nowhars enuf, go fetch more men. Man on the gray better titen his girth or heel have him a sorebacked hoss.

"Why, that . . . !" Short swore softly. "He was lyin' within fifty yards of us when he come by. Had him a rifle, too, I see it in a saddle scabbard on that buckskin in town. He could have got one of us, anyway!"

"Two or three most likely," Kimmel commented. The men stared at the paper then looked back into the wash. The sand showed a trail, but cattle had walked here, too. It would make the going a little slower.

Neill, his face flushed and his ears red, was tightening his saddle girth. The others avoided his eyes. The insult to him, even if the advice was good, was an insult to them all. Their jaws tightened. The squatter was playing Indian with them, and none of them liked it.

"Fair shootin', yeah!" Sutter exploded. "Right in the back!"

The trail led down the wash now, and it was slower going. The occasional puffs of wind they had left on the desert above were gone and the heat in the bottom of the wash was ovenlike. They rode into it, almost seeming to push their way through flames that seared. Sweat dripped into their eyes until they smarted, and trickled in tiny rivulets through their dust-caked beards, making their faces itch maddeningly.

The wash spilled out into a wide, flat bed of sand left by the rains of bygone years, and the tracks were plainer now. Neill tightened his bandanna and rode on, sodden with heat and weariness. The trail seemed deliberately to lead them into the worst regions, for now he was riding straight toward an alkali lake that loomed ahead.

At the edge of the water, the trail vanished. Lock had ridden right into the lake. They drew up and stared at it, unbelieving.

"He can't cross," Hardin stated flatly. "That's deep out to the middle. Durned treacherous, too. A horse could get bogged down mighty easy."

They skirted the lake, taking it carefully, three going one way, and three the other. Finally, glancing back, Neill caught sight of Kesney's uplifted arm.

"They found it," he said, "let's go back." Yet as he rode he was thinking what they all knew. This was a delay, for Lock knew they would have to scout the shores both ways to find his trail, and there would be a delay while the last three rejoined the first. A small thing, but in such a chase it was important.

"Why not ride right on to the ranch?" Short suggested.

"We might," Hardin speculated. "On the other hand he might fool us an' never go nigh it. Then we could lose him."

The trail became easier, for now Lock was heading straight into the mountains.

"Where's he goin'?" Kesney demanded irritably. "This don't make sense, nohow!"

There was no reply, the horsemen stretching out in single file, riding up the draw into the mountains. Suddenly Kimmel, who was now in the lead, drew up. Before him a thread of water trickled from the rock and spilled into a basin of stones.

"Huh!" Hardin stared. "I never knowed about this spring afore. Might's well have a drink." He swung down.

They all got down and Neill rolled a smoke.

"Somebody sure fixed her up nice," he said. "That wall of stone makin' that basin ain't so old."

"No, it ain't."

Short watched them drink and grinned.

"He's a fox, right enough. He's an old ladino, this one. A reg'lar mossy horn. It don't take no time for one man to drink, an' one hoss. But here we got six men an' six horses to drink an' we lose more time."

"You think he really planned it that way?" Neill was skeptical.

Hardin looked around at him. "Sure. This Lock knows his way around."

When they were riding on, Neill thought about that. Lock was shrewd. He was desert wise. And he was leading them a chase. If not even Hardin knew of this spring, and he had been twenty years in the Spring Valley country, then Lock must know a good deal about the country. Of course, this range of mountains was singularly desolate, and there was nothing in them to draw a man.

So they knew this about their quarry. He was a man wise in the ways of desert and trail, and one who knew the country. Also, Neill reflected, it was probable he had built that basin himself. Nobody lived over this way but Lock, for now it was not far to the Sorenson place.

Now they climbed a single horse trail across the starkly eroded foothills, sprinkled with clumps of Joshua and Spanish bayonet. It was a weird and broken land, where long fingers of black lava stretched down the hills and out into the desert as though clawing toward the alkali lake they had left behind. The trail mounted steadily and a little breeze touched their cheeks. Neill lifted his hand and wiped dust from his brow and it came away in flakes, plastered by sweat.

The trail doubled and changed, now across the rock face of the burnt red sandstone, then into the lava itself, skirting hills where the exposed ledges mounted in layers like a vast cake of many colors. Then the way dipped down, and they wound among huge boulders, smooth as so many water-worn pebbles. Neill sagged in the saddle, for the hours were growing long, and the trail showed no sign of ending.

"Lucky he ain't waitin' to shoot," Kimmel commented, voicing the first remark in over an hour. "He could pick us off like flies."

As if in reply to his comment, there was an angry whine above them, and then the crack of a rifle.

As one man they scattered for shelter, whipping rifles from their scabbards, for all but two had replaced them when they reached the lake. Hardin swore, and Kimmel wormed his way to a better view of the country ahead.

Short had left the saddle in his scramble for shelter, and his horse stood in the open, the canteen making a large lump behind the saddle. Suddenly the horse leaped to solid thud of a striking bullet, and then followed the crack of the rifle, echoing over the mountainside.

Short swore viciously. "If he killed that horse . . . !" But the horse, while shifting nervously, seemed uninjured.

"Hey!" Kesney yelled. "He shot your canteen!"

It was true enough. Water was pouring onto the ground, and swearing, Short started to get up. Sutter grabbed his arm.

"Hold it! If he could get that canteen, he could get you!"

They waited, and the trickle of water slowed, then faded to a drip. All of them stared angrily at the unrewarding rocks ahead of them. One canteen the less. Still they had all filled up at the spring and should have enough. Uncomfortably, however, they realized that the object of their chase, the man called Chat Lock, knew where he was taking them, and he had not emptied that canteen by chance. Now they understood the nature of the man they followed. He did nothing without object.

Lying on the sand or rocks they waited, peering ahead.

"He's probably ridin' off now!" Sutter braked.

Nobody showed any disposition to move. The idea appealed to none of them, for the shot into the canteen showed plainly enough the man they followed was no child with a rifle. Kimmel finally put his hat on a rifle muzzle and lifted it. There was no response. Then he tried sticking it around a corner.

Nothing happened, and he withdrew it. Almost at once, a shot hit the trail not far from where the hat had been. The indication was plain. Lock was warning them not only that he was still there, but that he was not to be fooled by so obvious a trick.

They waited, and Hardin suddenly slid over a rock and began a flanking movement. He crawled, and they waited, watching his progress. The cover he had was good, and he could crawl almost to where the hidden marksman must be. Finally, he disappeared from their sight and they waited. Neill tasted the water in his canteen, and dozed.

At last they heard a long yell, and looking up, they saw Hardin standing on a rock far up the trail, waving them on. Mounting, they led Hardin's horse and rode on up the trail. He met them at the trail side, and his eyes were angry.

"Gone!" he said, thrusting out a hard palm. In it lay three brass cartridge shells. "Found 'em standing up in a line on a rock. An' look here." He pointed, and they stared down at the trail where he indicated. A neat arrow made of stones pointed down the trail ahead of them, and scratched on the face of the sand stone above it were the words: FOLLER THE SIGNS.

Kesney jerked his hat from his head and hurled it to the ground.

"Why, that dirty . . . !" He stopped, beside himself with anger. The contempt of the man they pursued was obvious. He was making fools of them, deliberately teasing them, indicating his trail as to a child or a tenderfoot.

"That ratty back-shootin' killer!" Short said. "I'll take pleasure in usin' a rope on him! Thinks he's smart!"

They started on, and the horse ahead of them left a plain trail, but a quarter of a mile further along, three dried pieces of mesquite had been laid in the trail to form another arrow.

Neill stared at it. This was becoming a personal matter now. He was deliberately playing with them, and he must know how that would set with men such as Kimmel and Hardin. It was a deliberate challenge, more, it was a sign of the utmost contempt.

The vast emptiness of the basin they skirted now was becoming lost in the misty purple light of late afternoon. On the right, the wall of the mountain grew steeper and turned a deeper red. The burnt red of the earlier hours was now a bright rust red, and here and there long fingers of quartz shot their white arrows down into the face of the cliff.

They all saw the next message, but all read and averted their eyes. It was written on a blank face of the cliff. First, there was an arrow, pointing ahead, and then the words, SHADE, SO'S YOU DON'T GET SUNSTROK.

They rode on, and for several miles as the shadows drew down, they followed the markers their quarry left at intervals along the trail. All six of the men were tired and beaten. Their horses moved slowly, and the desert air was growing chill. It had been a long chase.

Suddenly, Kimmel and Kesney, who rode side by side, reined in. A small wall or rock was across the trail, and an arrow pointed downward into a deep cleft.

"What do you think, Hardin? He could pick us off man by man."

Hardin studied the situation with misgivings, and hesitated, lighting a smoke.

"He ain't done it yet."

Neill's remark fell into the still air like a rock into a calm pool of water. As the rings of ripples spread wider into the thoughts of the other five, he waited.

Lock could have killed one or two of them, perhaps all of them by now. Why had he not? Was he waiting for darkness and an easy getaway? Or was he leading them into a trap?

"The devil with it!" Hardin exclaimed impatiently. He wheeled his horse and pistol in hand, started down into the narrow rift in the dark. One by one, they followed. The darkness closed around them, and the air was damp and chill. They rode on, and then the trail mounted steeply toward a grayness ahead of them, and they came out in a small basin. Ahead of them they heard a trickle of running water and saw the darkness of trees.

Cautiously they approached. Suddenly, they saw the light of a fire. Hardin drew up sharply and slid from his horse. The others followed. In a widening circle, they crept toward the fire. Kesney was the first to reach it, and the sound of his swearing rent the stillness and shattered it like thin glass. They swarmed in around him.

The fire was built close and beside a small running stream, and nearby was a neat pile of dry sticks. On a paper, laid out carefully on a rock, was a small mound of coffee, and another of sugar. Nobody said anything for a minute, staring at the fire and the coffee. The taunt was obvious, and they were bitter men. It was bad enough to have a stranger make such fools of them on a trail, to treat them like tenderfeet, but to prepare a camp for them. . . .

"I'll be cussed if I will!" Short said violently. "I'll go sleep on the desert first!"

"Well—" Hardin was philosophical. "Might's well make the most of it. We can't trail him at night, no way."

Kimmel had dug a coffee pot out of his pack and was getting water from the stream which flowed from a basin just above their camp. Several of the others began to dig out grub, and Kesney sat down glumly, staring into the fire. He started to pick a stick of the pile left for them, then jerked his hand as though he had seen a snake and getting up, he stalked back into the trees, and after a minute, he returned.

Sutter was looking around, and suddenly he spoke. "Boys, I know this place! Only I never knew about that crack in the wall. This here's the Mormon Well!"

Hardin sat up and looked around. "Durned if it ain't," he said. "I ain't been in here for six or seven years."

Sutter squatted on his haunches. "Look!" He was excited and eager. "Here's Mormon Well, where we are. Right over here to the northwest there's an old saw mill an' a tank just above it. I'll bet a side of beef that durned killer is holed up for the night in that sawmill!"

Kesney, who had taken most to heart the taunting of the man they pursued, was on his knees staring at the diagram drawn in the damp sand. He was nodding thoughtfully.

"He's right! He sure is. I remembered that old mill! I holed up there one time in a bad storm. Spent two days in it. If that sidewinder stays there tonight, we can get him!"

As they ate, they talked over their plan. Travelling over the rugged mountains ahead of them was almost impossible in the darkness, and besides, even if Lock could go the night without stopping, his horse could not. The buckskin must have rest. Moreover, with all the time Lock had been losing along the trail, he could not be far ahead. It stood to reason that he must have planned just this, for them to stop here, and to hole up in the sawmill himself.

"We'd better surprise him," Hardin suggested. "That sawmill is heavy timber an' a man in there with a rifle an' plenty of ammunition could stand us off for a week."

"Has he got plenty?"

"Sure he has," Neill told them. "I was in the Bon Ton when he bought his stuff. He's got grub and he's got plenty of .44's. They do for either his Colt or his Winchester."

Unspoken as yet, but present in the mind of each man, was a growing respect for their quarry, a respect and an element of doubt. Would such a man as this shoot another in the back? The evidence against him was plain enough, or seemed plain enough.

Yet beyond the respect there was something else, for it was no longer simply a matter of justice to be done, but a personal thing. Each of them felt in some measure that his reputation was at stake. It had not been enough for Lock to leave an obvious trail, but he must leave markers, the sort to be used for any tenderfoot. There were men in this group who could trail a woodtick through a pine forest.

"Well," Kimmel said reluctantly, and somewhat grimly, "he left us good coffee, anyway!"

They tried the coffee, and agreed. Few things in this world are so comforting and so warming to the heart as hot coffee on a chilly night over a campfire when the day has been long and weary. They drank, and they relaxed. And as they relaxed, the seeds of doubt began to sprout and put forth branches of speculation.

"He could have got more'n one of us today," Sutter hazarded. "This one is brush wise."

"I'll pull that rope on him!" Short stated positively. "No man makes a fool out of me!" But in his voice there was something lacking.

"You know," Kesney suggested, "if he knows these hills like he seems to, an' if he really wanted to lose us, we'd have to burn the stump and sift the ashes before we found him!"

There was no reply. Hardin drew back and eased the leg of his pants away from the skin, for the cloth had grown too hot for comfort.

Short tossed a stick from the neat pile into the fire.

"That mill ain't so far away," he suggested, "shall we give her a try?"

"Later." Hardin leaned back against a log and yawned. "She's been a hard day."

"Both them bullets go in Johnny's back?"

The question moved among them like a ghost. Short stirred uneasily, and Kesney looked up and glared around. "Sure they did! Didn't they, Hardin?"

"Sure." He paused thoughtfully. "Well, no. One of them was under his left arm. Right between the ribs. Looked like a heart shot to me. The other one went through near his spine."

"The heck with it!" Kesney declared. "No slick, rustlin' squatter can come into this country and shoot one of our boys! He was shot in the back, an' I seen both holes. Johnny got that one nigh the spine, an' he must have turned and tried to draw, then got that bullet through the heart!"

Nobody had seen it. Neill remembered that, and the thought rankled. Were they doing an injustice? He felt like a traitor at the thought, but secretly he had acquired a strong tinge of respect for the man they followed.

The fire flickered and the shadows danced a slow, rhythmic quadrille against the dark background of trees. He peeled bark from the log beside him and fed it into the fire. It caught, sparked brightly, and popped once or twice. Hardin leaned over and pushed the coffee pot nearer the coals. Kesney checked the loads in his Winchester.

"How far to that saw mill, Hardin?"

"About six miles, the way we go."

"Let's get started." Short got to his feet and brushed off the sand. "I want to get home. Got my boys buildin' fence. You either keep a close watch or they are off gal hootin' over the hills."

They tightened their saddle girths, doused the fire, and mounted up. With Hardin in the lead once more, they moved off into the darkness.

Neill brought up the rear. It was damp and chill among the cliffs, and felt like the inside of a cavern. Overhead the stars were very bright. Mary was going to be worried, for he was never home so late. Nor did he like leaving her alone. He wanted to be home, eating a warm supper and going to bed in the old four poster with the patchwork quilt Mary's grandmother made, pulled over him. What enthusiasm he had had for the chase was gone. The warm fire, the coffee, his own weariness, and the growing respect for Lock had changed him.

Now they all knew he was not the manner of man they had supposed. Justice can be a harsh taskmaster, but Western men know their kind, and the lines were strongly drawn. When you have slept beside a man on the trail, worked with him, and with others like him, you come to know your kind. In the trail of the man Chat Lock, each rider of the posse was seeing the sort of man he knew, the sort he could respect. The thought was nagging and unsubstantial, but each of them felt a growing doubt, even Short and Kesney who were most obdurate and resentful.

They knew how a backshooter lived and worked. He had his brand on everything he did. The mark of this man was the mark of a man who did things, who stood upon his own two feet, and who if he died, died facing his enemy. To the unknowing, such conclusions might seem doubtful, but the men of the desert knew their kind.

The mill was dark and silent, a great looming bulk beside the stream and the still pool of the mill pond. They dismounted and eased close. Then according to a prearranged plan, they scattered and surrounded it. From behind a lodgepole pine, Hardin called out.

"We're comin' in, Lock! We want you!"

The challenge was harsh and ringing. Now that the moment had come something of the old suspense returned. They listened to the water babbling as it trickled over the old dam, and then they moved. At their first step, they heard Lock's voice.

"Don't come in here, boys! I don't want to kill none of you, but you come an' I will! That was a fair shootin'! You've got no call to come after me!"

Hardin hesitated, chewing his mustache. "You shot him in the back!" he yelled.

"No such thing! He was a-facin' the bar when I come in. He seen I was heeled, an' he drawed as he turned. I beat him to it. My first shot took him in the side an' he was knocked back against the bar. My second hit him in the back an' the third missed as he was a fallin'. You hombres didn't see that right."

The sound of his voice trailed off and the water chuckled over the stones, then sighed to a murmur among the trees. The logic of Locke's statement struck them all. It could have been that way.

A long moment passed, and then Hardin spoke up again.

"You come in an' we'll give you a trial. Fair an' square!"

"How?" Lock's voice was a challenge. "You ain't got no witness. Neither have I. Ain't nobody to say what happened there but me, as Johnny ain't alive."

"Johnny was a mighty good man, an' he was our friend!" Short shouted. "No murderin' squatter is goin' to move into this country an' start shootin' folks up!"

There was no reply to that, and they waited, hesitating a little. Neill leaned disconsolately against the tree where he stood. After all, Lock might be telling the truth. How did they know? There was no use hanging a man unless you were sure.

"Gab!" Short's comment was explosive. "Let's move in, Hardin! Let's get him! He's lyin'! Nobody could beat Johnny, we know that!"

"Webb was a good man in his own country!" Lock shouted in reply. The momentary silence that followed held them, and then, almost as a man they began moving in. Neill did not know exactly when or why he started. Inside he felt sick and empty. He was fed up on the whole business and every instinct he had told him this man was no backshooter.

Carefully, they moved, for they knew this man was handy with a gun. Suddenly, Hardin's voice rang out.

"Hold it, men! Stay where you are until daybreak! Keep your eyes open an' your ears. If he gets out of here he'll be lucky, an' in the daylight we can get him, or fire the mill!"

Neill sank to a sitting position behind a log. Relief was a great warmth that swept over him. There wouldn't be any killing tonight. Not tonight, at least.

Yet as the hours passed, his ears grew more and more attuned to the darkness. A rabbit rustled, a pine cone dropped from a tree, the wind stirred high in the pine tops and the few stars winked through, lonesomely peering down upon the silent men.

With daylight they moved in and they went through the doors and up to the windows of the old mill, and it was empty and still. They stared at each other, and Short swore viciously, the sound booming in the echoing, empty room.

"Let's go down to the Sorenson place," Kimmel said. "He'll be there."

And somehow they were all very sure he would be. They knew he would be because they knew him for their kind of man. He would retreat no further than his own ranch, his own hearth. There, if they were to have him and hang him, they would have to burn him out, and men would die in the process. Yet with these men there was no fear. They felt the drive of duty, the need for maintaining some law in this lonely desert and mountain land. There was only doubt which had grown until each man was shaken with it. Even Short, whom the markers by the trail had angered, and Kesney, who was the best tracker among them, even better than Hardin, and had been irritated by it, too.

The sun was up and warming them when they rode over the brow of the hill and had looked down into the parched basin where the Sorenson place lay.

But it was no parched basin. Hardin drew up so suddenly his startled horse almost reared. It was no longer the Sorenson place.

The house had been patched and rebuilt. The roof had spots of new lumber upon it, and the old pole barn had been made water tight and strong. A new corral had been built, and to the right of the house was a fenced in garden of vegetables, green and pretty after the desert of the day before.

Thoughtfully, and in a tight cavalcade, they rode down the hill. The stock they saw was fat and healthy, and the corral was filled with horses.

"Been a lot of work done here," Kimmel said. And he knew how much work it took to make such a place attractive.

"Don't look like no killer's place!" Neill burst out. Then he flushed and drew back, embarrassed by his statement. He was the youngest of these men, and the newest in the country.

No response was forthcoming. He had but stated what they all believed. There was something stable, lasting, something real and genuine in this place.

"I been waitin' for you."

The remark from behind them stiffened every spine. Chat Lock was here, behind them. And he would have a gun on them, and if one of them moved, he could die.

"My wife's down there fixin' breakfast. I told her I had some friends comin' in. A posse huntin' a killer. I've told her nothin' about this trouble. You ride down there now, you keep your guns. You eat your breakfast and then if you feel bound and determined to get somebody for a fair shootin', I'll come out with anyone of you or all of you, but I ain't goin' to hang.

"I ain't namin' no one man because I don't want to force no fight on anybody. You ride down there now."

They rode, and in the dooryard, they dismounted. Neill turned them, and for the first time he saw Chat Lock.

He was a big man, compact and strong. His rusty brown hair topped a brown, sun-hardened face but with the warmth in his eyes it was friendly sort of face. Not at all what he expected.

Hardin looked at him. "You made some changes here."

"I reckon." Lock gestured toward the well. "Dug by hand. My wife worked the windlass." He looked around at them, taking them in with one sweep of his eyes. "I've got the grandest woman in the world."

Neill felt hot tears in his eyes suddenly, and busied himself loosening his saddle girth to keep the others from seeing. That was the way he felt about Mary.

The door opened suddenly, and they turned. The sight of a woman in this desert country was enough to make any man turn. What they saw was not what they expected. She was young, perhaps in her middle twenties, and she was pretty, with brown wavy hair and gray eyes and a few freckles on her nose. "Won't you come in? Chat told me he had some friends coming for breakfast, and it isn't often we have anybody in."

Heavy footed and shamefaced they walked up on the porch. Kesney saw the care and neatness with which the hard hewn planks had been fitted. Here, too, was the same evidence of lasting, of permanence, of strength. This was the sort of man a country needed. He thought the thought before he fixed his attention to it, and then he flushed.

Inside, the room was as neat as the girl herself. How did she get the floors so clean? Before he thought, he phrased the question. She smiled.

"Oh, that was Chat's idea! He made a frame and fastened a piece of pumice stone to a stick. It cuts into all the cracks and keeps them very clean."

The food smelled good, and when Hardin looked at his hands, Chat motioned to the door.

"There's water an' towels if you want to wash up."

Neill rolled up his sleeves and dipped his hands in the basin. The water was soft, and that was rare in this country, and the soap felt good on his hands. When he had dried his hands, he walked in. Hardin and Kesney had already seated themselves and Lock's wife was pouring coffee.

"Men," Lock said, "this is Mary. You'll have to tell her your names. I reckon I missed them."

Mary. Neill looked up. She was Mary, too. He looked down at his plate again and ate a few bites. When he looked up, she was smiling at him.

"My wife's name is Mary," he said, "she's a fine girl!"

"She would be! But why don't you bring her over? I haven't talked with a woman in so long I wouldn't know how it seemed! Chat, why haven't you invited them over?"

Chat mumbled something, and Neill stared at his coffee. The men ate in uncomfortable silence. Hardin's eyes kept shifting around the room. That pumice stone. He'd have to fix up a deal like that for Jane. She was always fussing about the work of keeping a board floor clean. That wash stand inside, too, with pipes made of hollow logs to carry the water out so she wouldn't have to be running back and forth. That was an idea, too.

They finished their meal reluctantly. One by one they trooped outside, avoiding each other's eyes. Chat Lock did not keep them waiting. He walked down among them.

"If there's to be shootin'," he said quietly, "let's get away from the house."

Hardin looked up. "Lock, was that right, what you said in the mill, was it a fair shootin'?"

Lock nodded. "It was. Johnny Webb prodded me. I didn't want trouble, nor did I want to hide behind the fact I wasn't packin' an iron. I walked over to the saloon not aimin' for trouble. I aimed to give him a chance if he wanted it. He drawed an' I beat him. It was a fair shootin'."

"All right." Hardin nodded. "That's good enough for me. I reckon you're a different sort of man than any of us figured."

"Let's mount up," Short said, "I got fence to build."

Chat Lock put his hand on Hardin's saddle. "You folks come over some time. She gets right lonesome. I don't mind it so much, but you know how women folks are."

"Sure," Hardin said, "sure thing."

"An' you bring your Mary over," he told Neill.

Neill nodded, his throat full. As they mounted the hill, he glanced back. Mary Lock was standing in the door way, waving to them, and the sunlight was very bright in the clean swept door yard.

TRAP OF GOLD

Wetherton had been three months out of Horsehead before he found his first color. At first it was a few scattered grains taken from the base of an alluvial fan where millions of tons of sand and silt had washed down from a chain of rugged peaks; yet the gold was ragged under the magnifying glass.

Gold that has carried any distance becomes worn and polished by the abrasive action of the accompanying rocks and sand, so this could not have been carried far. With caution born of harsh experience he seated himself and lighted his pipe, yet excitement was strong within him.

A contemplative man by nature, experience had taught him how a man may be deluded by hope, yet all his instincts told him the source of the gold was somewhere on the mountain above. It could have come down the wash that skirted the base of the mountain, but the ragged condition of the gold made that improbable.

The base of the fan was a half-mile across and hundreds of feet thick, built of silt and sand washed down by centuries of erosion among the higher peaks. The point of the wide V of the fan lay between two towering upthrusts of granite, but from where Wetherton sat he could see that the actual source of the fan lay much higher.

Wetherton made camp near a tiny spring west of the fan, then picketed his burros and began his climb. When he was well over two thousand feet higher he stopped, resting again, and while resting he dry-panned some of the silt. Surprisingly, there were more than a few grains of gold even in that first pan, so he continued his climb, and passed at last between the towering portals of the granite columns.

Above this natural gate were three smaller alluvial fans that joined at the gate to pour into the greater fan below. Dry-panning two of these brought no results, but the third, even by the relatively poor method of dry-panning, showed a dozen colors, all of good size.

The head of this fan lay in a gigantic crack in a granite upthrust that resembled a fantastic ruin. Pausing to catch his breath, his gaze wandered along the base of this upthrust, and right before him the crumbling granite was slashed with a vein of quartz that was liberally laced with gold!

Struggling nearer through the loose sand, his heart pounding more from excitement than from altitude and exertion, he came to an abrupt stop. The band of quartz was six feet wide and that six feet was cobwebbed with gold.

It was unbelievable, but here it was.

Yet even in this moment of success, something about the beetling cliff stopped him from going forward. His innate caution took hold and he drew back to examine it at greater length. Wary of what he saw, he circled the batholith and then climbed to the ridge behind it from which he could look down upon the roof. What he saw from there left him dry-mouth and jittery.

The grantic batholith was obviously a part of a much older range, one that had weathered and worn, suffered from shock and twisting until finally this tower of granite had been violently upthrust, leaving it standing, a shaky ruin among younger and sturdier peaks. In the process the rock had been shattered and riven by mighty forces until it had become a miner's horror.

Wetherton stared, fascinated by the prospect. With enormous wealth here for the taking, every ounce must be taken at the risk of life.

One stick of powder might bring the whole crumbling mass down in a heap, and it loomed all of three hundred feet above its base in the fan. The roof of the batholith was riven with gigantic cracks, literally seamed with breaks like the wall of an ancient building that has remained standing after heavy bombing. Walking back to the base of the tower. Wetherton found he could actually break loose chunks of the quartz with his fingers.

The vein itself lay on the downhill side and at the very base. The outer wall of the upthrust was sharply tilted so that a man working at the vein would be cutting his way into the very foundations of the tower, and any single blow of the pick might bring the whole mass down upon him. Furthermore, if the rock did fall, the vein would be hopelessly buried under thousands of tons of rock and lost without the expenditure of much more capital than he could command. And at this moment Wetherton's total of money in hand amounted to slightly less than forty dollars.

Thirty yards from the face he seated himself upon the sand and filled his pipe once more. A man might take tons out of there without trouble, and yet it might collapse at the first blow. Yet he knew he had no choice. He needed money and it lay here before him. Even if he were at first successful there were two things he must avoid. The first was tolerance of danger that might bring carelessness; the second, that urge to go back for that 'little bit more' that could kill him.

It was well into the afternoon and he had not eaten, yet he was not hungry. He circled the batholith, studying it from every angle only to reach the conclusion that his first estimate had been correct. The only way to get to the gold was to go into the very shadow of the leaning wall and attack it at its base, digging it out by main strength. From where he stood it seemed ridiculous that a mere man with a pick could topple that mass of rock, yet he knew how delicate such a balance could be.

The batholith was situated on what might be described as the military crest of the ridge, and the alluvial fan sloped steeply away from its lower side, steeper than a steep stairway. The top of the leaning wall over-shadowed the top of the fan, and if it started to crumble and a man had warning, he might run to the north with a bare chance of escape. The soft sand in which he must run would be an impediment, but that could be alleviated by making a walk from flat rocks sunken into the sand.

It was dark when he returned to his camp. Deliberately, he had not permitted himself to begin work, not by so much as a sample. He must be deliberate in all his actions, and never for a second should he forget the mass that towered above him. A split second of hesitation when the crash came—and he accepted it as inevitable—would mean burial under tons of crumbled rock.

The following morning he picketed his burros on a small meadow near the spring, cleaned the spring itself and prepared a lunch. Then he removed his shirt, drew on a pair of gloves and walked to the face of the cliff. Yet even then he did not begin, knowing that upon this habit of care and deliberation might depend not only his success in the venture, but life itself. He gathered flat stones and began building his walk. "When you start moving," he told himself, "you'll have to be fast."

Finally, and with infinite care, he began tapping at the quartz, enlarging cracks with the pick, removing fragments, then prying loose whole chunks. He did not swing the pick, but used it as a lever. The quartz was rotten, and a man might obtain a considerable amount by this method of picking or even pulling with the hands. When he had a sack filled with the richest quartz he carried it over his path to a safe place beyond the shadow of the tower. Returning, he tamped a few more flat rocks into his path, and began on the second sack. He worked with greater care than was, perhaps, essential. He was not and had never been a gambling man.

In the present operation he was taking a carefully calculated risk in which every eventuality had been weighed and judged. He needed the money and he intended to have it; he had a good idea of his chances of success, but knew that his gravest danger was to become too greedy, too much engrossed in his task.

Dragging the two sacks down the hill, he found a flat block of stone and with a single jack proceeded to break up the quartz. It was a slow and a hard job but he had no better means of extracting the gold. After breaking or crushing the quartz much of the gold could be separated by a knife blade, for it was amazingly concentrated. With water from the spring Wetherton panned the remainder until it was too dark to see.

Out of his blankets by daybreak he ate breakfast and completed the extraction of the gold. At a rough estimate his first day's work would run to four hundred dollars. He made a cache for the gold sack and took the now empty ore sacks and climbed back to the tower.

The air was clear and fresh, the sun warm after the chill of night, and he liked the feel of the pick in his hands.

Laura and Tommy awaited him back in Horse-head, and if he was killed here, there was small chance they would ever know what had become of him. But he did not intend to be killed. The gold he was extracting from this rock was for them, and not for himself.

It would mean an easier life in a larger town, a home of their own and the things to make the home a woman desires, and it meant an education for Tommy. For himself, all he needed was the thought of that home to return to, his wife and son—and the desert itself. And one was as necessary to him as the other.

The desert could be the death of him. He had been told that many times, and did not need to be told, for few men knew the desert as he did. The desert was to him what an orchestra is to a fine conductor, what the human body is to a surgeon. It was his work, his life, and the thing he knew best. He always smiled when he looked first into the desert as he started a new trip. Would this be it?

The morning drew on and he continued to work with an even-paced swing of the pick, a careful filling of the sack. The gold showed bright and beautiful in the crystalline quartz which was so much more beautiful than the gold itself. From time to time as the morning drew on, he paused to rest and to breathe deeply of the fresh, clear air. Deliberately, he refused to hurry.

For nineteen days he worked tirelessly, eight hours at day at first, then lessening his hours to seven, and then to six. Wetherton did not explain to himself why he did this, but he realized it was becoming increasingly difficult to stay on the job. Again and again he would walk away from the rock face on one excuse or another, and each time he would begin to feel his scalp prickle, his steps grow quicker, and each time he returned more reluctantly.

Three times, beginning on the thirteenth, again on the seventeenth and finally on the nineteenth day, he heard movement within the tower. Whether that whispering in the rock was normal he did not know. Such a natural movement might have been going on for centuries. He only knew that it happened now, and each time it happened a cold chill went along his spine.

His work had cut a deep notch at the base of the tower, such a notch as a man might make in felling a tree, but wider and deeper. The sacks of gold, too, were increasing. They now numbered seven, and their total would, he believed, amount to more than five thousand dollars—probably nearer to six thousand. As he cut deeper into the rock the vein was growing richer.

He worked on his knees now. The vein had slanted downward as he cut into the base of the tower and he was all of nine feet into the rock with the great mass of it above him. If that rock gave way while he was working he would be crushed in an instant with no chance of escape. Nevertheless, he continued.

The change in the rock tower was not the only change, for he had lost weight and he no longer slept well. On the night of the twentieth day he decided he had six thousand dollars and his goal would be ten thousand. And the following day the rock was the richest ever! As if to tantalize him into working on and on, the deeper he cut the richer the ore became. By nightfall of that day he had taken out more than a thousand dollars.

Now the lust of the gold was getting into him, taking him by the throat. He was fascinated by the danger of the tower as well as the desire for the gold. Three more days to go—could he leave it then? He looked again at the batholith and felt a peculiar sense of foreboding, a feeling that here he was to die, that he would never escape. Was it his imagination, or had the outer wall leaned a little more?

On the morning of the-twenty-second day he climbed the fan over a path that use had built into a series of continuous steps. He had never counted those steps but there must have been over a thousand of them. Dropping his canteen into a shaded hollow and pick in hand, he started for the tower.

The forward tilt did seem somewhat more than before. Or was it the light? The crack that ran behind the outer wall seemed to have widened and when he examined it more closely he found a small pile of freshly run silt near the bottom of the crack. So it had moved!

Wetherton hesitated, staring at the rock with wary attention. He was a fool to go back in there again. Seven thousand dollars was more than he had ever had in his life before, yet in the next few hours he could take out at least a thousand dollars more and in the next three days he could easily have the ten thousand he had set for his goal.

He walked to the opening, dropped to his knees and crawled into the narrowing, flat-roofed hole. No sooner was he inside than fear climbed up into his throat. He felt trapped, stifled, but he fought down the mounting panic and began to work. His first blows were so frightened and feeble that nothing came loose. Yet, when he did get started, he began to work with a feverish intensity that was wholly unlike him.

When he slowed and then stopped to fill his sack he was gasping for breath, but despite his hurry the sack was not quite full. Reluctantly, he lifted his pick again, but before he could strike a blow, the gigantic mass above him seemed to creak like something tired and old. A deep shudder went through the colossal pile and then a deep grinding that turned him sick with horror. All his plans for instant flight were frozen and it was not until the groaning ceased that he realized he was lying on his back, breathless with fear and expectancy. Slowly, he edged his way into the air and walked, fighting the desire to run, away from the rock.

When he stopped near his canteen he was wringing with cold sweat and trembling in every muscle. He sat down on the rock and fought for control. It was until some twenty minutes had passed that he could trust himself to get to his feet.

Despite his experience, he knew that if he did not go back now he would never go. He had but one sack for the day and wanted another. Circling the batholith, he examined the widening crack, endeavoring again, for the third time, to find another means of access to the vein.

The tilt of the outer wall was obvious, and it could stand no more without toppling. It was possible that by cutting into the wall of the column and striking down he might tap the vein at a safer point. Yet this added blow at the foundation would bring the tower nearer to collapse and render his other hole untenable. Even this new attempt would not be safe, although immeasurably more secure than the hole he had left. Hesitating, he looked back at the hole.

Once more? The ore was now fabulously rich, and the few pounds he needed to complete the sack he could get in just a little while. He stared at the black and undoubtedly narrower hole, then looked up at the leaning wall. He picked up his pick and, his mouth dry, started back, drawn by a fascination that was beyond all reason.

His heart pounding, he dropped to his knees at the tunnel face. The air seemed stifling and he could feel his scalp tingling, but once he started to crawl it was better. The face where he now worked was at least sixteen feet from the tunnel mouth. Pick in hand, he began to wedge chunks from their seat. The going seemed harder now and the chunks did not come loose so easily. Above him the tower made no sound. The crushing weight was now something tangible. He could almost feel it growing, increasing with every move of his. The mountain seemed resting on his shoulder, crushing the air from his lungs.

Suddenly he stopped. His sack almost full, he stopped and lay very still, staring up at the bulk of the rock above him.

No.

He would go no further. Now he would quit. Not another sackful. Not another pound. He would go out now. He would go down the mountain without a backward look, and he would keep going. His wife waiting at home, little Tommy, who would run gladly to meet him—these were too much to gamble.

With the decision came peace, came certainty. He sighed deeply, and relaxed, and then it seemed to him that every muscle in his body had been knotted with strain. He turned on his side and with great deliberation gathered his lantern, his sack, his hand-pick.

He had won. He had defeated the crumbling tower, he had defeated his own greed. He backed easily, without the caution that had marked his earlier movements in the cave. His blind, trusting foot found the projecting rock, a piece of quartz that stuck out from the rough-hewn wall.

The blow was too weak, too feeble to have brought forth the reaction that followed. The rock seemed to quiver like the flesh of a beast when stabbed; a queer vibration went through that ancient rock, then a deep, gasping sigh.

He had waited too long!

Fear came swiftly in upon him, crowding him, while his body twisted, contracting into the smallest possible space. He tried to will his muscles to move beneath the growing sounds that vibrated through the passage. The whispers of the rock grew into a terrifying groan, and there was a rattle of pebbles. Then silence.

The silence was more horrifying than the sound. Somehow he was crawling, even as he expected the avalanche of gold to bury him. Abruptly, his feet were in the open. He was out.

He ran without stopping, but behind him he heard a growing roar that he couldn't outrace. When he knew from the slope of the land that he must be safe from falling rock, he fell to his knees. He turned and looked back. The muted, roaring sound, like thunder beyond mountains, continued, but there was no visible change in the batholith. Suddenly, as he watched, the whole rock formation seemed to shift and tip. The movement lasted only seconds, but before the tons of rock had found their new equilibrium, his tunnel and the area around it had utterly vanished from sight.

When he could finally stand. Wetherton gathered up his sack of ore and his canteen. The wind was cool upon his face as he walked away; and he did not look back again.

DESERT DEATH-SONG

When Jim Morton rode up to the fire three unshaven men huddled there warming themselves and drinking hot coffee. Morton recognized Chuck Benson from the Slash Five. The other men were strangers.

"Howdy, Chuck!" Morton said. "He still in there?"

"Sure is!" Benson told him. "An' it don't look like he's figurin' on comin' out."

"I don't reckon to blame him. Must be a hundred men scattered about."

"Nigher two hundred, but you know Nat Bodine. Shakin' him out of these hills is going to be tougher'n shaking a possum out of a tree."

The man with the black-beard stubble looked up sourly. "He wouldn't last long if they'd let us go in after him! I'd sure roust him out of there fast enough!"

Morton eyed the man with distaste. "You think so. That means you don't know Bodine. Goin' in after him is like sendin' a houn' dog down a hole after a badger. That man knows these hills, ever' crack an' crevice! He can hide places an Apache would pass up."

The black-bearded man stared sullenly. He had thick lips and small, heavy-lidded eyes. "Sounds like maybe you're a friend of his'n. Maybe when we get him you should hang alongside of him."

91

Somehow the long rifle over Morton's saddle bows shifted to stare warningly at the man, although Morton made no perceptible movement. "That ain't a handy way to talk, stranger," Morton said casually. "Ever'body in these hills knows Nat, an' most of us been right friendly with him one time or another. I ain't takin' up with him, but I reckon there's worse men in this posse than he is."

"Meanin'?" The big man's hand lay on his thigh,

"Meanin' anything you like." Morton was a Tennessee mountain man before he came west and gun talk was no stranger to him. "You call it your ownself." The long rifle was pointed between the big man's eyes and Morton was building a cigarette with his hands only inches away from the trigger.

"Forget it!" Benson interrupted. "What you two got to fight about? Blackie, this here's Jim Morton. He's lion hunter for the Lazy S."

Blackie's mind underwent a rapid readjustment. This tall, lazy stranger wasn't the soft-headed drink of water he had thought him, for everybody knew about Morton. A dead shot with rifle and pistol, he was known to favor the former, even in fairly close combat. He had been known to go up trees after mountain lions and once, when three hardcase rustlers had tried to steal his horses, the three had ended up in Boothill.

"How about it, Jim?" Chuck asked. "You know Nat. Where'd you think he'd be?"

Morton squinted and drew on his cigarette. "Ain't no figurin' him. I know him, an' I've hunted along of him. He's almighty knowin' when it comes to wild country. Moves like a cat an' got eyes like a turkey buzzard." He glanced at Chuck. "What's he done? I heard some talk down to the Slash Five, but nobody seemed to have it clear."

"Stage robbed yestiddy. Pete Daley of the Diamond D was ridin' it, an' he swore the robber was Nat. When they went to arrest him, Nat shot the sheriff."

"Kill him?"

"No. But he's bad off, an' like to die. Nat only fired once an' the bullet took Larabee too high."

"Don't sound reasonable," Morton said slowly. "Nat ain't one to miss somethin' he aims to kill. You say Pete Daley was there?"

"Yeah. He's the on'y one saw it."

"How about this robber? Was he masked?"

"Uh huh, an' packin' a Winchester .44 an' two tied-down guns. Big black-headed man, the driver said. He didn't know Bodine, but Pete identified him."

Morton eyed Benson. "I shouldn't wonder," he said, and Chuck flushed.

Each knew what the other was thinking. Pete Daley had never liked Bodine. Nat married the girl Pete wanted, even though it was generally figured Pete never had a look-in with her, anyway, but Daley had worn his hatred like a badge ever since. Mary Callahan had been a pretty girl, but a quiet one, and Daley had been sure he'd win her.

But Bodine had come down from the hills and changed all that. He was a tall man with broad shoulders, dark hair and a quiet face. He was a good-looking man, even a handsome man, some said. Men liked him, and women too, but the men liked him best because he left their women alone. That was more than could be said for Daley, who lacked Bodine's good looks but made up for it with money.

Bodine had bought a place near town and drilled a good well. He seemed to have money, and that puzzled people, so hints began to get around that he had been rustling as well as robbing stages. There were those, like Jim Morton, who believed most of the stories stemmed from Daley, but no matter where they originated, they got around.

Hanging Bodine for killing the sheriff—the fact that he was still alive was overlooked, and considered merely a technical question, anyway—was the problem before the posse. It was a self elected posse, inspired to some extent by Daley, and given a semi-official status by the presence of Burt Stoval, Larrabee's jailer.

Yet to hang a man he must first be caught and Bodine had lost himself in that broken, rugged country known as Powder Basin. It was a region of some ten square miles backed against an even rougher and uglier patch of waterless desert, but the basin was bad enough itself.

Fractured with gorges and humped with fir-clad hogbacks, it was a maze where the juniper region merged into the fir and spruce, and where the canyons were liberally overgrown with manzanita. There were at least two cliff dwellings in the area, and a ghost mining town of some dozen ramshackle structures, tumbled-in and wind-worried.

"All I can say," Morton said finally, "is that I don't envy those who corner him—when they do and if they do."

Blackie wanted no issue with Morton, yet he was still sore. He looked up. "What do you mean, if we do? We'll get him!"

Morton took his cigarette from his lips. "Want a suggestion, friend? When he's cornered, don't you be the one to go in after him."

Four hours later, when the sun was moving toward noon, the net had been drawn tighter, and Nat Bodine lay on his stomach in the sparse grass on the crest of a hogback and studied the terrain below.

There were many hiding places, but the last thing he wanted was to be cornered and forced to fight it out. Until the last moment he wanted freedom of movement.

Among the searchers were friends of his, men with whom he rode and hunted, men he had admired and liked. Now, they believed him wrong, they believed him a killer, and they were hunting him down.

They were searching the canyons with care, so he had chosen the last spot they would examine, a bald hill with only the foot high grass for cover. His vantage point was excellent, and he had watched with appreciation the care with which they searched the canyon below him.

Bodine scooped another handful of dust and rubbed it along his rifle barrel. He knew how far a glint of sunlight from a rifle barrel can be seen, and men in that posse were Indian fighters and hunters.

No matter how he considered it, his chances were slim. He was a better woodsman than any of them, unless it was Jim Morton. Yet that was not enough. He was going to need food and water. Sooner or later they would get the bright idea of watching the waterholes, and after that. . . .

It was almost twenty-four hours since he had eaten, and he would soon have to refill his canteen.

Pete Daley was behind this, of course. Trust Pete not to tell the true story of what happened. Pete had accused him of the holdup right to his face when they had met him on the street. The accusation had been sudden, and Nat's reply had been prompt. He'd called Daley a liar, and Daley moved a hand for his gun. The sheriff sprang to stop them and took Nat's bullet. The people who rushed to the scene saw only the sheriff on the ground, Daley with no gun drawn, and Nat gripping his six-shooter. Yet it was not that of which he thought now. He thought of Mary.

What would she be thinking now? They had been married so short a time, and had been happy despite the fact that he was still learning how to live in civilization and with a woman. It was a mighty different thing, living with a girl like Mary.

Did she doubt him now? Would she, too, believe he had held up the stage and then killed the sheriff? As he lay in the grass he could find nothing on which to build hope.

Hemmed in on three sides, with the waterless mountains and desert behind him, the end seemed inevitable. Thoughtfully, he shook his canteen. It was nearly empty. Only a little water sloshed weakly in the bottom. Yet he must last the afternoon through, and by night he could try the waterhole at Mesquite Springs, no more than a half mile away.

The sun was hot, and he lay very still, knowing that only the faint breeze should stir the grass where he lay if he were not to be seen.

Below him he heard men's voices, and from time to time could distinguish a word or even sentence. They were cursing the heat, but their search was not relaxed. Twice men mounted the hill and passed near him. One man stopped for several minutes, not more than a dozen yards away, but Nat held himself still and waited. Finally the man moved on, mopping sweat from his face. When the sun was gone he wormed his way off the crest and into the manzanita. It took him over an hour to get within striking distance of Mesquite Springs. He stopped just in time. His nostrils caught the faint fragrance of tobacco smoke.

Lying in the darkness, he listened, and after a moment heard a stone rattle, then the faint chink of metal on stone.

When he was far enough away he got to his feet and worked his way through the night toward Stone Cup, a spring two miles beyond. He moved more warily now, knowing they were watching the waterholes.

The stars were out, sharp and clear, when he snaked his way through the reeds toward the cup. Deliberately, he chose the route where the overflow from the Stone Cup kept the earth soggy and high-grown with reeds and dank grass. There would be no chance of a watcher waiting there on the wet ground, nor would the wet grass rustle. He moved close, but here, too, men waited.

He lay still in the darkness, listening. Soon he picked out three men, two back in the shadows of the rock shelf, one over under the brush but not more than four feet from the small pool's edge.

There was no chance to get a canteen filled here, for the watchers were too wide awake. Yet he might manage a drink.

He slid his knife from his pocket and opened it carefully. He cut several reeds, allowing no sound. When he had them cut, he joined them and reached them toward the water. Lying on his stomach within only a few feet of the pool, and no farther from the nearest watcher, he sucked on the reeds until the water started flowing. He drank for a long time, then drank again. The trickle doing little, at first to assuage his thrist. After a while he felt better.

He started to withdraw the reeds, then grinned and let them lay. With care he worked his way back from the cup and got to his feet. His shirt was muddy and wet, and with the wind against his body he felt almost cold. With the waterholes watched there would be no chance to fill his canteen, and the day would be blazing hot. There might be an unwatched hole, but the chance of that was slight and if he spent the night in fruitless search of water he would exhaust his strength and lose the sleep he needed. Returning like a deer, to a resting place near a ridge, he bedded down in a clump of manzanita. His rifle cradled in his arm, he was almost instantly asleep. . . .

Dawn was breaking when he awakened, and his nostrils caught a whiff of wood smoke. His pursuers were at their breakfasts. By now they would have found his reeds, and he grinned at the thought of their anger at having had him so near without knowing. Morton, he reflected, would appreciate that. Yet they would all know he was short of water.

Worming his way through the brush, he found a trail that followed just below the crest, and moved steadily along in the partial shade, angling toward a towering hogback.

Later, from well up on the hogback, he saw three horsemen walking their animals down the ridge where he had rested the previous day. Two more were working up a canyon, and wherever he looked they seemed to be closing in. He abandoned the canteen, for it banged against brush and could be heard too easily. He moved back, going from one cluster of boulders to another, then pausing short of the ridge itself.

The only route that lay open was behind him, into the desert, and that way they were sure he would not go. The hogback on which he lay was the highest ground in miles, and before him the jagged scars of three canyons running off the hogback stretched their ugly length into the rocky, brush blanketed terrain. Up those three canyons groups of searchers were working. Another group had cut down from the north and come between him and the desert ghost town.

The far-flung skirmishing line was well disposed, and Nat could find it in himself to admire their skill. These were his brand of men, and they understood their task. Knowing them as he did, he knew how relentless they could be. The country behind him was open. It would not be open long. Knowing themselves, they were sure he would fight it out rather than risk dying of thirst in the desert. They were wrong.

Nat Bodine learned that suddenly. Had he been asked, he would have accepted their solution, yet now he saw that he could not give up.

The desert was the true Powder Basin. The Indians had called it The Place of No Water, and he had explored deep into it in the past years, and found nothing. While the distance across was less than twenty miles, a man must travel twice that or more, up and down and around, if he would cross it, and his sense of direction must be perfect. Yet, with water and time a man might cross it. And Nat Bodine had neither. Moreover, if he went into the desert they would soon send word and have men waiting on the other side. He was fairly trapped, and yet he knew that he would die in that waste alone, before he'd surrendered to be lynched. Nor could he hope to fight off this posse for long. Carefully he got to his feet and worked his way to the maw of the desert. He nestled among the boulders and watched the men below. They were coming carefully, still several yards away. Cradling his Winchester against his cheek, he drew a bead on a rock ahead of the nearest man, and fired.

Instantly the searchers vanished. Where a dozen men had been in sight, there was nobody now. He chuckled. "That made 'em eat dirt!" he said. "Now they won't be so anxious."

The crossing of the crest was dangerous, but he made it, and hesitated there, surveying the scene before him. Far away to the horizon stretched the desert. Before him the mountain broke sharply away in a series of sheer precipices and ragged chasms, and he scowled as he stared down at them, for there seemed no descent could be possible from here.

*　*　*

Chuck Benson and Jim Morton crouched in the lee of a stone wall and stared up at the ridge from which the shot had come. "He didn't shoot to kill," Morton said, "or he'd have had one of us. He's that good."

"What's on his mind?" Benson demanded. "He's stuck now. I know that ridge an' the only way down is the way he went up."

"Let's move in," Blackie protested. "There's cover enough."

"You don't know Nat. He's never caught until you see him down. I know the man. He'll climb cliffs that would stop a hoss fly."

Pete Daley and Burt Stoval moved up to join them, peering at the ridge before them through the concealing leaves. The ridge was a gigantic hogback almost a thousand feet higher than the plateau on which they waited. On the far side it fell away to the desert, dropping almost two thousand feet in no more than two hundred yards, and most of the drop in broken cliffs.

Daley's eyes were hard with satisfaction. "We got him now!" he said triumphantly. "He'll never get off that ridge! We've only to wait a little, then move in on him. He's out of water, too!"

Mortion looked with distaste at Daley. "You seem powerful anxious to get him, Pete. Maybe the sheriff ain't dead yet. Maybe he won't die. Maybe his story of the shootin' will be different."

Daley turned on Morton, his dislike evident. "Your opinion's of no account, Morton. I was there, and I saw it. As for Larabee, if he ain't dead he soon will be. If you don't like this job, why don't you leave?"

Jim Morton stoked his pipe calmly. "Because I aim to be here if you get Bodine," he said, "an' I personally figure to see he gets a fair shake. Furthermore, Daley, I'm not beholdin' to you, no way, an' I ain't scared of you. Howsoever, I figure you've got a long way to go before you get Bodine."

High on the ridge, flat on his stomach among the rocks, Bodine was not so sure. He mopped sweat from his brow and studied again the broken cliff beneath him. There seemed to be a vaguely possible route but at the thought of it his mouth turned dry and his stomach empty.

A certain bulge in the rock looked as though it might afford handholds, although some of the rock was loose, and he couldn't see below the bulge where it might become smooth. Once over that projection, getting back would be difficult if not impossible. Nevertheless, he determined to try.

Using his belt for a rifle strap, he slung the Winchester over his back, then turned his face to the rock and slid feet first over the bulge, feeling with his toes for a hold. If he fell from here, he could not drop less than two hundred feet, although close in there was a narrow ledge only sixty feet down.

Using simple pull holds, and working down with his feet, Bodine got well out over the bulge. Taking a good grip, he turned his head and searched the rock below him. On his left the rock was cracked deeply, with the portion of the face to which he clung projecting several inches farther into space than the other side of the crack. Shifting his left foot carefully, he stepped into the crack, which afforded a good jam hold. Shifting his left hand, he took a pull grip, pulling away from himself with the left fingers until he could swing his body to the left, and get a grip on the edge of the crack with his right fingers. Then lying back, his feet braced against the projecting far edge of the crack, and pulling toward himself with his hands, he worked his way down, step by step and grip by grip, for all of twenty feet. There the crack widened into a chimney, far too wide to be climbed with a lie back, its inner sides slick and smooth from the scouring action of wind and water.

Working his way into the chimney, he braced his feet against one wall and his back against the other, and by pushing against the two walls and shifting his feet carefully, he worked his way down until he was well past the sixty-foot ledge. The chimney ended in a small cavern-like hollow in the rock, and he sat there, catching his breath.

Nat ran his fingers through his hair and mopped sweat from his brow. Anyway, he grinned at the thought, they wouldn't follow him down here!

Carefully, he studied the cliff below him, then to the right and left. To escape his present position he must make a traverse of the rock face, working his way gradually down. For all of forty feet of climb he would be exposed to a dangerous fall, or to a shot from above if they had dared the ridge. Yet there were precarious handholds and some inch-wide ledges for his feet.

When he had his breath, he moved out, clinging to the rock face and carefully working across it and down. Sliding down a steep slab, he crawled out on a knife-edge ridge of rock and, straddling it, worked his way along until he could climb down a further face, hand over hand. Landing on a wide ledge, he stood there, his chest heaving, staring back up at the ridge. No one was yet in sight, and there was a chance that he was making good his escape. At the same time his mouth was dry and the effort expended in climbing and descending had increased his thirst. Unslinging his rifle, he completed the descent without trouble, emerging at last upon the desert below.

Heat lifted against his face in a stifling wave. Loosening the buttons of his shirt, he pushed back his hat and stared up at the towering height of the mountain, and even as he looked up, he saw men appear on the ridge. Lifting his hat, he waved to them.

Benson was the first man on that ridge, and involuntarily he drew back from the edge of the cliff, catching his breath at the awful depth below. Pete Daley, Burt Stoval and Tim Morgan moved up beside him, and then the others. It was Morgan who spotted Bodine first.

"What did I tell you?" he snapped. "He's down there on the desert!"

Daley's face hardened. "Why, the dirty—"

Benson stared. "You got to hand it to him!" he said. "I'd sooner chance a shootout than try that cliff!"

A bearded man on their left spat and swore softly. "Well, boys, this does it! I'm quittin! No man that game deserves to hang! I'd say, let him go!"

Pete Daley turned angrily, but changed his mind when he saw the big man and the way he wore his gun. Pete was no fool. Some men could be bullied, and it was a wise man who knew which and when. "I'm not quitting," he said flatly. "Let's get the boys, Chuck. We'll get our horses and be around there in a couple of hours. He won't get far on foot."

*   *   *

Nat Bodine turned and started off into the desert with a long swinging stride. His skin felt hot, and the air was close and stifling, yet his only chance was to get across this stretch and work into the hills at a point where they could not find him.

All this time Mary was in the back of his mind, her presence always near, always alive. Where was she now? And what was she doing? Had she been told?

Nat Bodine had emerged upon the desert at the mouth of a boulder-strewn canyon slashed deep into the rocky flank of the mountain itself. From the mouth of the canyon there extended a wide fan of rock, coarse gravel, sand and silt flushed down from the mountain by torrential rains. On his right the edge of the fan of sand was broken by the deep scar of another wash, cut at some later date when the water had found some crevice in the rock to give it an unexpected hold. It was toward this wash that Bodine walked.

Clambering down the slide, he walked along the bottom. Working his way among the boulders, he made his way toward the shimmering basin that marked the extreme low level of the desert. Here, dancing with heat waves, and seeming from a distance to be a vast blue lake, was one of those dry lakes that collect the muddy runoff from the mountains. Yet as he drew closer he discovered he had been mistaken in his hope that it was a playa of the dry type. Wells sunk in the dry type of playa often produce fresh cool water, and occasionally at shallow depths. This, however, was a pasty, water-surfaced salinas, and water found here would be salty and worse than none at all. Moreover, there was danger that he might break through the crust beneath the dry powdery dust and into the slime below.

The playa was such that it demanded a wide detour from his path, and the heat here was even more intense than on the mountain. Walking steadily, dust rising at each footfall, Bodine turned left along the desert, skirting the playa. Beyond it he could see the edge of a rocky escarpment, and this rocky ledge stretched for miles toward the far mountain range bordering the desert.

Yet the escarpment must be attained as soon as possible, for knowing as he was in desert ways and lore, Nate understood in such terrain there was always a possibility of stumbling upon one of those desert tanks, or tinajas, which contain the purest water any wanderer of the dry lands could hope to find. Yet he knew how difficult these were to find, for hollowed by some sudden cascade, or scooped by wind, they are often filled to the brim with gravel or sand, and must be scooped out to obtain the water in the bottom.

Nat Bodine paused, shading his eyes toward the end of the playa. It was not much farther. His mouth was powder dry now, and he could swallow only with an effort.

He was no longer perspiring. He walked as in a daze, concerned only with escaping the basin of the playa, and it was with relief that he stumbled over a stone and fell headlong. Clumsily, he got to his feet, blinking away the dust and pushing on through the rocks. He crawled to the top of the escarpment through a deep crack in the rock and then walked on over the dark surface.

It was some ancient flow of lava, crumbling to ruin now, with here and there a broken blister of it. In each of them he searched for water, but they were dry. At this hour he would see no coyote, but he watched for tracks, knowing the wary and wily desert wolves knew where water could be found.

The horizon seemed no nearer, nor had the peaks begun to show their lines of age, or the shapes into which the wind had carved them. Yet the sun was lower now, its rays level and blasting as the searing flames of a furnace. Bodine plodded on, walking toward the night, hoping for it, praying for it. Once he paused abruptly at a thin whine of sound across the sun-blasted air.

Waiting, he listened, searching the air about him with eyes suddenly alert, but he did not hear the sound again for several minutes, and when he did hear it there was no mistaking it. His eyes caught the dark movement, striking straight away from him on a course diagonal with his own.

A bee!

Nat changed his course abruptly, choosing a landmark on a line with the course of the bee, and then followed on. Minutes later he saw a second bee, and altered his course to conform with it. The direction was almost the same, and he knew that water could be found by watching converging lines of bees. He could afford to miss no chance, and he noted the bees were flying deeper into the desert, not away from it.

Darkness found him suddenly. At the moment the horizon range had grown darker, its crest tinted with old rose and gold, slashed with the deep fire of crimson, and then it was night, and a coyote was yapping myriad calls at the stars.

In the coolness he might make many miles by pushing on, and he might also miss his only chance at water. He hesitated, then his weariness conformed with his judgment, and he slumped down against a boulder and dropped his chin on his chest. The coyote voiced a shrill complaint, then satisfied with the echo against the rocks, ceased his yapping and began to hunt. He scented the man smell and skirted wide around, going about his business.

* * *

There were six men in the little cavalcade at the base of the cliff, searching for tracks. The rider found them there. Jim Morton calmly sitting his horse and watching with interested eyes, but lending no aid to the men who tracked his friend, and there were Pete Daley, Blackie, Chuck Benson and Burt Stoval. Farther along were other groups of riders.

The man worked a hard-ridden horse and he was yelling before he reached them. He raced up and slid his horse to a stop, gasping, "Call it off! It wasn't him!"

"What?" Daley burst out. "What did you say?"

"I said . . . it wa'n't Bodine! We got our outlaw this mornin' out east of town! Mary Bodine spotted a man hidin' in the brush below Wenzel's place, an' she come down to town. It was him, all right. He had the loot on him, an' the stage driver identified him!"

Pete Daley stared, his little eyes tightening. "What about the sheriff?" he demanded.

"He's pullin' through." The rider stared at Daley. "He said it was his fault he got shot. His an' your'n. He said if you'd kept your fool mouth shut nothin' would have happened, an' that he was a another fool for not lettin' you get leaded down like you deserved!"

Daley's face flushed, and he looked around angrily like a man badly treated. "All right, Benson. We'll go home."

"Wait a minute." Jim Morton crossed his hands on the saddle horn. "What about Nat? He's out there in the desert an' he thinks he's still a hunted man. He's got no water. Far's we know, he may be dead by now."

Daley's face was hard. "He'll make out. My time's too valuable to chase around in the desert after a no-account hunter."

"It wasn't too valuable when you had an excuse to kill him," Morton said flatly.

"I'll ride with you, Morton," Benson offered.

Daley turned on him, his face dark. "You do an' you'll hunt you a job!"

Benson spat. "I quit workin' for you ten minutes ago. I never did like coyotes."

He sat his horse, staring hard at Daley, waiting to see if he would draw, but the rancher merely stared back until his eyes fell. He turned his horse.

"If I were you," Morton suggested, "I'd sell out an' get out. This country don't cotton to your type, Pete."

Morton started his horse. "Who's comin'?"

"We all are." It was Blackie who spoke. "But we better fly some white. I don't want that salty Injun shootin' at me!"

It was near sundown of the second day of their search and the fourth since the holdup, that they found him. Benson had a shirt tied to his rifle barrel, and they took turns carrying it.

They had given up hope the day before, knowing he was out of water, and knowing the country he was in.

The cavalcade of riders were almost abreast of a shoulder of sandstone outcropping when a voice spoke out of the rocks. "You huntin' me?"

Jim Morton felt relief flood through him. "Huntin' you peaceful," he said. "They got their outlaw, an' Larrabee owes you no grudge."

His face burned red from the desert sun, his eyes squinting at them, Nat Bodine swung his long body down over the rocks. "Glad to hear that," he said. "I was some worried about Mary."

"She's all right." Morton stared at him. "What did you do for water?"

"Found some. Neatest tinaja in all this desert."

The men swung down and Benson almost stepped on a small, red spotted toad.

"Watch that, Chuck. That's the boy who saved my life."

"That toad?" Blackie was incredulous. "How d' you mean?"

"That kind of toad never gets far from water. You only find them near some permanent seepage or spring. I was all in, down on my hands and knees, when I heard him cheeping.

"It's a noise like a cricket, and I'd been hearing it sometime before I remembered that a Yaqui had told me about these frogs. I hunted, and found him, so I knew there had to be water close by. I'd followed the bees for a day and a half, always this way, and then I lost them. While I was studyin' the lay of the land, I saw another bee, an' then another. All headin' for this bunch of sand rock. But it was the toad that stopped me."

They had a horse for him, and he mounted up. Blackie stared at him. "You better thank that Morton," he said dryly. "He was the only one was sure you were in the clear."

"No, there was another," Morton said. "Mary was sure. She said you were no outlaw, and that you'd live. She said you'd live through anything." Morton bit off a chew, then glanced again at Nat. "They were wonderin' where you make your money, Nat."

"Me?" Bodine looked up, grinning. "Minin' turquoise. I found me a place where the Indians worked. I been cuttin' it out an' shippin' it east." He stooped and picked up the toad, and put him carefully in the saddlebag.

"That toad," he said emphatically, "goes home to Mary an' me. Our place is green an' mighty purty, an' right on the edge of the desert, but with plenty of water. This toad has got him a good home from here on, and I mean a good home!"

RIDING FOR THE BRAND

CHAPTER ONE: The Lone Wrecked Wagon

He had been watching the covered wagon for more than an hour. There was no movement, no sound. The bodies of two of the animals that had drawn the wagon lay in the grass, plainly visible. Farther away, almost two miles, stood a lone buffalo bull, black against the gray distance.

Nothing moved near the wagon, but Jed Ashbury had lived too long in Indian country to risk his scalp on appearances, and an Indian could lie ghost-still for hours on end. He had no intention of taking a chance, stark naked, and without weapons.

Two days before he had been stripped to the hide by Indians and forced to run the gauntlet, but he had run better than they had dreamed, and had escaped with only a few minor wounds.

Now, miles away, he had reached the limit of his endurance. Despite little water, and less food, he was still in good traveling shape except for his feet. They were lacerated and swollen, and caked with dried blood.

Finally, he started to move warily, taking advantage of every bit of cover, and moving steadily nearer the wagon. When he was no more than fifty feet away he settled in the grass and studied the situation.

Here was the scene of an attack. Evidently the wagon had been alone, and the bodies of two men and a woman lay stretched on the prairie.

Clothing, papers, and cooking utensils were scattered, evidence of hasty looting. Yet Jed saw relief for himself. Whatever the dreams of these people, they were finished now, another sacrifice to the westward march of empire. And they would not begrudge him the things he needed.

Rising, he moved cautiously up to the wagon, a tall, powerfully muscled young man, unshaven and untrimmed.

He avoided the bodies. Oddly, they were not mutilated, which was unusual. The men still wore their boots, and as a last resort, he would take a pair of them. First, he must look over the wagon.

Whatever Indians had looted the wagon had done so hurriedly. The wagon was in the wildest state of confusion, but in the bottom of a big trunk he found a fine black broadcloth suit. Also a new pair of handworked leather boots, a woolen shirt, and several white shirts.

"Somebody's Sunday-go-to-meetin' clothes," he muttered. "Hadn't better try them boots now, the way my feet's swole."

He found some clean underwear, and got into the clothes, pulling on the woolen shirt. When he was dressed he got water from a half-empty barrel and bathed his feet, then bandaged them with strips of clean white cloth torn from a freshly laundered dress.

His feet felt better then, and as the boots were a size larger than he wore, he tried them. There was some discomfort, but he decided to wear them.

With a shovel that was tied to the side of the wagon he dug a shallow grave, laid the three bodies in it side by side, covered them, and said a hasty prayer. Then he returned to the wagon. The savages had made only a hasty search, and there might be something they had overlooked that would help him.

There were some legal papers, a will, and a handful of letters. He put these aside over a poncho he found, then spotted a sewing basket. Remembering his grandmother's habits, he emptied out the needles and thread aind sewing. In the bottom was a large sealed envelope.

Ripping it open, he gave a grunt of satisfaction. Wrapped in carefully folded tissue paper were twenty twenty-dollar gold pieces. He pocketed them, then delved deeper into the trunk. At the bottom were some carefully folded clothes. The Indians had not gone this deep.

Several times he returned to the end of the wagon for a careful survey of the prairie, but it remained empty and still.

Then, in the very bottom of the trunk, he struck pay dirt. He found a steel box and, with a pick that was strapped to the wagon, he broke it open. Inside it, in some folded cloth, was a magnificent set of pistols. They were silver-plated and beautifully engraved, with pearl stocks and black leather holsters and belt, inlaid with mother of pearl. What was more to the point, there were several boxes of shells!

Grinning, he strapped on the guns, then filled the loops of the belt with shells, and pocketed a box of loose cartridges. The remaining two boxes he placed on the poncho.

In another fold of the cloth was a pearl-handled knife of beautifully tempered steel—a Spanish fighting knife, and a splendid piece of work. He slung the scabbard around his neck, the hilt just below his collar. Then he packed two white shirts, a string tie, and the black broadcloth coat in a bundle. He wrapped the poncho around it, and slung it over his shoulder.

In an inside pocket of the coat he had stowed the papers and letters he had found, while in his hip pocket he stuffed a small, leather-bound book that had been among the scattered contents of the wagon. He read little, but knew the value of a good book.

He had had three years of intermittent schooling, and had learned to read and write, and to solve sums, if not too intricate.

There had been no hat around the wagon, but he could do without one. What he needed now was a good horse.

There had been a canteen, and he had filled that, and slung it over his shoulder. Also, in his pack, he had put a tin cup and some coffee that had been spilled on the ground. He glanced at the sun, and started out.

Jed Asbury was accustomed to fending for himself. That there could be anything wrong in appropriating what he had found never entered his head. Likely it would not have entered the head of any man, at that time when life was short and hard, and one lived as best one might. Nor did one man begrudge another what he needed.

Jed had been born on an Ohio farm, but when his parents had died when he was only ten years old, he had been sent to a crabbed old uncle in a Maine fishing village. For three years his uncle had worked him like a slave, then he had gone out to the banks with a fishing boat, but on its return to New Bedford Jed Asbury had abandoned the boat, his uncle, and deep sea fishing.

He had walked to Boston, and then by devious methods, got to Philadelphia. He had run errands, worked in a mill, and finally got a job as a printer's devil in a small shop. He had grown to like a man who came there often, a quiet man with black hair and large gray eyes, his head curiously wide across the temples. The man wrote stories and literary criticism for some magazines, and occasionally loaned Jed books to read. His name was Edgar Poe, and he was reported to be the foster son of John Allan, the Virginia millionaire.

When Jed left the print shop he had shipped on a windjammer and sailed around the Horn. From San Francisco he had gone to Australia for a year in the gold fields, then to South Africa, and finally back to New York. He had been twenty then, and a big young man, over six feet tall and hardened by the life he had lived. He had gone West on a river boat, then down the Mississippi to Natchez and New Orleans.

In New Orleans an Englishman named Jem Mace had taught him to box. Until then all the fighting he had known had been learned the hard way. From New Orleans he had gone to Havana, to Brazil, and back to the States. In Natchez he caught a card shark cheating and both had gone for their guns. Jed Asbury had been the quickest and the gambler had died. Jed got a river boat out of town a few minutes ahead of the gambler's irate friends, and left it in St. Louis.

On a Missouri river boat he had gone to Fort Benton, then overland to Bannack, where he had joined a wagon train to Laramie, then gone on to Dodge.

In Tascosa he had run into a brother of the dead gambler and two friends, and in the battle that followed, had come out with a bullet in the leg. He had killed one of his enemies and wounded the other two. He had left town for Santa Fe.

He had been twenty-four, weighing almost two hundred pounds, and known much about the iniquities of the world. As a bull whacker he made one roundtrip to Council Bluffs then started out with a wagon train to Cheyenne. The Comanches had interfered, and he had been the sole survivor.

He knew approximately where he was now—somewhere south and west of Dodge, but closer to Santa Fe than to the Kansas trail town. However, not far away was the trail that led north from Tascosa, and he headed that way. Along the creek bottoms there might be stray cattle, and at least he could eat until a trail herd came along.

It was hot, and his feet hurt. Yet he kept going, shifting his burden from shoulder to shoulder.

On the morning of the third day he caught sight of a trail herd, headed for Kansas. As he walked toward the herd, two of the three riders riding point swung to meet him.

One was a lean, red-faced man with a yellowed mustache and a gleam of quizzical humor in his blue eyes. The other was a stocky, friendly rider on a paint horse.

"Howdy!" the older man said pleasantly. "Out for a mornin' stroll?"

"Sort of," Jed agreed, and noticed their curious glance at his new broadcloth suit. "Reckon it ain't entirely my choosin', though. I was bullwhackin' with a wagontrain out of Santa Fe for Cheyenne, and run smack into the Comanches."

Briefly, he explained.

The old man nodded. "Reckon yuh'll want a hoss," he said. "Ever do any ridin'?"

"A mite. Yuh need a hand?"

"Shore do. Forty a month and all yuh can eat!"

"The coffee's tumble!" the short rider said, grinning. "That dough wrangler we've got never could learn to make coffee that didn't taste like strong lye!"

CHAPTER TWO: Casa Grande

Wearing some borrowed jeans, and with his broadcloth packed away, Jed Asbury got out the papers he had found the moment he was alone. With narrowed eyes he read the first letter he opened:

Dear Michael:

When you get this you will know George is dead. He was thrown from a horse near Willow Springs last week, and died next day. The home ranch comprises 60,000 acres, and the other ranches twice that. This is to be yours, or your heirs if you have married since we last heard from you, if you or the heirs reach the place within one year of George's death. If you do not reach here on time, it will fall to the next of kin, and you may remember what Walt is like, from the letters.

Naturally, we hope you will come at once for all of us know what it would be if Walt came here. You should be around twenty-six now, and able to handle Walt, but be careful. He is dangerous, and has killed several men around Noveno.

Things are in good shape, but there is bad trouble impending with Besovi, a neighbor of ours. The least thing might start a cattle war, and if Walt takes over, that will happen. Also, those of us who have lived here so long will be thrown out. Can you come quickly?

Tony Costa

The letter was addressed to "Michael Latch, St. Louis, Mo." Thoughtfully, Jed folded the letter, then glanced through the others. He learned much, yet little.

Michael Latch had been the nephew of George Baca, a half-American, half-Spanish rancher who owned a huge hacienda in California. Neither Baca nor Tony Costa had ever seen Michael. Nor had the man known as Walt, who seemed to be the son of George's half-brother.

The will was that of Michael's father, Thomas Latch, the deed was to a small California ranch.

From other papers, and an unmailed letter, Jed learned that the younger of the two men he had buried was Michael Latch. The man and woman had been two friends of Michael's—Randy and May Kenner. There was also a mention in the letter of a girl named Arden who had accompanied them.

"Them Indians must have taken that girl with 'em," Jed thought.

He considered trying to find her, but dismissed the idea as impractical. Looking for a needle in a haystack would at least be a local job; searching for the girl captured by a roving band of Indians could cover a couple of thousand square miles.

Then he had another idea.

Michael Latch was dead. A vast estate awaited him—a fine, comfortable life, a constructive life which young Latch would have loved. Now the estate would fall to Walt, whoever he was—unless he, Jed Asbury, took the name of Michael Latch and claimed the estate!

The old man who was his new boss rode in from a ride around the herd. He glanced at Jed, squatting near the fire.

"Say, stranger," he said, "what did yuh say your name was?"

Only for an instant did Jed hesitate. "Latch," he said quietly. "Mike Latch. . . ."

Warm sunlight lay upon the hacienda at Casa Grande. The hounds sprawling in drowsy peace under the smoke trees scarcely opened their eyes when a tall stranger turned his horse in at the gate. Many strangers came to Casa Grande, and the uncertainty that hung over the vast ranch had not reached the dogs.

Tony Costa straightened his lean frame from the door where he leaned and studied the stranger from under an eye-shielded hand.

"Senorita," he said softly, "someone comes!"

"Is it Walt?" Sharp, quick heels sounded on the stone-flagged floor. "If he comes, what will we do? Oh, if Michael were only here."

"Today is the last day," Costa said gloomily.

"Look!" The girl grasped his sleeve. "Turning in the gate behind him! That's Walt Seever!"

"Two of his boys with him," Tony agreed. "We will have trouble if we try to stop him, senorita. He would never lose the ranch to a woman."

The stranger on the black horse swung down at the steps. He wore a flat-crowned black hat and a black broadcloth suit. His boots were almost new and hand-tooled, but when the girl's eyes dropped to the guns, she caught her breath.

"Tony!" she gasped. "The guns!"

The young man came up the steps, swept off his hat, and bowed. She looked at him, her eyes curious and alert.

"You are Tony Costa?" he said to the Mexican. "The foreman of Casa Grande?"

The three other horsemen clattered into the yard and the leader, a big man with bold, hard eyes, swung down. He brushed past the stranger and confronted the foreman.

"Well, Costa," he said triumphantly, "today this becomes my ranch! You're fired!"

117

"No!"

All eyes turned to the stranger, the girl's startled. This man was strong, she thought incongruously. He had a clean-cut face, pleasant gray eyes, hair that was black and curly.

"If you're Walt," the stranger continued, "you can ride back where you came from. This ranch is mine. I am Michael Latch!"

Fury and shocked disbelief shook Walt Seever. "You? Michael Latch?" Anger and disappointment struggled in his face as he stared. "You couldn't be!"

"Why not?" Jed spoke calmly. Eyes on Seever, he could not see the effect of his words on the girl or Costa. "George sent for me. Here I am."

Mingled with the baffled rage there was something else in Walt's face, some ugly suspicion or knowledge. Suddenly Jed had a suspicion that Walt knew he was not Michael Latch. Or doubted it vehemently.

Tony Costa shrugged.

"Why not?" he repeated. "We have been expecting him. His uncle wrote for him, and after Baca's death, I wrote to him. If you doubt him, look at the guns. Are there two such pairs of guns in the world? Are there two men in the world who could make such guns?"

Seever's eyes dropped to the guns, and Jed saw doubt and puzzlement replace the angry certainty.

"I'll have to have more proof than a set of guns!" he said.

Cooly, Jed drew a letter from his pocket and passed it over.

"From Tony, here. I also have my father's will, and other letters."

Walt Seever glanced at the letter, then hurled it into the dust. He turned furiously.

"Let's get out of here!" he snarled.

Jed Asbury watched them go, but he was puzzling over that expression in Walt Seever's eyes. Until Walt had seen the letter he had been positive Jed was not Mike Latch; now he was no longer sure. But what could have made him so positive in the beginning? What could he know?

The girl was whispering something to the foreman. Jed smiled at her.

"I don't believe Walt is too happy about my bein' here!" he said.

"No—" Costa's face was stiff—"he isn't. He expected to get this ranch himself." He turned toward the girl. "Señor Latch. I would like to introduce Senorita Carol James, a—a ward of Señor Baca's, and his good friend!"

Jed acknowledged the introduction.

"You must give me all the information," he said to Tony Costa. "I want to know all you can tell me about Walt Seever."

Costa exchanged a glance with Carol. "Si, señor. Walt Seever is a malo hombre, señor. He has killed several men, and the two you saw with him—Harry Strykes and Gin Feeley—are notorious gunmen, and believed to be thieves."

Jed Asbury listened attentively, wondering about that odd expression in Carol's eyes. Could she suspect he was not Michael Latch? If so, why didn't she say something? He was a little unsure of himself because they had accepted him so readily. For even after the idea had come to him suddenly that he might take the dead man's place he had not been sure he would go through with it. He had a feeling of guilt, yet the real Mike Latch was dead, and the heir was a killer, perhaps a thief. All the way on his wild ride to reach here before the date that ended the year of grace Latch had been given, Jed had debated with himself.

At one moment he had been convinced that it was the wrong thing to do, yet he could not see how he could be doing Latch any harm. And certainly, Costa and Carol seemed pleased to have him there, and the expression on Seever's face had been worth the ride even if Jed did not persist in his claim.

119

Yet there was another undercurrent here that disturbed him. That was Walt Seever's baffled anger.

"You say Seever seemed sure he would inherit?" Jed asked.

Carol looked at him curiously. "Yes, until three months ago he was hating George Baca for leaving his ranch to you, then he changed and became sure he would inherit."

It had been three months ago that Jed Asbury had come upon the lone covered wagon which had been attacked and three people, one of them Michael Latch, had been killed. Could Walt Seever have known of that?

The idea took root. Seever must have known. If that was so, then those three people had not been killed by Indians, or if so the Indians had been set upon the wagon. A lot remained to be explained. How had the wagon happened to be out there alone? And what had become of the girl, Arden?

If it had not been Indians, or if it had been Indians operating for white men, they must have taken Arden prisoner. And she would know the real Michael Latch! She would know Jed Asbury was an imposter, and might know who the killers were.

Walking out on the wide terrace that overlooked the green valley beyond the hacienda, Jed stared down the valley with his mind filled with doubts and apprehension.

In the valley, trees lined the banks of the streams, and on the higher mountains the forest crept down almost to the edge of the valley. It was lovely land, well-watered and rich. Here, with what he knew, he could carry on the work that old George Baca had begun. He could do what Michael Latch might have done. And he might even do it better.

There was danger, but when had he not known danger? And these people at the ranch were good people, honest people. If he did no more than keep Seever and his lawless crowd away, it would be adequate reason for taking the dead man's place. Yet he knew he was only finding excuses for something that might be entirely wrong.

The guns he wore meant something, too. The girl and Costa had recognized them, and so had Seever. What significance had they?

He was in deep water here. Every remark he made must be guarded, also making sure that he did not unconsciously fall into western idiom. And even though they had not seen him before, they would have memories or knowledge in common. He must watch for any trap.

CHAPTER THREE: The Interloper

A movement behind Jed Asbury made him turn. In the gathering dusk he saw Carol. He could hear Costa whistling as he walked toward the corrals.

"You like it?" Carol gestured toward the valley.

"It's splendid!" he said. "I reckon I never seen—saw anything prettier."

She glanced up at him, but said nothing. Then after they had stood there for a few minutes, she said:

"Somehow you're different than I expected."

"I am?" He was careful, waiting for her to say more.

"Yes, you're much more assured than I'd ever expected Mike Latch to be. Mike was quiet, Uncle George used to say. Read a lot, but didn't get around much. That was why you startled me by the way you handled Walt Seever."

He scarcely knew what to say. He shrugged finally.

"A man grows older," he said. "And coming West, to a new life, makes a man more sure of himself."

She noticed the book in his pocket.

"What's the book?" she asked curiously.

It was the battered copy of Plutarch he had found in the wagon. He drew it from his pocket and showed it to her. He was on safe ground here, for inside the book was inscribed, "To Michael, from Uncle George."

"It was a favorite of his," Carol said. "Uncle George used to say that next to the Bible more great men had read Plutarch than any other book."

"I like it," Jed agreed. "I've been reading it nights."

He turned to face her more directly. "Carol, what do you think Walt Seever will do?"

"Try to kill you, or have you killed," she said honestly. She gestured toward the guns. "You had better learn to use those."

"I can, a little," he admitted.

He did not dare admit how well he could use them. A man did not come by such skill as his in a few weeks. It would be better to retain such knowledge until time to display it. "Seever has counted on having this place, hasn't he?"

"He has made a good many plans, and a good deal of big talk." She glanced up at him again. "You know, Walt was no blood relation of Uncle George. Walt Seever was the son of a woman of the gold camps who married George Baca's half-brother."

"I see." Actually, Jed decided, Walt's claim was scarcely better than his own. He added tentatively, "I know from the letters that Uncle George wanted me to have the estate, but never having seen my uncle, or not within any reasonable time, I feel like an outsider. I am afraid I may be doing wrong to take a ranch that has been the work of other people. Perhaps Walt has more right than I have. Perhaps he is not as bad as you believe and I may be doing wrong to assert my claim."

He was aware of her searching gaze. When she spoke it was deliberately, and as though she had reached some decision.

"Michael, I don't know you. But you would have to be very bad indeed, to be as dangerous and as evil as Walt Seever. I would say that no matter what the circumstances, you should stay and see this through."

Was there a hint that she might know more than she was implying? No, it was only natural that he should be looking for suspicion behind every bush. But he had to do that, to keep from being trapped.

"However," Carol went on, "it is only fair to warn you that you have let yourself in for more than you bargained for. Uncle George understood what you would be facing, for he knew the viciousness of Walt Seever. He was doubtful if you were strong enough and clever enough to defeat Walt. So I must warn you, Michael Latch, that if you do stay, and I believe you should, you will probably be killed."

He smiled into the darkness. Since his early boyhood he had lived in proximity to death. He was not foolhardy nor reckless, for a truly brave man was never reckless. Yet he knew that he could skirt the ragged edge of death, if need be, as he had in the past.

He was an interloper here. He was stealing, and there was no other way to look at it. Yet the man whose place he had taken was dead, and perhaps he could carry on, taking that man's place, making this ranch safe for the people who loved it. Then after a while, he could step out and leave the ranch to this girl.

He turned very slowly. "I'm tired," he said. "I've been riding hard, and I think I'll go to bed. But I'm going to stay. . . ."

Jed Asbury was fast asleep when Carol went into the long dining room and stood looking at Tony Costa. Without him, what would she have done? He had been with her father for thirty years, and was past fifty now, but he was as erect and slender as a young man. And he was shrewd.

Costa looked up as she walked to where he sat drinking coffee by the light of a candle.

"Well, senorita," he said, "for better or worse, it is begun. What do you think now?"

"He told me, after I warned him of what to expect, that he was staying."

Costa studied the coffee in his cup. "You are not afraid?" he asked finally.

"No," she said honestly. Her decision had been made out there in the darkness. "He faced Walt Seever, and that was enough for me. I think anything is to be preferred to Seever."

"Si." Costa's agreement was positive. "Senorita, did you notice his hands when he faced Seever? They were ready, carolita, to draw. This man has used the gun before. He is a strong man, carolita!"

"I think you are right. He is a strong man. . . ."

For two days nothing happened from the direction of town. Walt Seever and his hard-bitten companions might have vanished from the earth, but on the Rancho Casa Grande much was happening, and Tony Costa was whistling most of the time.

Jed Asbury's formal education was slight but he knew men, and how to lead them, to get the results he wanted and he had practical knowledge.

He got up at five the morning after his conference with Carol, and when she awakened, old Maria, the cook, hastened to tell her that the señor was hard at work in the office. The door was open a crack, and when she came by she saw Jed, his curly hair on end, deep in the accounts of the ranch. Pinned up before him was a map of the Casa Grande holdings, and as he checked the disposition of cattle and horses he studied the map.

He ate a hurried breakfast and at eight o'clock was in the saddle. He ate his other meals at one of the line camps in the mountains, and rode in after dark.

In two days he spent twenty hours in the saddle.

On the third day he called Costa to the office, and asked Maria to request the presence of Carol. Puzzled and curious, she joined them.

Jed wore a white shirt, the black broadcloth trousers, and the silver guns. His face seemed to have hardened in those past two days, but when he smiled, it lighted up.

"You have been here longer than I," he said to Carol, "and are in a sense, a partner." Before she could speak he turned on Costa. "And you have been foreman here. I want you to remain foreman. However, I asked you both to be here because I am making some changes."

He indicated a point on the map. "That narrow passage leads over the border of our land into open country and then the desert. I found cattle tracks there, going out. It might be rustlers. A little blasting up on the rocks above the gap will close it tight."

Costa nodded. "You are correct, señor. That is a good move."

"This field—" Jed indicated a large area in a broad valley not far from the house—"must be fenced off. We will plant it to flax."

"Flax, señor?" Costa was puzzled.

"Yes. There will be a good market for it." He indicated a smaller area. "This piece we will plant to grapes, and all that hillside will support them. There will be times when we cannot depend entirely upon cattle or horses, and we must have other sources of income."

Carol studied him in wonderment. He was moving fast, this new Michael Latch. He was getting things done. Already he had grasped the situation, accomplishing much.

"Also, Costa, we must have a roundup. Gather all the cattle, weed out all those over four years old and we'll sell them. I found a lot of cattle back in the timber that run five to eight years old. . . ."

A few hours after he had ridden away, Carol walked down toward the blacksmith shop to talk with Pat Flood. He was an old seafaring man with a peg leg whom Uncle George had found on the beach in San Francisco, and he was a marvel with tools.

He glanced up from under his bushy gray brows as she drew near. He was cobbling a pair of boots.

Before she could speak he said:

"This here new boss, Latch—been to sea, ain't he?"

She looked at him quickly. "What gave you that idea?"

"Seen him throw a bowline on a bight yesterday. Purtiest job I seen since I come ashore. He made that rope fast like he'd been doin' it for years."

"I expect many men handle ropes well," she said.

126

"But not sailor fashion. He called it a line, too. 'Hand me that line!' he says. Me, I been ashore so long I'm callin' them ropes myself, but not him. I'd stake my dinner he's walked a deck. . . ."

Jed Asbury was riding to Noveno. He wanted to do several things he might not do so well, unless alone.

In the first place, he wanted to assay the feeling of the town toward the ranch, toward George Baca, and toward Walt Seever. He thought he might talk with a few people before they discovered who he was. Also, he was growing irritated at the delay in a showdown with Seever. His appearance in town alone might force that showdown, or allow Seever an opportunity if he felt he needed one.

Jed had never avoided trouble. He always went right to the heart of it. For this trip he was dressed for it, wearing a pair of worn gray trousers, boots, his silver guns, and a battered black hat. He hoped to pass as a drifting puncher.

Already, in his riding around the ranch and his conversations with the riders he had learned a good deal. He knew that the place to go in Noveno was the Gold Strike. He swung down and tied his horse to the hitching-rail and walked inside.

Three men were loafing against the bar. Immediately he recognized the big man with the hard face and the scar on his lip as Harry Strykes, the gunslick who had ridden with Seever. As Jed stepped up to the bar and ordered a drink, a man who was seated at a table got up slowly and walked up to Strykes.

"Never saw him afore," he said.

Strykes walked around the man and stopped in front of Jed.

"So?" he sneered. "A smart trick of yore own, huh? Well, nobody cuts in on my boss. Go for yore gun, or go back to Texas!"

Jed did not move.

"I've no reason to kill you," he said calmly. "I don't like your tone, but I'm not going to touch a gun, because if I drew I'd shoot you so you'd take a long time to die. Instead, I'm going to teach you to have better sense than to speak to strangers as you have me."

His right hand grabbed Strykes by the belt. He shoved back, then lifted, and his left toe hooked Strykes's knee with a sharp kick. Strykes's feet flew up and Jed jerked him free of the floor, his arms pawing wildly at the air. Jed dropped him flat on his back.

Strykes had been caught unawares, and he hit the floor so hard that for an instant he was stunned. Then with a curse he came off the floor.

CHAPTER FOUR: Cut Down to Size

Jed Asbury held his drink in his left hand, leaning carelessly against the bar. Harry Strykes stared at him, too furious for words. Then he lunged.

Jed's left foot was on the brass rail, but as Strykes lunged and swung, Jed moved out from the bar to the full length of his straightened left leg. Strykes's swing missed and the force of it threw his chest against the edge. Jed lifted the remainder of the glass of rye and tossed it in the man's eyes.

Coolly he put the glass down and stepped away. He made no move to hit Strykes, merely waiting for him to paw the liquor out of his eyes. When he seemed about to get that done, Jed leaned forward and, with a sudden jerk, whipped open the man's belt. Strykes's trousers slid toward his knees, and he grabbed at them wildly. Jed pushed him, with the tips of his fingers. Strykes couldn't stagger with his trousers around his knees, so he fell.

Jed turned and smiled.

"Sorry to have disturbed you, gentlemen! The name is Mike Latch. If you are ever out to Casa Grande, please call."

Abruptly he walked out of the saloon, and behind him he heard roars of laughter as the men stared at Harry Strykes sprawling ludicrously on the floor.

Yet Jed had not forgotten the man who had stepped up to Strykes and said that he had never seen Jed before. Did that man know the real Michael Latch? If Walt Seever did know something of the covered wagon and the three murdered people, he would know that Jed Asbury was an impostor, and would be searching for the evidence. The vast and beautiful acres of Rancho Casa Grande were reason enough.

Riding homeward later, Jed Asbury mulled over the problem. There was every chance of eventual exposure, yet no one might ever come near who actually knew him.

His brief altercation with Strykes had got him nowhere. He probably had been observed when he had ridden into town, and that the stranger had known Latch, and had been ready to identify him. But the fight might have won Jed a few friends who enjoyed seeing a bully put in his place, and friends might be valuable in the months to come. The town as a whole had been noncommittal or frankly friendly with Seever, although Walt's friends were the tough element.

Seever would fight, and Jed might be killed. So somehow he must find a way to give Carol a strong claim to the ranch. Failing in that, he must kill Walt Seever.

Jed Asbury had never killed a man except to protect himself or those dear to him. Deliberately to hunt a man down and shoot him was something he had never dreamed of doing. Yet it might be the only way. With a shock he realized he was thinking more of the girl than himself, and he scarcely knew her.

Apparently the stranger had identified him. Next time it might be a direct accusation in front of witnesses. Jed considered the problem all the way home. . . .

Unknown to Jed, Jim Pardo, one of the toughest hands on the ranch had followed him to Noveno. On his return Pardo reined in before the blacksmith shop and looked down at gigantic old Pat Flood. The blacksmith would have weighed three hundred pounds with two legs, and little of it fat. He loomed five inches over six feet and his hands were enormous. He rarely left his shop, his wooden leg giving him trouble.

Pardo squinted after Jed and nodded. "He'll do," he said, swinging down.

Flood lighted his corncob pipe.

"Had him a run-in with Harry Strykes," said Pardo.

Flood looked at Pardo, his gaze searching.

"Made a fool of Harry," said Pardo.

"Whup him?"

"Not like he should of. But it was worse. He got him laughed at."

"Strykes will kill him for that."

"Mebbe." Pardo rolled a smoke and related the events of the brief visit in town.

"Mebbe Strykes will get smart and leave Latch alone," he finished. "This here Mike Latch is no greenhorn. No man who's green takes things easy like this hombre. Never even turned a hair when Strykes braced him. Harry didn't have no idea what to do. Nossiree, yuh can place yore bets on this here boss of our'n. He's got sand in his gizzard, and I'm bettin' he's a hand with a shootin' iron. He's braced trouble afore."

Flood chewed on his pipe stem. "He's deep," he said.

"Old George always said young Latch was a book-readin' hombre. Quiet-like."

"Well," Flood said thoughtfully, "this Latch is quiet enough, and he reads books. . . ."

Tony Costa learned of the incident from Pardo, and Maria related the story to Carol. Jed made no reference to it at supper.

Costa hesitated as he arose from the table.

"Señor," he said, "since Señor Baca's death the senorita has allowed me to eat in the ranchhouse. If you wish, I can—"

Jed glanced up. "Forget it," he said. "And unless you're in a hurry, sit down."

When Costa had seated himself, Jed lit a cigarette and leaned back.

"Yesterday I was over in Fall Valley," he said, "and I saw some cattle over there, quite a lot of them, with a Bar O brand."

Costa's eye flared. "Bar O? Ah, then they try again! This brand, señor, belongs to a man with a big ranch—Frank Besovi. He is a big man, ver' ugly man. Señor Baca has much troubles with him. Always he tries to take that valley, and if he gets that, he will try to take more. He has taken many ranches so."

"Take some of the boys up there and throw that bunch of cattle back on his own range," ordered Jed.

"There will be trouble, señor."

"You afraid of trouble, Costa?" Jed Asbury asked quietly.

The foreman's face sharpened. "No, señor!"

"Neither am I. Throw them back."

When the punchers moved out in the morning, Jed mounted his own horse and, keeping to the timber, followed them. And there was going to be trouble. Jed saw that when they neared the valley.

Several punchers were grouped near a big man with a black beard. Their horses had a Bar O brand.

Jed rode out of the trees.

"I'll take over, Costa," he said. "I want to hear what Besovi has to say."

"Besovi, he ver' bad man!" Costa warned.

Jed Asbury knew trouble when he saw it and he knew that Besovi and his men had ridden in here for a showdown. He rode directly to them and pushed his big black right up against Besovi's gray. The big man's face flamed with rage.

"What yuh tryin' to do?" he roared.

"Listen, Besovi!" Jed's voice was cold and even. "Have your boys round up those cattle and run them back over that line—right now! If you don't, I'll make you run 'em over afoot!"

"What?" Besovi's voice was an incredulous bellow.

"You heard me. Give the order."

"I'll see you in Tophet first!" Besovi roared.

Jed Asbury knew this could be settled in two ways. If he went for a gun there would be shooting on both sides and men would be killed. He chose the other way.

He grabbed Besovi by the beard and jerked the rancher sharply toward him. He kicked the big man's foot free of the stirrup, then shoved hard. Besovi, caught by the sheer unexpectedness of the attack, went off his horse, and Jed hit the ground and was around the horses in a flash.

Besovi, his face white with anger, was lunging to his feet, his hand clawing for a gun.

"Afraid to fight with your hands?" Jed taunted.

Besovi glared, then unbuckled his gunbelts and handed them to the nearest horseman. Without hesitation, Jed unbuckled the silver guns and handed them to Costa.

Besovi started toward him with a sort of crabwise movement that made Jed's eyes sharpen. He circled warily, looking the big man over.

Jed was at least thirty pounds lighter than Besovi, and the big man had power in those mighty shoulders. Yet it took more than power to win in this kind of a fight. Jed moved in, feinting. Besovi grabbed at his wrist and Jed pushed the hand aside and stiffened a left in his face.

Blood showed, and the Casa Grande men yelled. Pardo rolled his chewing in his jaws and watched. He had seen Besovi fight before. The big man kept moving in, and Jed was wary. Besovi had some plan of action. He was no wild, hit-or-miss fighter. Jed feinted, then stabbed two lefts to Besovi's face so fast one punch had scarcely landed before the other smacked home. Pardo was surprised to see how Besovi's head jerked under the impact.

Besovi moved in and when Jed led again, the bigger man went under the punch and leaped close, encircling Jed with his mighty arms. Jed's quick leap back had been too slow, and he felt the power in that quick, grasping clutch. If those huge arms ever closed on him he would be in for trouble, so he kicked up both feet and fell.

The fall, sudden and unexpected, caught Besovi off balance, and he lunged on, losing his grip. Quickly he spun, but Jed was already on his feet. Besovi swung, however, and the punch caught Jed on the cheek bone. He took it standing, and Pardo's mouth dropped open. Nobody had ever stood up under such a Besovi punch before.

Jed struck then, a left and right that cracked home solidly. The left opened the gash over Besovi's eye a little more. The right landed on the chin, and the big man staggered. Jed moved in fast, threw both hands to the head. As the big rancher's hands came up to protect his face, Jed slugged him in the stomach.

Besovi got an arm around Jed and smashed him twice on the face with stiff, short-arm blows. Jed butted him hard, breaking free.

He was faster, and he caught the rancher behind the head and jerked Besovi's face down to meet the right uppercut that broke his nose. Jed pushed him away then and hit him seven times before he could set himself. Besovi tried, like a huge blind bear, to swing, but Jed went under the punch and hit him in the stomach again.

Besovi staggered back, and Jed drew back and dropped his hands.

"You've had plenty, Besovi, and you're too good a fighter to kill. You'd never quit. I could kill you but I'd probably break my hands. Did you take those cattle out of here?"

Besovi, standing unsteadily, wiped the blood from his eyes. He stared at Jed, unbelievingly.

"Well, I'll be hanged!" he said. He blinked, then turned. "You heard the man," he said. "Round up them cows. The fun's over."

He turned back to Jed. "Yuh're a fighter, by the eternal! Yuh could have beat me to death! Want to shake?"

"I'd never shake with a better man, or a tougher one!"

Their hands gripped, and suddenly Besovi began to laugh. He slapped his thigh and roared. His eyes twinkled at Jed.

"Come over for supper some night, will yuh? Ma's been telling me this would happen. She'll be right pleased to see yuh!"

CHAPTER FIVE: At Bay

The big rancher's lips were split, there was a cut over his right eye, his cheek bone was cut under it. The other eye was slowly swelling shut. There was one bruise on Jed's cheek bone. It would be bigger tomorrow, but it wasn't enough to know he had been in a fight. Pardo studied his new boss carefully.

"Can't figger him," he told Flood later. "Is he scared to use them guns? Or does he just like to fight with his hands?"

"He's smart," Flood said. "Look, he's made a friend of Besovi. If he'd beaten him to the ground, Besovi never would forgive him. He was savin' face for Besovi, like they call it over China way. And what if he'd reached for guns?"

"Likely seven or eight wouldn't have rode home tonight."

"Shore. This hombre is smart, that's what he is!"

Jed, soaking his battered hands, was not so sure. Besovi might have gone for a gun, or one of his men might have. He had been lucky. He might not be so lucky next time.

Anyhow there was now one less enemy for the Casa Grande ranch. And perhaps a good friend.

If anything happened to him, Carol would need friends. Walt Seever was ominously quiet, and Jed had a feeling the man was waiting for proof that the man who called himself Michael Latch was not Michael Latch.

That gave Jed an idea. It was a game at which two could play.

Carol was saddling her own horse when he walked out in the morning. She glanced at him quickly, noting the bruise on his face.

"You seem to have a faculty of getting into trouble!" she said, smiling at him.

He grinned at her as he led his black gelding out. "I don't aim to hunt for trouble," he said, "but it don't pay to try to duck it, then it just piles up bigger and bigger until a lot of little troubles become one great big one. Sometimes too big to handle."

"You seem to have made a friend of Besovi," she suggested, looking at him curiously.

"Why not? He's a good man, just too used to taking all he can put his hands on, but he'll be a good neighbor." He hesitated, not looking at her, afraid his eyes might give him away. "If anything should happen to me, you'd need friends. I think Besovi would help you."

Her eyes softened. "Thank you—Mike." She hesitated just a little over the name. "You have already done so much that Uncle George talked of doing."

Costa was out gathering the herd Jed wanted to sell, and Pardo had gone with Tony. Jed did not ask Carol where she was going, but watched her ride away toward the valley. Then he threw the saddle on his own horse and cinched up. At the sound of horses' hoofs, he turned.

Walt Seever was riding into the yard, and with him were Harry Strykes, Gin Feeley, and the man who had spoken to Strykes in the bar. Realizing suddenly that he wore no guns, Jed felt naked and helpless and there was no one around the ranch-house that he knew of.

Seever drew rein and leaned on the pommel of his saddle.

"Howdy!" he said slowly, savoring his triumph. "Howdy, Jed!"

No muscle changed on Jed Asbury's face. He stood, hands at his sides, waiting. If it came to trouble, he was going right at Seever.

"Purty smart play," Seever said, "if it hadn't been for me suspicionin' yuh might have got away with it."

Jed waited, watching.

"Now," Seever said, "yore play's finished. I suppose we should let yuh get on yore hoss and ride, but we ain't goin' to."

"You mean to kill me like you did Latch and his friends?"

Seever's face tightened. "Purty smart hombre, ain't yuh? But when yuh said that, yuh signed yore death warrant, sonny!"

"I suppose your yellow-faced friend there was one of the men you sent to kill Latch," Jed said. "He looks the kind."

"Let me kill him, Walt!" begged the man with the yellow complexion. "Just let me kill him!"

"What I want to know is where you got them guns?" Walt demanded.

"Out of the wagon, of course!" Jed smiled. "The men you sent to stop Latch before he could get here to claim the estate, messed things up. The Indians had me, but I got away. I found clothes at the wagon. It was as simple as that."

Seever nodded. "Like I figgered. Now when we get rid of you, nobody'll know what happened, and I'll claim Casa Grande!"

Jed chuckled. "Thieves like you always forget the important things. Like I said, that outfit you sent messed up the deal. What are you going to do about Arden?"

"Arden?" Walt Seever's face tightened. "Who the devil is Arden?"

Jed laughed softly. He had worked inches nearer, merely shifting his feet and his weight, They might get him, but he was going to kill Walt Seever.

He chuckled. "Why, Seever, Arden is a girl, and a mighty nice one! She was with Latch when he was killed!"

"A girl?" Seever turned sharply. "Clark, yuh said there was two men and a middle-aged woman!"

"That's all there was!" Clark said flatly.

"You killed three of them," said Jack, "but Arden had gone out on the prairie to gather some wild onions. When you opened up on the wagon, she hid in the grass. I found her."

"That's a lie!" Clark bellowed. "There was only the three of them!"

"What about those fancy clothes you threw around huntin' in the wagon?" Jed asked coolly. "Think they were old woman's clothes?"

Walt's face darkened with fury. "Cuss you, Clark! Yuh said yuh got all of 'em!"

"There wasn't no girl!" Clark said feebly. "Anyway, I didn't see none!"

"There was, and she's in Santa Fe, plenty safe there, waitin' for word from me. Somebody will have to answer if I turn up missing, and it looks like you, Walt! You can't win! You ain't got a chance."

Seever's face was ugly. "Anyway," he said, "we've got yuh dead to rights, and yuh die now!"

His hand moved back for his gun, but before Jed Asbury could move a muscle, a shot rang out. Seever yelled in surprise.

From behind Jed came Pat Flood's voice.

"Better keep yore hands away from yore guns, Walt. I can shoot the buttons off yore shirt with this here rifle. And in case it ain't enough, I got me a scattergun right alongside me. You hombres unbuckle yore belts real careful. You first, Seever!"

Jed dropped back swiftly and picked up the sawed-off, double-barreled shotgun.

The men shed their guns.

"Now get off them hosses!" Flood ordered.

They dismounted and Flood, without shifting his eyes, asked:

"What yuh want done with 'em, Boss? Should we shoot the pack of coyotes?"

"No." Jed smiled. "Let them walk back to town. All except Clark. I want to talk to Clark."

"You can't get away with this!" Seever's face turned an ugly red.

"Ssh!" Jed said gently. "Just look at this shotgun again! It's mighty persuasive."

Three men started trooping back to town. Clark, his face ashen, stood with his hands up and his jaw slack.

"Let me go!" he pleaded abjectly. "They'll kill me!"

Jed gathered up the guns and strolled back to the blacksmith shop. Flood was holding the rifle on the trembling Clark as they followed.

"How much did you hear?" Jed asked Flood.

"All of it," the big blacksmith said bluntly. "But my memory's mighty poor. I judge a man by the way he handles himself in a rough sea. You've been workin' for the good of the ship—ridin' for the brand, as they say it in cattle country. I ain't interested in anything else."

"Thanks," Jed turned to Clark. "You've got one chance to live, and you shouldn't have that. Tell us what happened, who sent you, what you did." Out of the side of his mouth he said, "Take this down."

"I got paper and pencil," the blacksmith said. "Always keep a log."

"All right, Clark," Jed said. "A complete confession."

"Seever will kill me, I tell yuh!" Clark pleaded.

Jed stared at him coldly. "You can die right here, or you can have your horse and thirty minutes' start. Make your choice."

Clark hesitated, and when he spoke his voice was so low they scarcely could hear.

"I was broke, and Seever came to Ogden and told me I was to find this wagon that was just startin' west from St. Louis. We was to head 'em off and make shore they never got here. I never knew there was no woman along. Not even one. I didn't want to kill no woman."

"Who was with yuh?" Flood demanded.

"Hombre name of Quindry. Another name of Cal Santon. I met up with 'em in Laramie."

Jed's exclamation brought Flood's head up. "You know 'em?"

"Yeah." Jed nodded grimly. "I killed Buck Santon, Cal's brother. He was a crooked gambler!"

"Then you was the hombre they was huntin'!" Clark said, astonished.

"Where are they now?"

"Headin' west. Seever sent for 'em for some reason. Guess he figured they'd come in here and prove you was somebody different than yuh said yuh was. He didn't guess you knowed 'em, though."

"Seever ordered the killing?"

"Shore."

A few more questions, and the confession was completed.

"All right," Jed told him. "Sign it."

Pat Flood had the paper spread, and Clark scratched his name on it.

"Now," Jed said, "much as I hate to let a killer go, I gave my promise. Get on your horse. You've got thirty minutes' start. Make the most of it."

"Do I get my gun!" Clark pleaded.

"No. Get out of here before I change my mind."

Clark fairly threw himself at the nearest horse. Bent low he spurred the horse and they went out of the ranchyard on a dead run.

Flood handed the confession to Jed. "Yuh goin' to use it?"

Jed hesitated. "Not right now. I'm going to put it in the safe in the house. Then if Carol ever needs it, she can use it. If I brought it out now it would also prove I'm not Michael Latch!"

Flood nodded. "I knowed yuh wasn't," he said. "Old George told me a good deal about his nephew, and he never went to sea. But the other day I spotted yuh tyin' a bowline on a bight, and yuh handled that line like a sailor. A few other things showed me yuh'd been around more'n Latch had."

"Does Carol know?"

"Don't reckon she does," Flood said thoughtfully. "But she's a mighty knowin' young lady! Smart, that's what she is!"

If Cal Santon and Quindry were headed west, Seever must have telegraphed them. They would certainly ally themselves with Seever against Jed Asbury. As if there wasn't trouble enough!

CHAPTER SIX: For the Brand

Costa and Jim Pardo rode into the yard and Costa trotted his horse over to Jed who was wearing the silver guns now.

"The cattle, señor, are many!" Costa said. "More than we think for! We come to see if the Willow Springs crew can help us."

"They should be through," Jed said. "Is Miss Carol still out there with you?"

"No, señor," Costa said. "She has gone to Noveno."

Jed turned abruptly toward his waiting horse. "Come on! We're goin' to town!"

Seever would stop at nothing now, and if Santon and Quindry had arrived, Jed's work would be cut out for him. Santon was a feudist. There was every chance he had been well on his way West, following Jed Asbury before Seever's message had intercepted him. No doubt Seever had known how to reach the gambler, and he must be here now, and seen him, Jed Asbury, since Seever twice had called him "Jed."

Noveno lay basking in a warm, pleasant sun. In the distance the Sierras lifted their snow-crowned ramparts against the sky, the white of snow and the gray of rock merging into the deep green of the pines.

A man who was loitering in front of the Gold Strike stepped through the doors as Jed and his companions rode into the street. Then Walt Seever appeared in the doorway, careless, nonchalant.

Seever was smiling. "Huntin' somethin'?" he asked. His small eyes glinted with cruel amusement. "Figgered yuh'd be in before long. We just sort of detained that girl so's yuh'd come in. We can turn her loose now. We got what we want—you and yore salty friends in town!"

Jed swung down without replying. His eyes swept the street and the windows. This was a trap, and they had walked right into it.

"There's a gent in front of the express office, Boss," Pardo said softly.

"Thanks."

Jed was watching Seever. The trouble would start with him. He moved away from his horse. There was no time to see what Costa and Pardo were doing, but he knew they would be where it was best for them to be.

Thinking of Pardo's long, leathery face and cold eyes, he smiled a little. Costa would take care of himself, but Jim Pardo would do more. That old ladino was battle-wise and tough.

"Well, Seever," Jed said. "I'm glad you saved me the trouble of hunting you up."

Seever was standing on the board walk, a big man with a stubble of black beard on his granite-hard, wide-jawed face.

"Figgered this would save us both trouble," he drawled. "Folks hereabouts don't take to outsiders, Jed, especially when the outsider tries to run a blazer on us. The folks around here would a mite sooner have a tough ranny like me runnin' that spread than an outsider. Shuck yore guns, get on yore horses, and ride out of town, and we'll let yuh go."

"Don't do that, Boss!" Pardo interrupted. "He'll kill yuh as soon as yore guns drop!"

"I know. That's the kind of a rat he is. Cal Santon's in town, too, and he can't forget I killed that card-shark brother of his . . . No, Seever, the ranch goes to Miss Carol. If we shoot it out, you may get me, but I promise you—you'll die first!"

Seever's voice dropped to a hoarse snarl. "I'll kill—"

"Look out!" Pardo yelled.

Jed sprang back as the rifle roared from the window over the livery barn, yet even as he moved his hands swept down for the silver guns. They came up, spouting flame and spraying death.

Seever, struck in the chest, staggered back, his own gunfire pounding the dust at his feet, the horses near him leaping and snorting, wild-eyed with fear.

Oblivious to the bellowing gunfire behind and around him, Jed centered his attention on Walt Seever who was bending slowly at the knees, his face still twisted with hatred. When he finally crumpled on the board walk, Jed Asbury, feeling cold inside, hating the sight of this thing he had done, waited, watching and ready.

Slowly the gun dribbled from Seever's fingers and the man rolled over, his arm and head hanging over the edge of the walk. Blood gathered on the parched gray boards, and discolored the dust.

Jed turned then and took in the whole scene in one swift glance. Costa was down on one knee, blood staining the left sleeve of his shirt. He held his six-gun in his right hand and the barrel rested on his right knee. He was ready and waiting. His face showed no sign of pain.

A man sprawled over the window sill above the livery barn, and another lay in the street some forty feet away. Even at that distance Jed recognized Quindry. The man sprawled over the sill had the sandy hair that reminded Jed of Santon.

Pardo was holstering his gun. There was no sign of Strykes or Gin Feeley.

"You all right, Boss?" Pardo asked.

"Uh-huh. How about you?"

"I'm all right." Pardo looked at Costa. "Got one, Tony?"

"Si, in the shoulder, but not bad." He was trying to staunch the flow of blood with a handkerchief.

Heads were beginning to appear in windows and doors, but nobody showed any desire to get outside.

A door slammed open down the street, and the next minute Carol was hurrying toward them, her eyes frightened.

"Are you hurt?" she cried to Jed. "Did you get shot?"

He slid an arm around her as she came up to him, and it was so natural that neither of them noticed.

"Better get that shoulder fixed, Costa," he said.

He glanced down at Carol. "Where did they have you?"

"Strykes and Feeley had me in a house across the street. They were to hold me until you got worried and came to town. They thought you would come alone. When Feeley saw you weren't alone, he wanted Strykes to leave. Feeley looked out of the door and then Pat Flood saw him."

"Flood? How did he get here?"

"He followed you. And when he saw Feeley, he slipped around behind the house and got the drop on Feeley and Strykes through the window. I took their guns and he came in. He was just going to tie them up and help you when the shooting began."

"Carol," Jed said suddenly, "I've got a confession to make."

"You have?" she stared at him with wide eyes in which amusement seemed to lurk.

"Yes. I—I'm not Mike Latch!"

"Oh? Is that all? Why, I've known that all the time!"

"What?" He stared at her. "You knew?"

"Of course. You see, I was Michael Latch's wife!"

"His what?"

"Yes. Before I married him I was Carol Arden James. He was the only one who ever called me Arden. I was coming west with him but was ill, so I stayed inside the wagon and Clark never saw me at all. When we got far out on the trail, he convinced Michael there was a wagon train going by way of Santa Fe that would get us to the coast sooner, and that if we could catch them, we could make it out here sooner. Of course it was all a lie to get us away from the wagon train, but Michael listened. The train we were with was going only as far as Laramie.

"After we got out on the trail, Clark left us and said he would ride on ahead and locate the wagon train, then return to guide us to it. When Randy Kenner and Michael decided to camp in the morning, I was much better and went over the hill to a small pool to bathe. When I was dressing, I heard shooting, and believing it was Indians, crept to the top of the hill.

"It was all over. Clark had ridden up with two men and Michael, who had been expecting nothing, was dead. It was terrible! Randy was not dead yet when I got to the top of the hill, and I saw one of the men kick a pistol from his hand and shoot him again. There was nothing I could do, and I knew if I showed myself, they would kill me, too, so I lay there in the grass and waited."

"But what happened to you? How did you get out here?"

"There was nothing I could do at the wagon, so I started over the prairie toward the other wagon train. It was almost twenty miles away, but it was all I could do. When I'd only gone a few miles I saw old Nellie, Mike's saddle mare. She must have become frightened and broke loose. Anyway, she knew me and when I called she came right up, so I rode her to the other wagon train.

"From Laramie I came on by stage."

He looked at her uneasily.

"Then you knew all the time I was faking!"

"Yes, but when you stopped Walt that first night, I whispered to Costa not to tell."

"He knew all the time, too?"

"Yes." She was smiling at him. "I'd showed him my marriage license, which I'd been carrying in the pocket of my dress."

"Why didn't you tell?" he protested. "Here I was having a battle with my conscience, trying to decide what was right, and all the time I knew I had to explain sooner or later."

"You were doing so much better with the ranch than Michael ever could have, and Costa liked it that way. Michael and I grew up together and were more like brother and sister than husband and wife, but when he heard from his Uncle George, we were married. We thought Uncle George would be pleased—and we liked each other."

Suddenly it dawned on Jed that they were standing in the middle of the street and that he had his arm around Carol. He withdrew it hastily and they started toward the horses.

"Why didn't you just claim the estate as Mike's wife?" he asked.

"Costa was afraid Seever would kill me. We hadn't decided what to do when you solved everything for the time being."

"What about these guns?"

"My father made them. He was a gunsmith, and he made guns for Uncle George, too. These were a present to Mike when we started West."

His eyes avoided hers.

"Carol," he said. "I'll get my gear an' move on. The ranch is yours now, and I'd better head out."

"I don't want you to go," she murmured.

He thought his ears were deceiving him. "You— what?"

"Don't go, Jed. Stay with us. I couldn't manage the ranch alone, and Costa has been happy since you've been there. We need you, Jed. I—I need you."

"Well," he said hesitantly, "there's those cattle to be sold, and there's a quarter section near Willow Springs that could be irrigated."

Pardo, watching, glanced at Flood. "I think he's goin' to stay, Pat."

"Shore," Flood said knowingly, "ships and women. They all like a handy man around the place!"

Carol caught Jed's sleeve. "Then you'll stay?"

He smiled. "What could Costa do without me?"

BIG MEDICINE

Old Billy Dunbar was down flat on his face in a dry wash swearing into his beard. The best gold-bearing gravel he had found in a year, and then the Apaches would have to show up!

It was like them, the mean, ornery critters. He hugged the ground for dear life and hoped they would not see him, tucked away as he was between some stones where an eddy of the water that once ran through the wash had dug a trench between the stones.

There were nine of them. Not many, but enough to take his scalp if they found him, and it would be just as bad if they saw his burros or any of the prospect holes he had been sinking.

He was sweating like a stuck hog bleeds, lying there with his beard in the sand, and the old Sharps .50 ready beside him. He wouldn't have much of a chance if they found him, slithery fighters like they were, but if that old Sharps threw down on them he'd take at least one along to the Happy Hunting Ground with him.

He could hear them now, moving along the desert above the wash. Where in tarnation were they going? He wouldn't be safe as long as they were in the country, and this was country where not many white men came. Those few who did come were just as miserable to run into as the Apaches.

There were nine of them, the leader a lean-muscled man with a hawk nose. All of them slim and brown without much meat on them the way Apaches were, and wearing nothing but breech clouts and headbands.

He lay perfectly still. Old Billy was too knowing in Indian ways to start moving until he was sure they were gone. He laid right there for almost a half hour after he had last heard them, and then came out of it cautious as a bear reaching for a honey tree.

When he got on his feet, he hightailed it for the edge of the wash and took a look. The Apaches had vanished. He turned and went down the wash, taking his time and keeping the old Sharps handy. It was a mile to his burros and to the place where his prospect holes were. Luckily, he had them back in a draw where there wasn't much chance of them being found.

Billy Dunbar pulled his old gray felt hat down a little tighter and hurried on. Jennie and Julie were waiting for him, standing head to tail so they could brush flies off each other's noses.

When he got to them he gathered up his tools and took them back up the draw to the rocks at the end. His canteens were full, and he had plenty of grub and ammunition. He was lucky that he hadn't shot that rabbit when he saw it. The Apaches would have heard the bellow of the Old Sharps and come for him, sure. He was going to have to be careful.

If they would just kill a man it wouldn't be so bad, but these Apaches liked to stake a man out on an ant hill and let the hot sun and ants do for him, or maybe the buzzards—if they got there soon enough.

This wash looked good, too. Not only because water had run there, but because it was actually cutting into the edge of an old river bed. If he could sink a couple of holes down to bedrock, he'd bet there'd be gold and gold aplenty.

When he awakened in the morning he took a careful look around his hiding place. One thing, the way he was located, if they caught him in camp they couldn't get at him to do much. The hollow was perhaps sixty feet across, but over half of it was covered by shelving rock from above, and the cliff ran straight up from there for an easy fifty feet. There was water in a spring and enough grass to last the burros for quite some time.

After a careful scouting around, he made a fire of dead mesquite which made almost no smoke, and fixed some coffee. When he had eaten, Dunbar gathered up his pan, his pick, shovel and rifle and moved out. He was loaded more than he liked, but it couldn't be helped.

The place he had selected to work was the inside of the little desert stream. The stream took a bend and left a gravel bank on the inside of the elbow. That gravel looked good. Putting his Sharps down within easy reach, Old Billy got busy.

Before sundown he had moved a lot of dirt, and tried several pans, loading them up and going over to the stream. Holding the pan under the water, he began to stir the gravel, breaking up the lumps of clay and stirring until every piece was wet. Then he picked out the larger stones and pebbles and threw them to one side. He put his hands on opposite sides of the pan and began to oscillate vigorously under water, moving the pan in a circular motion so the contents were shaken from side to side.

With a quick glance around to make sure there were no Apaches in sight, he tipped the pan slightly, to an angle of about 30 degrees so the lighter sands, already buoyed up by the water, could slip out over the side.

He struck the pan several good blows to help settle the gold, if any, and then dipped for more water and continued the process. He worked steadily at the pan, with occasional glances around until all the refuse had washed over the side but the heavier particles. Then with a little clean water, he washed the black sand and gold into another pan which he took from the brush where it had been concealed the day before.

For some time he worked steadily, then as the light was getting bad, he gathered up his tools, and concealing the empty pan, carried the other with him back up the wash to his hideout.

He took his Sharps and crept out of the hideout and up the wall of the canyon. The desert was still and empty on every side.

"Too empty, durn it!" he grumbled. "Them Injuns'll be back. Yuh can't fool an Apache!"

Rolling out of his blankets at sunup, he prepared a quick breakfast and then went over his takings of the day with a magnet. This black sand was mostly particles of magnetite, ilmenite, and black magnetic iron oxide. What he couldn't draw off, he next eliminated by using a blow box.

"Too slow, with them Apaches around," he grumbled. "A man workin' down there could mebbe do sixty, seventy pans a day, in that sort of gravel, but watchin' for Injuns ain't goin' t' help much!"

Yet he worked steadily, and by nightfall, despite interruptions, had handled more than fifty pans. When the second day was over, he grinned at the gold he had. It was sufficient color to show he was on the right track. Right here, by using a rocker, he could have made it pay, but he wasn't looking for peanuts.

He had cached his tools along with the empty pan in the brush at the edge of the wash. When morning came, he rolled out and was just coming out of the hideout when he saw the Apache. He was squatted in the sand staring at something, and despite his efforts to keep his trail covered, Dunbar had a good idea what that something would be. He drew back into the hideout.

Lying on his middle, he watched the Indian get to his feet and start working downstream. When he got down there a little further, he was going to see those prospect holes. There would be nothing Dunbar could do then. Nor was there anything he could do now. So far as he could see, only one Apache had found him. If he fired, to kill the Indian, the others would be aware of the situation and come running.

Old Billy squinted his eyes and pondered the question. He had a hunch that Indian wasn't going to go for help. He was going to try to get Dunbar by himself, so he could take his weapons and whatever else he had of value.

The Indian went downstream further, and slipped out of sight. Billy instantly ducked out into the open and scooted down the canyon into the mesquite. He dropped flat there, and inched along in the direction the Indian had gone.

He was creeping along, getting nearer and nearer to his prospect holes, when suddenly, instinct or the subconscious hearing of a sound warned him. Like a flash, he rolled over, just in time to see the Indian leap at him, knife in hand!

Billy Dunbar was no longer a youngster, but he had lived a life in the desert, and he was hard and tough as whalebone. As the Apache leaped, he caught the knife wrist in his left hand, and stabbed at the Indian's ribs with his own knife. The Apache twisted away, and Billy gave a heave. The Indian lost balance. They rolled over, then fell over the eight-foot bank into the wash!

Luck was with Billy. The Indian hit first, and Billy's knife arm was around him, with the point gouging at the Indian's back. When they landed, the knife went in to the hilt.

Billy rolled off, gasping for breath. Hurriedly, he glanced around. There was no one in sight. Swiftly, he clawed at the bank, causing the loosened gravel to cave down and in a few minutes of hot, sweating work the Indian was buried.

Turning, Billy lit out for his hideaway and when he made it, he lay there gasping for breath, his Sharps ready. There would be no work this day. He was going to lie low and watch. The other Indians would come looking, he knew.

After dark he slipped out and covered the Indian better, and then used a mesquite bush to wipe out, as well as possible, the signs of their fighting. Then he catfooted it back to the hollow and tied a rawhide string across the entrance with a can of loose pebbles at the end to warn him if Indians found him. Then he went to sleep.

At dawn he was up. He checked the Sharps and then cleaned his .44 again. He loaded his pockets with cartridges just in case, and settled down for a day of it.

Luckily, he had shade. It was hot out there, plenty hot. You could fry an egg on those rocks by ten in the morning—not that he had any eggs. He hadn't even seen an egg since the last time he was in Fremont, and that had been four months ago.

He bit off a chew of tobacco and rolled it in his jaws. Then he studied the banks of the draw. An Apache could move like a ghost and look like part of the landscape. He had known them to come within fifteen feet of a man in grassy country without being seen, and no tall grass at that.

It wouldn't be so bad if his time hadn't been so short. When he left Fremont, Sally had six months to go to pay off the loan on her ranch, or out she would go. Sally's husband had been killed by a bronc down on the Sandy. She was alone with the kids and that loan about to take their home away.

When the situation became serious, Old Billy thought of this wash. Once, several years before, he had washed out some color here, and it looked rich. He had left the country about two jumps ahead of the Apaches and swore he'd never come back. Nobody else was coming out of here with gold, either, so he knew it was still like he remembered. Several optimistic prospectors had tried it, and were never heard of again. However, Old Billy had decided to take a chance. After all, Sally was all he had, and those-two grandchildren of his deserved a better chance than they'd get if she lost the place.

The day moved along, a story told by the shadows on the sides of the wash. You could almost tell the time by those shadows. It wasn't long before Dunbar knew every bush, every clump of greasewood or mesquite along its length, and every rock.

He wiped the sweat from his brow and waited. Sally was a good girl. Pretty, too, too pretty to be a widow at twenty two. It was almost midafternoon when his questing eye halted suddenly on the bank of the wash. He lay perfectly still, eyes studying the bank intently. Yet his eyes had moved past the spot before they detected something amiss. He scowled, trying to remember. Then it came to him.

There had been a torn place there, as though somebody had started to pull up a clump of greasewood, then abandoned it. The earth had been exposed, and a handful of roots. Now it was blotted out. Straining his eyes he could see nothing, distinguish no contours that seemed human, only that the spot was no longer visible. The spot was mottled by shadows and sunlight through the leaves of the bush.

Then there was a movement, so slight that his eye scarcely detected it, and suddenly the earth and torn roots were visible again. They had come back. Their stealth told him they knew he was somewhere nearby, and the logical place for him would be right where he was.

Now he was in for it. Luckily, he had food, water, and ammunition. There should be just eight of them unless more had come. Probably they had found his prospect holes and trailed him back this way.

There was no way they could see into his hollow, no way they could shoot into it except through the narrow entrance which was rock and brush. There was no concealed approach to it. He dug into the bank a little to get more earth in front of himself.

No one needed to warn him of the gravity of his situation. It was one hundred and fifty miles to Fremont, and sixty miles to the nearest white man, young Sid Barton, a cowhand turned rancher who started running some cattle on the edge of the Apache country.

Nor could he expect help. Nobody ever came into this country, and nobody knew where he was but Sally, and she only knew in a general way. Prospectors did not reveal locations where they had found color.

Well, he wasn't one of these restless young coots who'd have to be out there tangling with the Apaches. He could wait. And he would wait in the shade while they were in the sun. Night didn't worry him much. Apaches had never cared much for night fighting, and he wouldn't have much trouble with them.

One of them showed himself suddenly—only one arm and a rifle. But he fired, the bullet striking the rock overhead. Old Billy chuckled. "Tryin' t' draw fire," he said, "get me located!"

Billy Dunbar waited, grinning through his beard. There was another shot, then more stillness. He lay absolutely still. A hand showed, then a foot. He rolled his quid in his jaws and spat. An Indian suddenly showed himself, then vanished as though he had never been there. Old Billy watched the banks cynically. An Indian showed again, hesitated briefly this time, but Dunbar waited.

Suddenly, within twenty feet of the spot where Dunbar lay, an Indian slid down the bank and with a shrill whoop, darted for the entrance to the hideaway. It was point blank, even though a moving target. Billy let him have it!

The old Sharps bellowed like a stricken bull and leaped in his hands. The Apache screamed wildy and toppled over backwards, carried off his feet by the sheer force of the heavy-caliber bullet. Yells of rage greeted this shot.

Dunbar could see the Indian's body sprawled under the sun. He picked up an edged piece of white stone and made a straight mark on the rock wall beside him, then seven more. He drew a diagonal line through the first one. "Seven t' go," he said.

A hail of bullets began kicking sand and dirt up around the opening. One shot hit overhead and showered dirt down almost in his face. "Durn you!" he mumbled. He took his hat off and laid it beside him, his six-shooter atop of it, ready to hand.

No more Indians showed themselves, and the day drew on. It was hot out there. In the vast brassy vault of the sky a lone buzzard wheeled.

He tried no more shots, just waiting. They were trying to tire him out. Doggone it—in this place he could outwait all the Apaches in the Southwest—not that he wanted to!

Keeping well below the bank, he got hold of a stone about the size of his head and rolled it into the entrance. Instantly, the shot smacked the dirt below it and kicked dirt into his eyes. He wiped them and swore viciously. Then he got another stone and rolled that in place, pushing dirt up behind them. He scooped his hollow deeper, and peered thoughtfully at the banks of the draw.

Jennie and Julie were eating grass, undisturbed and unworried. They had been with Old Billy too long to be disturbed by these—to them—meaningless fusses and fights. The shadow from the west bank reached farther toward the east, and Old Billy waited, watching.

He detected an almost indiscernible movement atop the bank, in the same spot where he had first seen an Indian. Taking careful aim, he drew a bead on the exposed roots and waited.

He saw no movement, yet suddenly he focused his eyes more sharply and saw the roots were no longer exposed. Nestling the stock against his shoulder, his finger eased back on the trigger. The old Sharps wavered, and he waited. The rifle steadied, and he squeezed again.

The gun jumped suddenly and there was a shrill yell from the Apache who lunged to full height, rose on his tiptoes, both hands clasping his chest. The stricken redskin then plunged face forward down the bank in a shower of gravel. Billy reloaded and waited. The Apache lay still lying in the shadow below the bank. After watching him for a few minutes, alternating between the still form and the banks of the draw, Dunbar picked up his white stone and marked another diagonal white mark across the second straight line.

He stared at the figures with satisfaction. "Six left," he said. He was growing hungry. Jennie and Julie had both decided to lie down and call it a day.

As luck would have it, his shovel and pick were concealed in the brush at the point where the draw opened into the wider wash. He scanned the banks suddenly, and then drew back. Grasping a bush, he pulled it from the earth under the huge rocks. He then took the brush and some stones and added to his parapet. With some lumps of earth and rock he gradually built it stronger.

Always he returned to the parapet, but the Apaches were cautious and he saw nothing of them. Yet his instinct told him they were there, somewhere. And that, he knew, was the trouble. It was the fact he had been avoiding ever since he holed up for the fight. They would always be around somewhere now. Three of their braves were missing—dead. They would never let him leave the country alive.

If he had patience, so had they, and they could afford to wait. He could not. It was not merely a matter of getting home before the six month period was up—and less than two months remained of that—it was a matter of getting home with enough money to pay off the loan. And with the best of luck it would require weeks upon weeks of hard, uninterrupted work.

And then he saw the wolf.

It was no more than a glimpse, and a fleeting glimpse. Billy Dunbar saw the sharply pointed nose, and bright eyes, then the swish of a tail! The wolf vanished somewhere at the base of the shelf of rock that shaded the pocket. It vanished in proximity to the spring.

Old Billy frowned and studied the spot. He wasn't the only one holed up here! The wolf evidently had a hole somewhere in the back of the pocket, and perhaps some young, as the time of year was right. His stillness after he finished work on the entrance had evidently fooled the wolf into believing the white man was gone.

Obviously, the wolf had been lying there, waiting for him to leave so it could come out and hunt. The cubs would be getting hungry. If there were cubs.

The idea came to him then. An idea utterly fantastic, yet one that suddenly made him chuckle. It might work! It could work! At least, it was a chance, and somehow, some way, he had to be rid of those Apaches!

He knew something of their superstitions and beliefs. It was a gamble, but as suddenly as he conceived the idea, he knew it was a chance he was going to take.

Digging his change of clothes out of the saddle bags, he got into them. Then he took his own clothing and laid it out on the ground in plain sight. The pants, then the coat, the boots and nearby, the hat.

Taking some sticks he went to the entrance of the wolf den and built a small fire close by. Then he hastily went back and took a quick look around. The draw was empty, but he knew the place was watched. He went back and got out of line of the wolf den, and waited.

The smoke was slight, but it was going into the den. It wouldn't take long. The wolf came out with a rush, ran to the middle of the pocket, took a quick, snarling look around and then went over the parapet and down the draw!

Working swiftly, he moved the fire and scattered the few sticks and coals in his other fireplace. Then he brushed the ground with a branch. It would be a few minutes before they moved, and perhaps longer.

Crawling into the wolf den he next got some wolf hair which he took back to his clothing. He put some of the hair in his shirt, and some near his pants. A quick look down the draw showed no sign of an Indian, but that they had seen the wolf, he knew, and he could picture their surprise and puzzlement.

Hurrying to the spring, he dug from the bank near the water a large quantity of mud. This was an added touch, but one that might help. From the mud, he formed two roughly human figures. About the head of each he tied a blade of grass.

Hurrying to the parapet for a stolen look down the draw, he worked until six such figures were made. Then, using thorns and some old porcupine quills he found near a rock, he thrust one or more through each of the mud figures.

They stood in a neat row facing the parapet. Quickly, he hurried for one last look into the draw. An Indian had emerged. He stood there in plain sight, staring toward the place!

They would be cautious, Billy knew, and he chuckled to himself as he thought of what was to follow. Gathering up his rifle, the ammunition, a canteen and a little food, he hurried to the wolf den and crawled back inside.

On his first trip he had ascertained that there were no cubs. At the end of the den there was room to sit up, topped by the stone of the shelving rock itself. To his right, a lighted match told him there was a smaller hole of some sort.

Cautiously, Billy crawled back to the entrance, and careful to avoid the wolf tracks in the dust outside, he brushed out his own tracks, then retreated into the depths of the cave. From where he lay he could see the parapet.

Almost a half hour passed before the first head lifted above the poorly made wall. Black straight hair, a red headband, and the sharp, hard features of their leader.

Then other heads lifted beside him, and one by one the six Apaches stepped over the wall and into the pocket. They did not rush, but looked cautiously about, and their eyes were large, frightened. They looked all around, then at the clothing, then at the images. One of the Indians grunted and pointed.

They drew closer, then stopped in an awed line, staring at the mud figures. They knew too well what that meant. Those figures meant a witch doctor had put a death spell on each one of them.

One of the Indians drew back and looked at the clothing. Suddenly he gave a startled cry and pointed—at the wolf hair!

They gathered around, talking excitedly, then glancing over their shoulders fearsomely.

They had trapped what they believed to be a white man, and knowing Apaches, Old Billy would have guessed they knew his height, weight, and approximate age. Those things they could tell from the length of his stride, the way he worked, the pressure of a footprint in softer ground.

They had trapped a white man, and a wolf had escaped! Now they find his clothing lying here, and on the clothing, the hair of a wolf!

All Indians knew of wolf-men, those weird creatures who changed at will from wolf to man and back again, creatures that could tear the throat from a man while he slept, and could mark his children with the wolf blood.

The day had waned, and as he lay there, Old Billy Dunbar could see that while he worked the sun had neared the horizon. The Indians looked around uneasily. This was the den of a wolf-man, a powerful spirit who had put the death spell on each of them, who came as a man and went as a wolf.

Suddenly, out on the desert, a wolf howled!

The Apaches started as if struck, and then as one man they began to draw back. By the time they reached the parapet they were hurrying.

Old Billy stayed the night in the wolf hole, lying at its mouth, waiting for dawn. He saw the wolf come back, stare about uneasily, then go away. When light came he crawled from the hole.

The burros were cropping grass and they looked at him. He started to pick up a pack saddle, then dropped it. "I'll be durned if I will!" he said.

Taking the old Sharps and the extra pan, he walked down to the wash and went to work. He kept a careful eye out, but saw no Apaches. The gold was panning out even better than he had dreamed would be possible. A few more days—suddenly, he looked up.

Two Indians stood in plain sight, facing. The nearest one walked forward and placed something on a rock, then drew away. Crouched, waiting, Old Billy watched them go. Then he went to the rock. Wrapped in a piece of tanned buckskin, was a haunch of venison!

He chuckled suddenly. He was big medicine now. He was a wolf-man. The venison was a peace offering, and he would take it. He knew now he could come and pan as much gold as he liked in Apache country.

A few days later he killed a wolf, skinned it, and then buried the carcass, but of the head he made a cap to fit over the crown of his old felt hat, and wherever he went, he wore it.

A month later, walking into Fremont behind the switching tails of Jennie and Julie, he met Sally at the gate. She was talking with young Sid Barton.

"Hi," Sid said, grinning at him. Then he looked quizzically at the wolfskin cap. "Better not wear that around here! Somebody might take you for a wolf!"

Old Billy chuckled. "I am!" he said. "Yuh're durned right, I am! Ask them Apaches!"

MAN RIDING WEST

CHAPTER ONE: The Man from Points Yonder

Three men were hunkered down by the fire when Jim Gary walked his buckskin up to their camp in the lee of the cliff. The big man across the fire had a shotgun lying beside him. It was the shotgun that made Gary uneasy, for cowhands do not carry shotguns, especially when on a trail drive as these men obviously were.

Early as it was, the cattle were already bedded down for the night in the meadow alongside the stream, and from their looks they had come far and fast. It was still light, but the clouds were low and swollen with rain.

"How's for some coffee?" Jim asked as he drew up. "I'm ridin' through, an' I'm sure hungry an' tuckered."

Somewhere off in the mountains, thunder rolled and grumbled. The fire crackled, and the leaves on the willows hung still in the lifeless air. There were three saddled horses nearby, and among the gear was an old Mother Hubbard style saddle with a wide skirt.

"Light an' set up," the man who spoke was lean jawed and sandy haired. "Never liked to ride on an empty stomach m'self."

More than ever, Gary felt uneasy. Neither of the others spoke. All were tough-looking men, unshaven and dirty, but it was their hard-eyed suspicion that made Jim wonder. However, he swung down and loosened his saddle girth, then slipped the saddle off and laid it well back under the overhang of the cliff. As he did so he glanced again at the old saddle that lay there.

The overhang of the cliff was deep where the fire was built for shelter from the impending rain. Jim dropped to an ancient log, gray and stripped of bark, and handed his tin plate over to the man who reached for it. The cook slapped two thick slabs of beef on the plate and some frying pan bread liberally touched with the beef fryings. Gary was hungry and he dove in without comment, and the small man filled his cup.

"Headed west?" The sandy-haired man asked, after a few minutes.

"Yeah, headed down below the Rim. Pleasant Valley way."

The men all turned their heads toward him but none spoke. Jim could feel their eyes on his tied down guns. There was a sheep and cattle war in the Valley.

"They call me Red Slagle. These hombres are Tobe Langer and Jeeter Dirksen. We're drivin' to Salt Creek."

Langer would be the big one. "My name's Gary," Jim replied, "Jim Gary. I'm from points yonder. Mostly Dodge an' Santa Fe."

"Hear they are hirin' warriors in Pleasant Valley."

"Reckon." Jim refused to be drawn, although he had the feeling they had warmed to him since he mentioned heading for the Valley.

"Ridin' thataway ourselves," Red suggested. "Wan to make a few dollars drivin' cattle? We're short handed."

"Might," Gary admitted, "the grub's good."

"Give you forty to drive to Salt Creek. We'll need he'p. From hereabouts the country is plumb rough an' she's fixin' to storm."

"You've hired a hand. When do I start?"

"Catch a couple of hours sleep. Tobe has the first ride. Then you take over. If you need he'p, just you call out."

Gary shook out his blankets and crawled into them. In the moment before his eyes closed he remembered the cattle had all worn a Double A brand, and the brands were fresh. That could easily be with a trail herd. But the Double A had been the spread that Mart Ray had mentioned.

It was raining when he rode out to the herd. "They ain't fussin'," Langer advised, "an' the rain's quiet enough. It should pass mighty easy. See you."

He drifted toward camp, and Gary turned up his slicker collar and studied the herd as well as he could in the darkness. They were lying quiet. He was riding a gray roped from the small remuda, and he let the horse amble placidly toward the far side of the meadow. A hundred yards beyond the meadow the bulk of the sloping hill that formed the opposite side of the valley showed blacker in the gloom. Occasionally there was a flash of heat lightning, but no thunder.

Slagle had taken him on because he needed hands, but none of them accepted him. He decided to sit tight in his saddle and see what developed. It could be plenty, for unless he was mistaken, this was a stolen herd, and Slagle was a thief, as were the others.

If this herd had come far and fast, he had come farther and faster, and with just as great a need. Now there was nothing behind him but trouble, and nothing before him but bleak years of drifting ahead of a reputation.

Up ahead was Mart Ray, and Ray was as much of a friend as he had. Gunfighters are admired by many, respected by some, feared by all and welcomed by none. His father had warned him of what to expect, warned him long ago before he himself had died in a gun battle. "You're right handy, Son," he had warned, "one of the fastest I ever seen, so don't let it be known. Don't never draw a gun on a man in anger, an' you'll live happy. Once you get the name of a gunfighter, you're on a lonesome trail, an' there's only one ending."

So he had listened, and he had avoided trouble. Mart Ray knew that. Ray was himself a gunman. He had killed six men of whom Jim Gary knew, and no doubt there had been others. He and Mart had been riding together in Texas, and then in a couple of trail drives, one all the way to Montana. He never really got close to Mart, but they had been partners, after a fashion.

Ray had always been amused at his eagerness to avoid trouble, although he had no idea of the cause of it. "Well," he had said, "they sure cain't say like father, like son. From all I hear your pappy was an uncurried wolf, an' you fight shy of trouble. You run from it. If I didn't know you so well, I'd say you was yaller."

But Mart Ray had known him well, for it had been Jim who rode his horse down in front of a stampede to pick Ray off the ground, saving his life. They got free, but no more, and a thousand head of mad cattle stampeded over the ground where Ray had stood.

Then, a month before, down in the Big Bend country, trouble had come, and it was trouble he could not avoid. It braced him in a little Mexican cantina just over the river, and in the person of a dark, catlike Mexican with small feet and dainty hands, but his guns were big enough and there was an unleashed devil in his eyes.

Jim Gary had been dancing with a Mexican girl and the Mexican had jerked her from his arms and struck her across the face. Jim knocked him down, and the Mexican got up, his eyes fiendish. Without a word, the Mexican went for his gun, and for a frozen, awful instant, Jim saw his future facing him, and then his own hand went down and he palmed his gun in a flashing, lightning draw that rapped out two shots. The Mexican, who had reached first, barely got his gun clear before he was dead. He died on his feet, then fell.

In a haze of powder smoke and anguish, Jim Gary had wheeled and strode from the door, and behind him lay dead and awful silence. It was not until two days later that he knew who and what he had killed.

The lithe-bodied Mexican had been Miguel Sonoma, and he had been a legend along the Border. A tough, dangerous man with a reputation as a killer.

Two nights later, a band of outlaws from over the Border rode down upon Gary's little spread to avenge their former leader, and two of them died in the first blast of gun fire, a matter of hand guns at point-blank range.

From the shelter of his cabin, Gary fought them off for three days before the smoke from his burning barn attracted help. When the help arrived, Jim Gary was a man with a name. Five dead men lay on the ground around the ranch yard and in the desert nearby. The wounded had been carried away. And the following morning, Jim turned his ranch over to the bank to sell, and lit a shuck—away from Texas.

Of this Mart Ray knew nothing. Half of Texas and all of New Mexico, or most of it, would lie behind him when he reached the banks of Salt Creek. Mart Ray was ramrodding the Double A, and he would have a job for him.

CHAPTER TWO: Ghost with the Night Herd

Jim Gary turned the horse and rode slowly back along the side of the herd. The cattle had taken their midnight stretch and after standing around a bit, were lying down once more. The rain was falling, but softly, and Gary let the gray take his own time in skirting the herd.

The night was pitch dark. Only the horns of the cattle glistened with rain, and their bodies were a darker blob in the blackness of the night. Once, drawing up near the willows along the stream, Jim thought he detected a vague sound. He waited a moment, listening. On such a night nobody would be abroad who could help it, and it was unlikely that a mountain lion would be on the prowl, although possible.

He started on again, yet now his senses were alert, and his hand slid under his slicker and touched the butt of a .44. He was almost at the far end of the small herd when a sudden flash of lightning revealed the hillside across the narrow valley.

Stark and clear, glistening with rain, sat a horseman! He was standing in his stirrups, and seemed amazingly tall, and in the glare of the flash, his face was stark white, like the face of a fleshless skull!

Startled, Gary grunted and slid his gun into his hand, but all was darkness again. And listen as he could, he heard no further sound. When the lightning flashed again, the hillside was empty and still. Uneasily, he caught himself staring back over his shoulder into the darkness, and he watched his horse. The gray was standing, head up and ears erect, staring off toward the darkness near the hill. Riding warily, Gary started in that direction, but when he got there, he found nothing.

It was almost daylight when he rode up to the fire which he had kept up throughout the night, and swinging down, he awakened Dirksen. The man sat up, startled. "Hey!" he exclaimed. "You forgot to call me?"

Jim grinned at him. "Just figured I was already up an' a good cook needed his sleep."

Jeeter stared at him. "You mean you rode for me? Say, you're all right!"

"Forget it!" Gary stretched. "I had a quiet night, mostly."

Red Slagle was sitting up, awakened by their talk. "What do you mean—mostly?"

Jim hesitated, feeling puzzled. "Why, to tell you the truth, I'm not sure whether I saw anything or not, but I sure thought I did. Anyway, it had me scared."

"What was it?" Slagle was pulling on his pants, but his eyes were serious. "A lion?"

"No, it was a man on a horse. A tall man with a dead white face, like a skull." Gary shrugged sheepishly. "Makes me sound like a fool, but I figured for a moment that I'd seen a ghost!"

Red Slagle was staring at him, and Jeeter's face was dead white and his eyes were bulging. "A ghost?" he asked, faintly. "Did you say, a ghost?"

"Shucks," Gary shrugged, "there ain't no such thing. Just some hombre on a big black horse, passin' through in the night, that was all! But believe me, seein' him in the lightnin' up on that hill like I did, it sure was scary!"

Tobe Langer was getting up, and he too, looked bothered. Slagle came over to the fire and sat down, boots in hand. Reaching down he pulled his sock around to get a hole away from his big toe, then he put his foot into the wet boot and began to struggle with it.

"That horse now," Langer asked carefully, "did it have a white star between the eyes?"

Gary was surprised. "Why, yes! Matter of fact, it did! You know him?"

Slagle let go of the boot and stomped his foot to settle it in the boot. "Yeah, feller we seen down the road a ways. Big black horse."

Slagle and Langer walked away from camp a ways and stood talking together. Jeeter was worried. Jim could see that without half trying, and he studied the man thoughtfully. Jeeter Dirksen was a small man, quiet, but inclined to be nervous. He had neither the strength nor the toughness of Slagle and Langer. If Gary learned anything about the cattle it would be through his own investigation or from Jeeter. And he was growing more and more curious.

Yet, if these were Double A cattle, and had been stolen, why were they being driven toward the AA ranch, rather than away from it? He realized suddenly that he knew nothing at all about Red Slagle nor his outfit, and it was time he made some inquiries.

"This Double A," he asked suddenly, "you been ridin' for them long?"

Dirksen glanced at him sharply, and bent over his fire. "Not long," he said. "It's a Salt Creek outfit. Slagle's segundo."

"Believe I know your foreman," Gary suggested, "I think this was the outfit he said. Hombre name of Mart Ray. Ever hear of him?"

Jeeter turned sharply, slopping coffee over the rim of the cup. It hissed in the fire, and both men looked around at the camp. Jeeter handed the cup to Gary and studied him, searching his face. Then he admitted cautiously, "Yeah, Ray's the foreman. Ranch belongs to a syndicate out on the coast. You say you know him?"

"Uh huh. Used to ride with him." Langer and Slagle had walked back to the fire, and Dirksen poured coffee for them.

"Who was that you rode with?" Slagle asked.

"Your boss, Mart Ray."

Both men looked up sharply, then Slagle's face cleared and he smiled. "Say! That's why the name was familiar! You're that Jim Gary! Son of Old Steve Gary. Yeah, Mart told us about you."

Langer chuckled suddenly. "You're the scary one, huh? The one who likes to keep out of trouble. Yeah, we heard about you!"

The contempt in his tone stiffened Jim's back, and for an instant he was on the verge of a harsh retort, then the memory of what lay behind him welled up within, and bitterly he kept his mouth shut. If he got on the prod and killed a man here, he would only have to drift farther. There was only one solution, and that was to avoid trouble. Yet irritating as it was to be considered lacking in courage, Langer's remark let him know that the story of his fights had not preceded him.

"There's no call," he said, after a minute, "to go around the country killin' folks. If people would just get the idea they can get along without all that. Me, I don't believe in fightin'."

Langer chuckled, but Slagle said nothing, and Dirksen glanced at him sympathetically.

All day the herd moved steadily west, but now Gary noticed a change, for the others were growing more watchful as the day progressed, and their eyes continued to search the surrounding hills, and they rode more warily approaching any bit of cover.

Once, when Jeeter rode near him, the little man glanced across the herd at the other riders, then said quietly, "That was no ghost you saw. Red rode up there on the hill, an' there was tracks, tracks of a mighty big black horse."

"Wonder why he didn't ride down to camp?" Jim speculated. "He sure enough saw the fire!"

Dirksen grunted. "If that hombre was the one Red thinks it is, he sure didn't have no aim to ride down there!"

Before Gary could question him further, Jeeter rode off after a stray and cutting him back into the herd, rode on further ahead. Jim dropped back to the drag, puzzled over this new angle. Who could the strange rider be? What did he want? Was he afraid of Slagle?

A big brindle steer was cutting wide of the herd and Jim swung out to get him, but dashing toward the stream, the steer floundered into the water and into quicksand. Almost at once, it was down, struggling madly, its eyes rolling.

Jim swung a loop and dropped it over the steers horns. If he could give the steer a little help now there was a chance he could get it out before it bogged in too deep.

He started the buckskin back toward more solid ground and with the pull on the rope and the struggling of the steer, he soon had it out on the bank of the stream. The weary animal stumbled and went down, and shaking his loop loose, Gary swung his horse around to get the animal up. Something he saw on the flank made him swing down beside the steer. Curiously, he bent over the brand.

It had been worked over! The Double A had been burned on over a Slash Four!

"Somethin' wrong?"

The voice was cold and level, and Jim Gary started guiltily, turning. Then his eyes widened. "Mart! Well, for cryin' out in the night time! Am I glad to see you!"

Ray stared. "For the luvva Pete, if it ain't Gary! Say, how did you get here? Don't tell me you're drivin' that herd up ahead?"

"That's right! Your outfit, ain't it? I hired on back down the line. This steer just got hisself bogged down an' I had a heck of a time gettin' him out. You seen Red an' the boys?"

"Not yet. I swung wide. Get that steer on his feet an' we'll join 'em."

Yet as they rode back, despite Ray's affability, Gary was disturbed. Something here was very wrong. This was a Slash

Four steer with the brand worked over to a Double A, the brand for which Ray was foreman. If these cattle were rustled, then Mart Ray was party to it, and so were Slagle, Langer and Dirksen! And, if caught with these men and cattle, so was he!

He replied to Ray's questions as well as he could, and briefly, aware that his friend was preoccupied and thinking of something else. Yet at the same time he was pleased that Ray asked him no questions about his reasons for leaving home.

Mart Ray rode up ahead and joined Slagle and he could see the two men riding on together, deep in conversation. When they bedded down for the night there had been no further chance to talk to him, and Gary was just as well satisfied, for there was much about this that he did not like. Nor was anything said about the midnight rider. When day broke, Mart Ray was gone. "Rode on to Salt Creek," Red said, "we'll see him there." He glanced at Jim, his eyes amused. "He said to keep you on, that you was a top-hand."

Despite the compliment, Jim was nettled. What else had Ray told Slagle? His eyes narrowed. Whatever it was, he was not staying on. He was going to get shut of this outfit just as fast as he could. All he wanted was his time. Yet by midday he had not brought himself to ask for it.

Dirksen had grown increasingly silent, and he avoided Langer and Slagle. Watching him, Jim was puzzled by the man, but could find no reason for his behavior unless the man was frightened by something. Finally, Jim pulled up alongside Jeeter.

The man glanced at him, and shook his head. "I don't like this. Not even a little. She's too quiet."

Gary hesitated, waiting for the cowhand to continue, but he held his peace. Finally, Gary said, speaking slowly, "It is mighty quiet, but I see nothin' wrong with that. I'm not hunting trouble."

"Trouble," Jeeter said dryly, "comes sometimes whether you hunt it or not. If anything breaks around this herd, take my advice an' don't ask no questions. Just scatter dust out of here!"

"Why are you warning me?" Gary asked.

Jeeter shrugged. "You seem like a right nice feller," he said quietly. "Shame for you to get rung in on somethin' as dirty as this when you had nothin' to do with it."

CHAPTER THREE: Boss of the Slash Four

Despite his questions, Jeeter would say no more, and finally Gary dropped back to the drag. There was little dust, due to the rains, but the drag was a rough deal for the herd was tired and they kept lagging back. Langer and Slagle, Jim observed, spent more time watching the hills than the cattle. Obviously, both men were as jumpy as Dirksen, and were expecting something. Toward dusk Red left the herd and rode up a canyon into the hills.

Slagle was still gone, and Jim was squatting by the fire watching Jeeter throw grub together when there was a sudden shot from the hills to the north.

Langer stopped his nervous pacing and faced the direction of the shot, his hand on his gun. Jim Gary got slowly to his feet, and he saw that Jeeter's knuckles gripping the frying pan were white and hard.

Langer was first to relax. "Red must have got him a turkey," he said, "few around here, and he was sayin' earlier he'd sure like some."

Nevertheless, Gary noted that Langer kept back from the firelight and had his rifle near at hand. There was a sound of an approaching horse and Langer slid his rifle across his knees, but it was Slagle, and he swung down, glancing toward the big man.

"Shot at a turkey, an' missed." Then he added, looking right at Langer, "Nothin' to worry about now. This time for sure."

Dirksen got suddenly to his feet. "I'm quittin', Red. I don't like this a-tall, not none. I'm gettin' out."

Slagle's eyes were flat and ugly. "Sit down an' shut up, Jeeter," he said impatiently, "tomorrow's our last day. We'll have a payday this side of Salt Creek an' then if you want to blow, why you can blow out of here."

Gary looked up. "I reckon you can have my time, then, too," he said quietly, "I'm ridin' west for Pleasant Valley."

"You?" Langer snorted. "Pleasant Valley? You better stay somewhere where you can be took care of. They don't side-step trouble out there."

Gray felt something rise within him, but he controlled his anger with an effort. "I didn't ask you for any comment, Tobe," he said quietly, "I can take care of myself."

Langer sneered. "Why, you yaller skunk! I heard all about you! Just because your pappy was a fast man, you must think folks are skeered of you! You're yaller as saffron! You ain't duckin' trouble, you're just scared!"

Gary was on his feet, his face white. "All you've got to do, Tobe, if you want to lose some teeth, is to stand up!"

"What?" Langer leaped to his feet. "Why, you dirty—"

Jim Gary threw a roundhouse left. The punch was wide, but it came fast, and Langer was not expecting Jim to fight. Too late, he tried to duck, but the fist caught him on the nose, smashing it and showering the front of his shirt with gore.

The big man was tough, and he sprang in, swinging with both hands. Gary stood his ground, and began to fire punches with both fists. For a full minute the two big men stood toe to toe and slugged wickedly, and then Gary deliberately gave ground. Over eager, Langer leaped after him, and Gary brought up a wicked right that stood Tobe on his boot toes, then a looping left that knocked him into the fire.

With a cry, he leaped from the flames, his shirt smoking. Ruthlessly, Gary grabbed him by the shirt front and jerked him into a right hand to the stomach, then a right to the head, and shoving him away he split his ear with another looping left, smashing it like an over ripe tomato. Langer went down in a heap.

Red Slagle had made no move to interfere, but his eyes were hard and curious as he stared up at Gary. "Now where," he said, "did Ray get the idea that you wouldn't fight?"

Gary spilled water from a canteen over his bloody knuckles. "Maybe he just figured wrong. Some folks don't like trouble. That don't mean they won't fight when they have to."

Langer pulled himself drunkenly to his feet and staggered toward the creek.

Red measured Jim with careful eyes. "What would you do," he asked suddenly, "if Langer reached for a gun?"

Gary turned his level green eyes toward Slagle. "Why, I reckon I'd have to kill him," he said, matter-of-factly. "I hope he ain't so foolish."

Dawn broke cold and gray and Jim Gary walked his horse up into the hills where he had heard the shot the night before. He knew that if Slagle saw him, he would be in trouble, but there was much he wanted to know.

Despite the light fall of rain the night before, there were still tracks. He followed those of Slagle's bay until he found where they joined those of a larger horse. Walking the buckskin warily, Jim followed the trail. It came to a sudden end.

A horse was sprawled in a clearing, shot through the head. A dozen feet away lay an old man, a tall old man, his sightless eyes staring toward the lowering skies, his arms flung wide. Jim bent over him and saw that he had been shot three times through the chest. Three times. And the wound lower down was an older wound, several days old at least.

The horse wore a Slash Four brand. Things were beginning to make sense now. Going through the old man's pockets, Jim found a worn envelope containing some tallies of cattle, and the envelope was addressed to Tom Blaze, Durango, Colo.

Tom Blaze . . . the Slash Four!

Tom Blaze, the pioneer Kiowa fighting cattleman who owned the Slash Four, one of the toughest outfits in the West! Why he had not connected the two Jim could not imagine, but the fact remained that the Slash Four had struck no responsive chord in his thoughts until now.

And Tom Blaze was dead.

Now it all fitted. The old Mother Hubbard saddle had been taken from Tom's horse, for this was the second time he had been shot. Earlier, perhaps when the cattle had been stolen, they had shot him and left him for dead, yet they had been unable to leave the saddle behind, for a saddle was two or three month's work for a cowhand, and not to be lightly left behind.

They had been sure of themselves, too. Sure until he saw Blaze, following them despite his wound. After that they had been worried, and Slagle must have sighted Blaze the afternoon before, then followed him and shot him down.

When the Slash Four found Tom Blaze dead all heck would break loose. Dirksen knew that, and that was why he wanted out, but fast. And it was why Red Slagle and Tobe Langer had pushed so hard to get the cattle to Salt Creek where they could be lost in larger herds, or in the breaks of the hills around the Double A.

When he rode the buckskin down to the fire the others were all up and moving around. Langer's face was swollen and there were two deep cuts, one on his cheekbone, the other over an eye. He was sullen and refused to look toward Gary.

Slagle stared at the buckskin suspiciously, noticing the wetness on his legs from riding in the high grass and brush.

Whatever the segundo had in mind he never got a chance to say. Jim Gary poured a cup of coffee, but held it in his left hand. "Red, I want my money. I'm takin' out."

"Mind if I ask why?" Red's eyes were level and waiting.

Gary knew that Slagle was a gun hand but the thought did not disturb him. While he avoided trouble, it was never in him to be afraid, nor did his own skill permit it. While he had matched gun speed with only one man, he had that sure confidence that comes from unerring marksmanship and speed developed from long practice.

"No, I don't mind. This morning I found Tom Blaze's body, right where you killed him yesterday afternoon. I know that Slash Four outfit, and I don't want to be any part of this bunch when they catch up to you."

His frankness left Slagle uncertain. He had been prepared for evasion. This was not only sincerity, but it left Slagle unsure as to Gary's actual stand. From his words Slagle assumed Gary was leaving from dislike of the fight rather than dislike of rustling.

"You stick with us, Jim," he said, "you're a good man, like Mart said. That Slash Four outfit won't get wise, and there'll be a nice split on this cattle deal."

"I want no part of it," Jim replied shortly. "I'm out. Let me have my money."

"I ain't got it," Red said simply. "Ray pays us all off. I carry no money around. Come on, Jim, lend us a hand. We've only today, then we'll be at the head of Salt Creek Wash and get paid off."

Gary hesitated. He did need the money, for he was broke and would need grub before he could go on west. Since he had come this far, another day would scarcely matter. "All right, I'll finish the drive."

Nothing more was said, and within the hour they moved out. Yet Gary was restless and worried. He could feel the tenseness in the others and knew they, too, were disturbed. There was no sign of Mart Ray, who should be meeting them soon.

To make matters worse, the cattle were growing restive. The short drives had given them time to recover some of their energy and several of them, led by one big red steer, kept breaking for the brush. It was hot, miserable work. The clouds still hung low, threatening rain, but the air was sultry.

Jim Gary started the day with the lean gray horse he had ridden before, but by midafternoon he exchanged the worn out animal for his own buckskin. Sweat streamed down his body under his shirt, and he worked hard, harrying the irritable animals down the trail that now was lined with piñon and juniper, with a sprinkling of huge boulders. Ahead, a wide canyon opened, and not far beyond would be the spot where he expected to find Ray with the payoff money.

The big red steer suddenly made another bolt for the brush and the buckskin unwound so fast that it almost unseated Gary. He swore softly and let the horse take him after the steer and cut it back to the herd. As it swung back, he glanced up to see Langer and Red Slagle vanishing into the brush. Where Dirksen was he could not guess until he heard a wild yell.

Swinging around, he saw a dozen hard riding horsemen cutting down from the brush on both sides, and a glance told him that flight was useless. Nevertheless, Jeeter Dirksen tried it.

Slamming the spurs into his bronc, he lunged for the brush in the direction taken by Slagle and Langer, but he made no more than a dozen yards when a rattle of gunfire smashed him from the saddle. His slender body hit the ground rolling, flopped over one last time, and lay sprawled and sightless under the low gray clouds.

Gary rested his hands on his saddlehorn and stared gloomily at the strange little man, so badly miscast in this outlaw venture. Then horsemen closed in around him; his six-guns were jerked from their holsters, and his rifle from its scabbard.

"What's the matter with you?" The voice was harsh. "Won't that horse of yours run?"

Jim looked up into a pair of cold gray eyes in a leatherlike face. A neat gray mustache showed above a firm lipped mouth.

Jim Gary smiled, although he had never felt less like it in his life. The horsemen surrounded him, and their guns were ready. "Never was much of a hand to run," Jim said, "an' I've done nothin' to run for."

"You call murderin' my brother nothin'? You call stealin' cattle nothin'? Sorry, friend, we don't see things things alike. I call it hangin'."

"So would I, on'y I haven't done those things. I hired onto this oufit back down the line. Forty bucks to the head of Salt Creek Wash . . . an' they ain't paid me."

"You'll get paid!" The speaker was a lean, hard-faced young man. "With a rope!"

Another rider pushed a horse through the circle. "Who is this man, Uncle Dan? Why didn't he try to get away?"

"Says he's just a hired hand," Uncle Dan commented.

"That's probably what that dead man would have said, too!" the lean puncher said. "Let me an' the boys have him under that cottonwood we seen. It had nice strong limbs."

Gary had turned his head to look at the girl. Uncle Dan would be Dan Blaze, and this must be the daughter of the murdered man. She was tall, slim but rounded of limb and undeniably attractive, with color in her cheeks and a few scattered freckles over her nose. Her eyes were hazel and now looked hard and stormy.

"Did you folks find Tom Blaze's body?" he asked. "They left him back yonder." Lifting a hand carefully to his shirt pocket he drew out the envelope and tally sheets. "These were his."

"What more do you need?" The lean puncher demanded. He pushed his horse against Jim's and grabbed at the buckskin's bridle. "Come on, boys!"

"Take it easy, Jerry!" Dan Blaze said sharply. "When I want him hung, I'll say so." His eyes shifted back to Jim. "You're a mighty cool customer," he said. "If your story's straight, what are you doing with these?"

Briefly as possible, Jim explained the whole situation, and ended by saying, "What could I do? I still had forty bucks comin', an' I did my work, so I aim to collect."

"You say there were three men with the herd? And the two who got away were Tobe Langer and Red Slagle?"

"That's right," Jim hesitated over Mart Ray, then said no more.

Blaze was staring at the herd, now he looked at Jim. "Why were these cattle branded AA? That's a straight outfit. You know anything about that?"

Gary hesitated. Much as he had reason to believe Ray was not only one of these men but their leader, he hated to betray him. "Not much. I don't know any of these outfits. I'm a Texas man."

Blaze smiled wryly. "You sound it. What's your handle?"

"Jim Gary."

The puncher named Jerry started as if struck. "Jim Gary?" he gasped, his voice incredulous. "The one who killed Sonoma?"

"Yeah, I reckon."

Now they were all staring at him with new interest, for the two fights he had were ample to start his name growing a legend on the plains and desert. These punchers had heard of him, probably from some grub line rider or drifting puncher.

"Jim Gary," Blaze mused, "we've heard about you. Old Steve's son, aren't you? I knew Steve."

Jim looked up his eyes cold."My father," he said grimly, "was a mighty good man!"

Dan Blaze's eyes warmed a little. "You're right. He was."

"What of it?" Jerry demanded sullenly. "The man's a killer. We know that. We found him with the cattle. We found him with some of Tom's stuff on him. What more do you want?"

The girl spoke suddenly. "There was another rider, one who joined you, then rode away. Who was he?"

There it was, and Jim suddenly knew he would not lie. "Mart Ray," he said quietly, "of the Double A."

"That's a lie!" The girl flashed back. "What are you saying?"

"You got any proof of that?" Jerry demanded hotly. "You're talkin' about a friend of our'n."

"He was a friend of mine, too." Gary explained about Mart Ray. "Why don't you turn me loose?" he suggested then. "I'll go get Ray and bring him to you. Chances are Slagle and Tobe will be with him."

"You'll get him?" Jerry snorted. "That's a good one, that is!"

"Tie him," Dan Blaze said suddenly. "We'll go into Salt Creek."

CHAPTER FOUR: Hoofmarked for Justice

Riding behind Dan Blaze and his niece, whom he heard them call Kitty, Jim Gary was suddenly aware, almost for the first time, of the danger he was in. The fact that it had been averted for the moment was small consolation, for these were hard, desperate men, and one of them, perhaps more, had been slain.

Fear was something strange to him, and while he had known danger, it had passed over him leaving him almost untouched. This situation conveyed only a sense of unreality, and until now the idea that he might really be in danger scarcely seemed credible. Listening to these men, his mind changed about that. He realized belatedly that he was in the greatest danger of his life. If he had none of their talk to warn him, the mute evidence of Jeeter's body was enough. And Jeeter had died yelling to him, trying to give him a warning so he might escape.

Now fear rode with him, a cold, clammy fear that stiffened his fingers and left his mouth dry and his stomach empty. Even the sight of the scattered buildings of the town of Salt Creek did not help, and when they rode up the street, the red of embarrassment crept up his neck at the shame of being led into the town, his hands tied behind him, like a cheap rustler.

Mart Ray was sitting on the steps and he shoved his hat back and got to his feet. Beside him was Red Slagle. There was no sign of Tobe Langer. "Howdy, Dan! What did you catch? A hoss thief?" Ray's voice was genial, his eyes bland. "Looks like a big party for such a small catch!"

Blaze reined in his horse and stopped the little cavalcade. His eyes went from Mart to Slagle. "How long have you been here, Red?" he demanded.

"Me?" Slagle was innocent. "No more'n about fifteen minutes, maybe twenty. Just rode in from the Double A. Somethin' wrong?"

Blaze turned his cold eyes on Jim Gary, then looked back to Ray. "We found a herd of Slash Four cattle east of here, Mart. They were wearin' a Double A brand worked over our Slash Four. How do you explain it?"

Ray shrugged. "I don't," he said simply. "How does that hombre you got with you explain it?"

Kitty Blaze spoke up quickly. "Mart, did you ever see this man before? Did you?"

Ray stared at Gary. "Not that I recall," he said seriously. "He sure don't look familiar to me!"

"Blaze," Gary said suddenly, "if you'll turn my hands loose and give me a gun I can settle this in three minutes! I can prove he's a liar! I can prove that he does know me, an' that I know him!"

"There's nothin' you can prove with a gun you can't prove without it!" Blaze said flatly. "Whatever you know, spill it! Else you're gettin' your neck stretched! I'm tired of this fussin' around!"

Jim Gary kneed his horse foreward. His eyes were hot and angry. "Mart," he said, "I always suspected there was a streak of coyote in you, but I never knowed you'd be this low down. I don't like to remind anybody of what I done for him, but I recall a stampede I hauled you out of. Are you goin' to talk?"

Ray shook his head smiling. "This is a lot of trouble, Dan. Take him away and stretch his neck before I get sore and plug him."

"You'd be afraid to meet me with a gun, Mart. You always were afraid!" Jim taunted. "That's why you left Red and Tobe with the cattle. You wanted the profit but none of the trouble! Well, you've got trouble now! If I had a gun I'd see you eat dirt!"

Mart Ray's face was ugly. "Shut up, you fool! You call me yellow? Why, everybody knows you're yellow as—!" He caught himself abruptly, his face paling under the tan.

"What was that, Ray?" Dan Blaze's face had sharpened. "Ever'body knows what about him? If you've never seen him before, how could you say ever'body calls him yellow?"

Ray shrugged. "Just talkin' too fast, that's all!" He turned and stepped up on the sidewalk. "He's your man. You settle your own war." Ray turned to go, but Jim yelled at him, and Ray wheeled.

"Mart, if I don't know you, how do I know you've got a white scar down your right side, a scar made by a steer's hoof?"

Ray laughed, but it was a strained laugh. He looked trapped now, and he took an involuntary step backward. "That's silly!" he scoffed. "I've no such scar!"

"Why not take off your shirt?" Jerry said suddenly. "That will only take a minute." The lean jawed cowhand's face was suddenly hard. "I think I remember you having such a scar, from one time I seen you swimmin' in the San Juan. Take off your shirt an' let's see!"

Mart Ray backed up another step, his face sharp and cold. "I'll be damned if I take off my shirt in the street for any low down rustler!" he snapped. "This here nonsense has gone far enough!"

"Loose my hands!" Jim pleaded in a whisper. "I'll take his shirt off!"

Kitty stared at him. Her face was white and strained, but in her eyes he now saw a shadow of doubt. Yet it was Jerry who acted suddenly, and jerked him around and before anyone realized what he had done, he severed the bonds with a razor sharp knife and jerked the ropes from his hands. With almost the same gesture, he slammed guns in Gary's holsters. "All right! Maybe I'm crazy!" he snapped. "But go to it!"

The whole action had taken less than a minute, and Mart Ray had turned his back and started away while Blaze waited in indecision. It was Red Slagle who saw Jim Gary hit the ground. "Boss!" he yelled. His voice was suddenly sharp with panic. "Look out!"

Ray wheeled, and when he saw Gary coming toward him, chafing his wrists, he stood still, momentarily dumbfounded. Then he laughed. "All right, Yellow! You're askin' for it! This is one bunch of trouble you can't duck! You've ducked your last fight!"

Furious, he failed to realize the import of his words, and he dropped into a half crouch, his hands ready above his gun butts. It was Jerry who shook him. Jerry who made the casual remark that jerked Mart Ray to realization of what he was facing.

"Looks like whatever Ray knows about him, he sure ain't heard about Jim Gary killin' Miguel Sonoma!"

Mart Ray was staggered. "Sonoma?" he gasped. "You killed Sonoma?"

Jim Gary was facing him now. Some of the numbness was gone from his hands, and something cold and terrible was welling up within him. He had ridden beside this man, shared food with him, worked with him, and now the man had tricked and betrayed him.

"Yes, Mart, I killed Sonoma. I ain't afraid. I never was. I just don't like trouble!"

Ray's tongue touched his lips and his eyes narrowed to slits, he sank a little deeper into the crouch, and men drew away to

189

the sides of the street. Scarcely twenty feet apart, the two faced each other. "Take off your shirt, Ray. Take it off and show them. Reach up slow and unbutton it. You take it off yourself, or I'll take it off your body!"

"Go to blazes!" Ray's voice was hoarse and strange. Then, with incredible swiftness, his hands dropped for the guns.

In the hot, dusty stillness of the afternoon street, all was deathly still. Somewhere a baby cried, and a foot shifted on the board walk. For what seemed an age, all movement seemed frozen and still as the two men in the street faced each other.

Kitty Blaze, her eyes wide with horror, seemed caught in that same breathless, time-frozen hush. The hands of the men were moving with flashing speed, but at that instant everything seemed to move hauntingly slow. She saw Mart Ray's gun swing up, she saw the killing eagerness in his face, his lips thinned and white, his eyes blazing.

And she saw the stranger, Jim Gary. Tall, lithe and strong, his dark face passionless, yet somehow ruthless. And she saw his lean brown hand flash in a blur of movement, saw flame leap from the black muzzles of his guns, and saw Mart Ray smashed back, back, back! She saw his body flung sideways into the hitching rail, saw a horse rear, his lashing hoofs within inches of the man, she saw the gun blaze again from the ground, and a leap of dust from the stranger's shoulder, and she saw Gary move coolly aside to bring his guns better to bear upon the man who was now struggling up.

As in a kind of daze, she saw Jim Gary holding his fire, letting Ray get to his feet. In that stark, incredible instant, she saw him move his lips and she heard the words, as they all heard them in the silence of the street. "I'm sorry, Mart. You shouldn't have played it this way. I'd rather it had been the stampede."

And then Ray's guns swung up. His shirt was bloody, his face twisted in a sort of leer torn into his cheek by a bullet, but his eyes were fiendish. The guns came up, and even as they came level, red flame stabbed from the muzzle of Gary's guns and Ray's body jerked, dust sprang from his shirt's back, and he staggered back, sat down on the edge of the walk, and then as though taken with a severe pain in the groin, he rolled over into the street and sprawled out flat. Somewhere thunder rolled.

For a long moment, the street was motionless. Then somebody said, "We better get inside. She's rainin'."

Jerry swung from his horse and in a couple of strides was beside the fallen man. Ripping back the shirt, he exposed the side, scarred by a steer's hoof.

Dan Blaze jerked around. "Slagle!" he yelled. "Where's Red Slagle! Get him!

"Here." Slagle was sitting against the building, gripping a bloody hand. "I caught a slug. I got behind Ray." He looked up at Blaze. "Gary's right. He's straight as a string. It was Ray's idea to ring him in and use him as the goat after he found him with us."

Dan Blaze knelt beside him. "Who killed my brother?" he demanded. "Was it you or Ray?"

"Ray shot him first. I finished it. I went huntin' for him an' he busted out of the brush. He had a stick he'd carried for walkin' an' I mistook it for a gun."

"What about Langer?" Gary demanded. "Where's he?"

Red grinned, a hard, cold grin. "He lit a shuck. That whuppin' you gave him took somethin' out of him. Once he started to run he didn't stop, not even for his money."

He dug into his pocket. "That reminds me. Here's the forty bucks you earned."

Jim Gary took the money, surprised speechless. Slagle struggled erect. Gary's expression seemed to irritate him. "Well, you earned it didn't you? An' I hired you, didn't I? Well, I never gypped no man out of honest wages yet!

"Anyway," he added wryly, "by the looks of that rope I don't reckon I'll need it. Luck to you, kid! An'," he grinned, "stay out of trouble!"

Thunder rumbled again, and rain poured into the street, a driving, pounding rain that would start the washes running and bring the grass to life again, green and waving for the grazing cattle, moving west, moving north.

MCQUEEN OF THE TUMBLING K

CHAPTER ONE: Ramrod

Ward McQueen reined in the strawberry roan and dug for the "makin's." His eyes squinted against the sun as he stared across the moving herd toward Kim Sartain, who was hazing a pair of restless steers back to the mass of tossing horns.

"Bud" Fox loped his horse out of the dust along the flank of the herd and then walked him up the slope. Digging out his papers, he reached for McQueen's tobacco.

"Recollect that old brindle ladino with the scarred side?" he said. "This here's his range, but we ain't seen hide nor hair of him."

"That mossyhorn?" Ward glanced cynically at Fox. "Reckon I won't forget him too quick. He's prob'ly back in one of them canyons. Yuh cleaned 'em out yet?"

"Uh-huh, we have. Baldy and me both worked in there. No sign of him. Makes a body plumb curious."

"Yeah." Ward's brow puckered. "Ain't like him not to be down here makin' trouble. Missed any other stock since I been gone?"

Fox shrugged. "If there's any missin' it can be only a few. But yuh can bet if that ol' crowbait's gone some others went with him. He ramrods a good-sized herd all by hisself."

"Baldly" Jackson joined them on the grassy slope. The cattle were moving steadily down the widening valley. Kim Sartain and the long-geared "Tennessee" were enough to keep the herd moving. Working them out of the cedar brakes and the canyons had been the job.

Baldy jerked his head back toward the nearest canyon mouth. "Seen some mighty queer tracks over yonder," he said. "Like a man afoot."

"We'll have a look." Ward McQueen touched a spur to the roan and loped it across the narrow valley. Jackson and Fox fell in behind him.

The canyon mouth was narrow and high-walled. It was choked with tumbled boulders and dense brush with only a dry watercourse making a winding trail down the canyon floor. In the spreading fan of sand where the watercourse emptied into the valley, Baldy swung down.

Ward, a big, wide-shouldered rider with keen eyes, stared thoughtfully at the tracks. "Yeah," he muttered, "they do look odd. Got him some home-made footgear. Wonder if that's man blood or critter blood?" Turning, he followed the tracks back up the narrow watercourse.

After a few minutes, he stopped. "Uh-huh, he's hurt. Look at them tracks headed thisaway. Fairly long, steady step. I reckon he's a tall man. Goin' back the steps are shorter, an' he's staggerin' some. He stopped twice in about twenty yards. Both times he leaned against somethin'."

"Reckon we better foller him?" Baldy squinted doubtfully at the jumble of boulders. "If'n he don't aim to git ketched he can make us a powerful lot of trouble!"

"Uh-huh," Ward agreed. "But we'll foller him. Baldy, you go back and help Kim. Tell him where we're at. Bud will stay with me. Mebbe we can trail this hombre down, an' he should be grateful. It looks like he's bad hurt."

They had moved along for a hundred yards or so when Bud Fox stopped, mopping perspiration from his face.

"He don't aim to be follered," he answered. "He's makin' a try at losin' his trail for us. Even tried to wipe out a spot of blood."

Ward McQueen drew thoughtfully on his cigarette and glanced up the watercourse with keen, probing eyes. There was something wrong about all this. He had been riding this range for almost a year now, and believed he knew it well. Yet he remembered no such man as this must be, and had seen no tracks.

They moved on, working along the trail in the close, hot air of the draw. The tracks ended suddenly on a wide ledge of stone where the canyon divided into two branches.

"We're stuck," Bud said, puzzled. "He won't leave no tracks with them makeshift shoes on this stone. There ain't nowheres he can go up either one of them canyons, that I know of."

The right-hand branch ended in a steep, rocky slide, impossible to climb in less than hours of struggle up the shifting rock. The left branch ended against the sheer faces of a cliff against whose base were a heaped-up jumble of boulders and rocky debris.

"He must've doubled back," Fox suggested doubtfully. "Mebbe hid in the brush."

Ward threw his cigarette down in disgust. "Reckon he don't aim t' be found," he remarked. "But wounded like he is, he'd better be. He'll die shore as shootin'!"

Turning their horses they rode back down the canyon to rejoin the herd. . . .

Ruth Kermitt was waiting on the ranchhouse steps when they left the grassy bottom and rode up to the bunkhouse. With her was a slender, dark man in a frock coat and black trousers. He wore a new white hat. As Ward McQueen walked his horse toward the steps he saw the man's quick, cold, all-encompassing glance take him in, then slide away.

"Ward," Ruth said, "this is Jim Yount. He's buying cattle, and wants to have a look at some of ours."

"Howdy," Ward said agreeably.

He glanced at Yount's horse and then, his eyes more speculative, at the man's tied-down guns."

Two more men were sitting on the steps of the bunkhouse. A big, square-bodied man in a checkered shirt, and a slim redhead with a rifle over his knees.

"We're wantin' to buy five hundred to a thousand head," Yount said. "Heard yuh had some good stock."

"Beef?"

"No. Stockin' a ranch. I'm locatin' on the other side of the Newton's."

Ward looked at him and nodded. "Well, we've got some cattle," he said. "Or rather, Miss Kermitt has. I'm just the foreman."

"Oh?" Yount looked around at the girl with a quick, flashing smile. "Widow?"

"No." She flushed a little. "My brother and I came here together. He was—killed."

"Kind of hard for a girl runnin' a cow ranch alone, ain't it?" He smiled sympathetically.

"Miss Kermitt does mighty well," Ward suggested drily, "and she ain't exactly alone!"

"Oh?" Jim Yount glanced at McQueen thoughtfully, one eyebrow lifted. "No," he said after a minute, "I don't expect one could rightly say she was alone as long as she had some cowhands on the place, or cattle."

Ruth's eyes widened a little at the sudden tightening of Ward's mouth. "Mr. Yount," she interrupted hastily, "wouldn't you like to come in for some coffee? Then we could talk business."

When they had gone inside, Ward turned on his heel and strode back to the bunkhouse. He was mad, and didn't care who knew it. The thin-faced rider with the red hair glanced at him as he drew near.

"What's the matter, friend?" he asked. "Somebody take yore girl?"

Ward McQueen halted and turned his head. Baldy Jackson got up hastily and moved out of line. It was a move which brought him alongside the corner of the bunkhouse and put Yount's two riders at the apex of a triangle of which McQueen and himself formed the other two corners.

"Miss Kermitt," McQueen said coldly, "is my boss. She's also a lady. Don't get any funny notions!"

The redhead chuckled. "Yeah, and the boss is a ladies' man! He knows how to handle 'em!" Deliberately, he turned his back on Baldy. "Ever been a foreman on a spread like this, Dodson? Mebbe you or me'll have us a new job."

For an instant Ward hesitated, then he turned on his heel and walked into the bunkhouse. Bud Fox was loitering by the window. He straightened as McQueen came in. Ward saw that he, too, had been watching the pair.

"Don't seem like they want to make friends," Bud suggested, pouring warm water into the wash basin. "Like they might even want to start trouble!"

Ward glanced at the young cowhand thoughtfully. "What would be the idea of that?" he demanded.

Yet curiously he wondered over it. Certainly the attitude of the two wasn't typical of the West. He glanced toward the house and his lips tightened. Jim Yount was a slick-looking gent. He was a smooth talker, and probably a woman would think him good-looking.

He sat down on his bunk and dug out the "makin's." Out there beyond the ranchhouse was a distant light. That light would be in Gelvin's store, down to Mannerhouse. Gelvin had ranched the country beyond the Newtons. Suddenly, McQueen made up his mind. After chow he would ride into Mannerhouse and have a talk with Gelvin.

Supper was a quiet meal except for Ruth and Jim Yount who talked and laughed at the head of the table. Ward, seated opposite Yount, had little to say. Baldy, Bud and Tennessee sat in strict silence, and "Red" Lund sat beside Pete Dodson, only occasionally venturing some comment. At the foot of the table, lean, wiry Kim Sartain let his eyes move from face to face.

Ward left the table early, and paused on the step to light a smoke. Kim moved up beside him.

"What goes on?" he asked softly. "Never seen everybody so quiet."

Briefly, Ward explained. Then he added, "Yount may be a cattle buyer, but the two hombres with him ain't ordinary punchers. That Red Lund is a gun slick if I ever saw one, and Dodson looks to me like an owlhooter." He drew on his cigarette. "I'm ridin' into town. Keep an eye on things, will yuh?"

"Shore thing!" Kim's voice was dry, cold. "That Lund, I don't like him, myself!" Then glancing at Ward. "Nor Yount," he said.

CHAPTER TWO: The Drygulch

Gelvin's store was closed, but McQueen knew where to find him. Swinging down from the roan he walked through the swinging doors into the saloon. Abel was polishing glasses behind the bar, and Gelvin was sitting at a table with Dave Cormack, Logan Keane, and a tall, lean-bodied stranger. They were playing poker.

Two stranger riders lounged at the bar. They turned and looked at him as he came in.

"Howdy, Ward!" Abel said. "How's things at the Tumblin' K?"

The two men at the bar turned abruptly and looked at him again, a quick searching glance. He had started to speak to Gelvin, and something warned him. Turning on his heel he strode to the bar.

"Purty good," he said. "Diggin' some stock out of the brakes today. Tough work. All right for a brushpopper, but me, I like open country!"

He tossed off his drink and watched the two strange riders in the bar mirror.

"They tell me there's good range over beyond the Newtons, Gelvin," he said. "Reckon I'll go over and see if there's any lyin' around loose."

Gelvin looked up sharply. He was a short, square-shouldered man with a keen, intelligent face.

"There's plenty lyin' around loose!" he said. "Yuh can have it for the takin'! That country's goin' back to desert just as fast as it can! Sand movin' in, streams dryin' up! Yuh can ride for a hundred miles and never find a drink . . . Why"—he picked up the cards and began to shuffle them—"old Coyote Benny Chait was in here, two, three weeks ago. He was headin' out of the country! Got euchred out of his ranch by some slick card handler! He was laughin' at the hombre that won it, said he'd get enough of it in a hurry!"

The two riders had stiffened now, and were glaring, eyes hard, at Gelvin.

"Yeah?" McQueen suggested. "Who was the hombre what got the ranch? Did he say?"

"Shore!" Gelvin said. "Some card shark name of—"

"Yuh talk too much!" The voice was cold and ugly. The larger of the two riders stepped toward Gelvin's chair. "What do you know about the Newton country?"

Startled, Gelvin turned in his chair. His eyes went from one man to the other, his face slowly turning pale. Ward McQueen had the bottle and was pulling it toward his whisky glass.

"What is this?" Gelvin demanded. "What did I say?"

"Yuh lied!" the big man said coldy. "Yuh lied! That country over there ain't goin' back! She's good as she ever was!"

Gelvin was a stubborn man. "I did not lie," he said sternly. "I lived in that country for ten years! I came in with the first white men! I know of what I speak!"

"Then yuh mean I'm a liar?" The big man's hand spread over his gun. "Reach, cuss yuh!"

Ward McQueen turned in one swift movement. His right hand knocked the bottle rolling toward the second rider as he turned, and he kept on swinging until his right hand grabbed the big rider by the belt. With a heave of his shoulders, he swung the big fellow off balance and whirled him, staggering, into the smaller man who had sprung back to avoid the bottle.

The big man hit the floor and came up with a grunt of fury. He came up, and then he froze and his hands moved wide away from his gun butts. Ward McQueen was standing with a gun in his right hand, watching them.

"When a man wants to talk in this town," Ward said, "he talks, and nobody interferes. Get me?"

"If'n yuh didn't have the drop on me yuh wouldn't talk so big!" the bigger man sneered.

Swiftly, Ward flipped his gun back into the holster.

"All right!" he said loudly. "Yuh want it . . . Draw!"

The two men stood facing him, their faces turning white under their beards. Neither of them liked the look of Ward McQueen. Both men knew gun handlers when they saw them, and suddenly they decided this was no time for bravery.

"We ain't lookin' for trouble," the big one said. "Hollier'n me just rode into town for a drink."

"Then ride out," Ward said coolly, "and don't butt into talk where yuh're not needed."

The two men walked sheepishly from the room, and Ward watched them go. Then he stepped back to the bar.

"Thanks, Gelvin," he said. "Yuh told me somethin' I wanted to know."

"I don't understand," Gelvin said. "What made 'em mad?"

"That card shark?" Ward asked. "His name wasn't Jim Yount, was it?"

Gelvin's mouth gaped. "Why, shore! That's right! How'd yuh know?"

McQueen smiled, but said nothing. The tall stranger playing cards with Gelvin looked up and their eyes met.

"Yuh wouldn't be the Ward McQueen from down Texas way, would yuh?" the tall man asked.

"That's right," McQueen looked at the man. "Why?"

The fellow smiled engagingly. "Just wondered. I been down Texas way. Yuh cut a wide swath down thataway. I heard about that gang yuh run out of Maravillas Canyon. . . ."

Watchfully McQueen took the trail toward the Tumbling K, but he saw nothing of the two riders with whom he'd had trouble. Hollier. That would be the smaller one. Ward nodded thoughtfully. He recalled the name. There had been a Hollier who got away from a lynching party down in Uvalde a few years back. He trailed with an hombre named Packer. And the bigger man had a P burned on his holster with a branding iron.

What was Jim Yount's game? These two were obviously in with him, as both had seemed anxious his name not be spoken, and had seemed eager to quiet the talk about the range beyond the Newtons.

The facts were simple enough. Yount had won a ranch in a poker game. Gelvin implied the game was crooked. The ranch he had won was going back to desert. He had, in other words, won nothing but trouble. What followed from that?

The logical thing would be for Yount to shrug it off and ride on. He was not doing this, which implied some sort of a plan. Lund and Dodson would make likely companions for Packer and Hollier. Yount was talking of buying cattle, but he was not one to run his cattle on a dead range. Did they plan to rustle the cattle? Or was it some even more involved plan?

One thing was sure with McQueen. It was time he was getting back to the ranch to put the others on the lookout for trouble. It would be coming now, probably sooner than it might have had he not stumbled on that information from Gelvin tonight.

The Tumbling K foreman was riding into the yard when the shot rang out.

Something struck him a wicked blow on the head and he felt himself falling backward into darkness, the sound of the shot ringing in his ears. . . .

His head felt tight, constricted as though a band were drawn about his temples. Slowly, fighting every inch of the way, he battled his way back to consciousness. His lids fluttered, then closed, too weak to force themselves open. Again he fought against the heaviness and got them open. He was lying on his back in a half-light, the air felt damp, cool.

When awareness moved over him, he knew suddenly that he was in a cave or mine tunnel. Turning his head slightly, he looked around. He was lying on a crude pallet on a sandy cave floor. Some twenty feet away he could see a long narrow shaft of light. Nearby his guns hung from a peg in the cave wall, and his rifle leaned against the wall.

Suddenly the narrow rift of light was blotted out, and he heard someone crawling into the cave. The man came up and threw down an armful of fire wood, then lighted a lantern. He came over.

"Come out of it, huh? Man, I thought yuh never would!"

The man was lean and old, with twinkling blue eyes and almost white hair. He was long and tall. Ward noted the foot gear suddenly. This was the man they had trailed up the canyon!

"Who are you?" he demanded.

The man smiled. "Charlie Quayle's the name. Used to ride for Chait, over the Newtons."

"Yuh're the hombre we trailed up the canyon a few days back. Yestiddy, I mean."

Quayle laughed. "Right the first time! Yuh been lyin' here all of two weeks, nearer dead then alive. Delirious, most of the time. Figgered yuh never would come out of it."

"Two weeks!" Ward McQueen struggled to sit up, then sank back. "Yuh mean I've been here two weeks? Why, they'll figger I'm dead back at the ranch! Why'd yuh bring me here? Who shot me?"

"Hold on!" Quayle chuckled. "Give me me time an' I'll answer all the questions I can. First place, two of them rustlin' hands of Jim

Yount's packed yuh to the canyon and dropped yuh into a wash. They kicked sand over yuh and then dropped on some brush. But they wasn't no hands to work, so they left off and went away.

"I was right curious as to who yuh was, and dug into that pile. Then I found yuh was alive. Don't reckon they knowed it. I packed yuh in here, and mister, yuh're the heaviest durned man I ever did pack! And me with a game leg!"

"Was yuh trailin' 'em when they shot me?"

"No. I was scoutin' the layout around the ranch, figgerin' to steal me some coffee, when I heard the shot. Then I seen them packin' yuh away, so I follered." Quayle lighted his pipe. "There's been some changes," he went on. "Yore friend Sartain has been fired. So have Fox an' the baldheaded gent. Tennessee had a run-in with the redhead, that one they call Lund, and Lund killed him. Outdrawed him in a picked fight. Yount, he's real friendly with Miss Kermitt, and he's runnin' the ranch. One or more of them tough gun hands around all the time."

Ward lay on his back staring up at the rocky roof of the cave. Kim Sartain fired! It didn't seem reasonable. Why, Kim had been with Ruth Kermitt longer than any of them! He had been with her when she and her brother had first come over the trail from Wyoming. He had helped her when she bought this ranch, had known her brother, had been with her even before the trouble at Pilot Range when Ward had first joined them. And now he was fired, run off the place!

And Tennessee killed!

What sort of a girl was Ruth Kermitt to fire her oldest hands and take on a bunch of gunslick rustlers led by a crooked gambler?

"Yuh got a hard head," Quayle said suddenly, "or yuh'd be dead right now. The bullet hit right over the eye, but she skidded around yore skull under the skin. Laid yore scalp right open. Sort of concussion, too. And yuh lost a sight of blood."

"I've got to get out of here!" Ward said suddenly. "I've got to see Ruth Kermitt!"

"Yuh better sit tight an' get well," Quayle said drily. "She's right busy with that Yount hombre. Rides with him all over the range. Holdin' hands more'n half the time. Everybody's seen 'em! If she fired the rest of her boys, she shore wouldn't want no foreman back!"

McQueen looked at Quayle. "Say! Where do you fit into this deal?"

Charlie Quayle shrugged. "I rode for Chait, like I told yuh. Yount rooked him out of his ranch, but Chait was glad to get shet of it. But when Yount found out what a heap of sand he got he was some sore. Me, I'd save me nigh on a year's wages and was fixin' to set up for myself. One of them rannies of Yount's saw the money, and they trailed me down. Said it was ranch money. We had us a fight, and they winged me. I got away and holed up in this here canyon."

CHAPTER THREE: Stacked Deck

All day McQueen rested in the cave. After dark, Quayle left the cave. He was gone for hours, but when he returned, he was eager to talk.

"That Yount," he said, "takin' over the country! He went into Mannerhouse last night lookin' for Gelvin, but he'd gone off with some stranger friend of his'n. This Yount had some words with Dave Cormack, and killed him. They do say this here. Yount is fast as greased lightnin' with a gun!

"Then Red Lund and Pete Dodson pistol-whipped Logan Keane. Yount, he told 'em he was ramroddin' the Tumblin' K, and was goin' to marry Ruth Kermitt, and he was sick of the talk goin' around about him and his men. They've got that town treed, believe you me!"

Ruth to marry Jim Yount! Ward McQueen felt a sudden emptiness inside him. He knew then that he was in love with Ruth. In fact, as he thought of it, he had been in love with her for a long time. And now she was to marry Yount! A crooked gambler and ramrod of a gunslick gang of outlaws!

It didn't seem possible. Lying there on the pallet, he shook his head as if to clear it of the whole idea.

"See anything of Sartain?" he demanded.

"No," Quayle admitted, "but hear tell he drifted over into the Newtons with Fox and that Baldy hombre."

The next day, Ward was up with daybreak. He rolled out of the blankets. His head still ached, but he felt better. His long period of illness had at least given him time to rest, and his strength was enough to help him recuperate rapidly. He oiled his guns and reloaded them. Quayle eyed his preparations thoughtfully, and said nothing until McQueen began to pull on his boots.

"Better wait till sundown if yuh're goin' out huntin' trouble,' he said. "I got yuh a hoss. Got him hid down the canyon in the brush."

"A hoss?" Ward's eyes glinted. "Good for you, old-timer! I'm goin' up to have a look-see at the ranch. This deal don't figger right to me."

"Nor me." Quayle knocked out his pipe. "I seen that gal's face today. They rid past me as I lay in the brush. She shore didn't look happy like she was with no man she loved. Mebbe she ain't willin'."

"That's a thought." Ward nodded. "Well, tonight I ride."

"We ride!" Quayle insisted. "I don't like gettin' shot up no better than you-all. I'm in this fight, too."

"Thanks," McQueen said grimly. "I can use help, but what yuh might do is try to trail down Kim Sartain and the others. Get 'em back here for a showdown."

Where Quayle had picked up the little buckskin McQueen did not know or care. He needed a horse desperately, and the buckskin was a horse. Whatever Yount's game was he had been fast and thorough. He had moved in on the Tumbling K, had had Ward McQueen drygulched, had had Miss Kermitt fire her old hands, and then, riding into Mannerhouse, had quieted all outward opposition by killing one man and beating another.

Tennessee, too, had been killed. Jim Yount had shown himself to be fast, ruthless, and quick of decision. And as he acted with the real or apparent consent of Ruth Kermitt, there was nothing to be done by any of the townspeople in the little village of Mannerhouse.

Probably none were inclined to do anything. There was no personal gain for anyone in bucking the killers Yount had around him. Obviously, the gambler was in complete control of the situation. He had erred in only two things—in failing to track down and kill Charlie Quayle and in thinking McQueen was dead, instead of making certain of it.

The buckskin was a quick-stepping little horse with a liking for the trail. Ward headed out toward the Tumbling K. Quayle had left earlier in the day, starting back into the Newtons to hunt for Kim. Baldy and Bud were good cowhands, but the slim, dark-faced youngster, Kim Sartain, was one of the fastest gunhands Ward had ever seen, and he had a continual drive toward trouble. Never beginning any fight, he loved a battle.

"With him," Ward told the buckskin, "I'd tackle an army!"

He left the buckskin in a clump of willows near the stream, then crossed it on stepping stones, and worked his way through the greasewood toward the Tumbling K ranchhouse.

He had no plan of action. He had nothing on which to base such a plan. If he could find Ruth and talk to her, or if he could figure out something of the plan on which Yount was operating, that would be a beginning.

The windows shone bright as he neared the house. For a long time he lay behind a clump of greasewood and studied the situation. An error now would be fatal. Quick and sudden death would be all that awaited him.

There would be someone around, he was sure. Yount had no reason to expect trouble, for he seemed to have quieted all opposition with neatness and dispatch. Yet the gambler was a careful man.

A cigarette gleamed suddenly from the steps of the bunkhouse. Somebody was seated there, on guard or just having a smoke.

Ward worked to the left until the house was between them, then he got up and moved swiftly to the wall of the house. He eased up to the window. It was a warm night, and the window was open at the bottom.

Jim Yount was playing solitaire at the dining room table. Red Lund was oiling a pistol. Packer was leaning his elbows on the table watching Yount's cards and smoking.

"I always wanted a ranch," Yount was saying, "and this is it. No use gallivantin' around the country when a man can hole up and live in style. I'd of had it over the Newtons if that durned sand bed I got from Chait had been any good. Then I seen this place—it was too good to be true.

"Yuh shore worked fast," Packer agreed. "And it was plumb lucky that Hollier and me got that McQueen. I hear tell he was a plumb salty hombre."

Yount shrugged. "Mebbe. All sorts of stories get started. He might have been fast with a gun, but he didn't have brains. It would take brains to win out." He glanced up at Lund. "Look," he said. "Logan Keane has that spread south of Hosstail Creek. Nice piece of land, thousands of acres with good water, runnin' right up to Mannerhouse. Keane's all scared now. Once this girl and me are married so the title to this place is cinched, we'll go to work on Keane. We'll rustle his stock, run off his hands, and force him to sell. I reckon we can do the whole job in a month, at the outside."

Red glanced up from his pistol.

"You get the ranches," he said. "Where do I come in?"

Yount smiled. "You don't want a ranch," he said, "I do. Well, I happen to know where Ruth Kermitt's got her money cached. There's ten thousand in the lot. You boys"—for a moment his eyes held those of Red Lund—"can split that up among yuh. I reckon yuh can work out some way of dividin' it even up!"

Lund's eyes glinted with understanding. Watching, McQueen glanced quickly at Packer, but the big horse thief showed no sign of having seen the exchange of glances. Ward could see, only too plainly, how the money would be divided. It would be a split made by Red Lund's six-guns. The others got lead, he got the cash.

It had the added advantage to Jim Yount of having only one actual witness to his own treachery.

Crouched in the darkness below the window, Ward McQueen calculated his chances. Jim Yount was reputed to be a fast man with a gun. Red Lund had proved himself so. Packer would be good, even if not the flash artist the other two were. Three to one in this case made odds much too long. And at the bunkhouse were Hollier and Pete Dodson, neither one a man to trifle with.

A clatter of horses hoofs sounded suddenly on the hard-packed trail from town, and a horseman showed briefly in the light from the door. Ward McQueen heard Hollier hail the rider, and could hear the mumble of voices. Then the door opened. Watching from a corner window, Ward saw the rider ushered into the room. It was the lean stranger who had played poker with Gelvin and Keane.

"You Jim Yount?" he asked. "They call me Rip. Just rode out here to say they got a express package at the station for Miss Kermitt. She can drop in and pick it up tomorrow if she likes."

Yount stared at him. "Express package? Why didn't yuh bring it out?"

The young rider shrugged. "Wouldn't let me. Seems like it's money. A package of dinero as payment on some property of hers back in Wyomin'. She's got to sign for it herself. They won't let nobody else have it."

Yount stared at him. "Money, is it? Well, Miss Kermitt's gone to sleep, but I'll tell her!"

The rider turned and went out and in a few minutes Ward heard his horse on the road.

"More dinero?" Packer grinned. "Not bad, Boss! She can pick it up for us, and well split it, huh?"

Red Lund was staring at his pistol. "I don't like it!" he said suddenly. "Looks like a chance to get us off the ranch and the girl into town!"

Yount shrugged. "So if they do? Who in town will tackle us?" He leaned forward, smiling. "I think it's probably the truth. But even if it ain't, why worry? We'll send Packer in ahead to look the ground over. If there's any strangers, he can warn us. No, I think it's all right. We'll go in tomorrow!"

An hour later, and far back on a brush-covered hillside, Ward McQueen bedded down for the night. From where he lay he could see any party that left the ranch. One thing he knew. Tomorrow was the pay-off. Ruth Kermitt would not be returning to that ranch.

With daylight he was awake. He smoked his breakfast, trying to work the chill from his bones. It had been a damp, uncomfortable night. The sunshine caught light from the ranch-house windows and slow smoke lifted from the kitchen. Hollier walked out and began roping horses. He saddled his own, Ruth Kermitt's brown mare, and the big gray horse that belonged to Jim Yount.

Smoking his second cigarette, Ward McQueen tried to foresee what would happen. There were only nine buildings on the town's main street, scarcely more than twenty houses scattered around them.

The express and stage office was next to the saloon. Gelvin's store was across the street.

Where did this young rider stand? The man who called himself "Rip?" He seemed to be merely a tramp rider, but he had known of Ward McQueen's shootout in Maravillas Canyon. Not many knew of that. Nor did Rip look like the casual drifter he was supposed to be. His eyes were too keen, too sharp. If he had baited a trap with money he had used the only bait to which these men would rise. But what was he hoping to accomplish?

There were no men in Mannerhouse who would draw a gun against Jim Yount and Red Lund.

Gelvin would, if he was there. But Gelvin had only courage, and no six-gun skill, and the one needed the backing of the other.

CHAPTER FOUR: Six-Gun Return

I t was an hour after daylight when Packer mounted his paint gelding and started off for town. Ward watched him go, his eyes narrow. He had resolved upon his own course of action. It was no elaborate plan. He was going to slip into town and at the right moment he was going to kill Jim Yount, and if possible, Red Lund.

The cigarette tasted bitter, suddenly. Ward McQueen was no fool. He knew what tackling that bunch meant. Even if he got the two, he would go down himself. There was no alternative. Yet if he succeeded and Kim Sartain came back, Kim might ride in and drive the others off Ruth's ranch. The girl would have her own back.

Thoughtfully, he saddled the buckskin. As always the little horse was eager to go. He checked his six-guns again. Then, his lips thin, he swung into the saddle and started working his way down through the greasewood and mesquite to the valley floor.

He had gone but a few hundred yards when he saw Jim Yount and the girl ride away from the ranch. A few feet behind them was Red Lund.

Pete Dodson, mounted on a sorrel horse, had taken the southerly trail and was skirting the town to approach from the other direction. Ward saw this, too, and his eyes were grim. Jim Yount was taking no chances. . . .

The dusty street of Mannerhouse was warm in the bright morning sun. On the steps of the Express office, Rip was sunning himself. Abel, behind the bar of his saloon looked nervously at the door. He was on edge and aware, aware as is a wild animal when a strange creature nears his lair. Trouble was in the wind. He wanted no part of it.

Gelvin's store was still closed. That was unusual for this time of the day. Abel glanced at Rip, and his brow puckered. Rip was wearing tied-down guns this morning.

Abel put the glass down and glanced at Packer who was sitting over a drink. Suddenly, Packer downed the drink and got up. He walked carefully to the door and glanced up and down the street. All was quiet. A man came out of the post-office and walked down to the barber shop. The sound of the door closing was the only noise. Packer stared at Rip, noting the guns.

He saw Pete Dodson stop his horse behind Gelvin's store, and his eyes sharpened. Pete was carrying a rifle.

Packer turned suddenly, staring at Abel.

"Give me that scattergun yuh got under the bar!"

"Huh?" Abel's face paled. "I ain't got—" he started to reply, but Packer cut him short.

"Don't give me that," Packer snarled. "I want that gun!"

When Abel put it on the bar, his tongue wetting dry lips, Packer picked it up with satisfaction. Then he walked back to the window and put the gun beside it. Carefully he eased the window up about three inches. His position covered Rip's side and back.

Jim Yount rode up the street with Ruth Kermitt beside him. Her face was pale and strained. Her eyes seemed unusually large. Red Lund trailed a few yards behind and reined in his horse across the street. Then he swung down.

From the bar, Abel could see it all. Jim Yount and the girl were approaching Rip from the west. North and west was Red Lund.

Due north, in the shadow of Gelvin's store, was Pete Dodson. In the saloon, southeast of the express office porch was Packer. Rip was boxed. Signed and sealed. All but delivered.

Jim Keane, Logan's much older brother, was express agent. He saw Jim Yount come, and his face paled as he glimpsed Red Lund across the street.

Rip got up lazily and smiled as Ruth Kermitt came up the steps with Jim Yount.

"Come for yore package, Miss Kermitt?" he asked politely. "While yuh're here, yuh might answer some questions."

"By whose authority?" Yount demanded sharply.

Ward McQueen, crouched behind the saloon, heard the answer clearly.

"The State of Texas, Yount," Rip replied, "I'm a Ranger!"

Jim Yount laughed shortly. "This ain't Texas, and she answers no questions!"

McQueen jumped inside his skin. A shotgun barrel was easing over the window sill of the saloon! Wheeling, he slipped to the back door. There was no reason now to be quiet. In fact, noise would help. He jerked open the door and jumped inside.

Parker, intent on the tableau on the porch, and getting Rip lined up with the shotgun, heard the door slam open. Startled, he spun on the balls of his feet. Ward McQueen stood just inside the door, and Packer's face blanched. Somehow his hand was dropping for a gun, but even as his hand moved, he knew it was hopeless.

Ward McQueen palmed his six-gun with a gesture deadly as a striking snake. The shot sounded flat and dead in the empty room.

Packer's gun slid from helpless fingers and he pitched forward on his face.

Outside, all perdition broke loose. Ruth Kermitt, aware of the danger Rip was in, had been tense and waiting. She knew she could not help him, only handicap, so when that shot sounded suddenly from the saloon, she dropped flat on the porch and rolled off into the dust by the steps.

Rip went for his gun, stepping quickly to the left as he did, trying to get Yount between him and Red Lund. Their guns all began barking at once, and even as the first shot sounded, Ward McQueen plunged through the saloon doors and caught himself with one of the posts on the edge of the saloon walk. He fired at Lund, and a bullet from Pete Dodson's rifle clipped slivers from the post, spitting them into his face.

Ward hit the dust on both feet and started toward Lund, both guns ready.

Red had wheeled away from Rip, his face snarling, and Ward held his fire, stepping quickly and carefully. The steps carried him forward, and Pete Dodson had to get out from the side of the building to get him in his sights again.

Red fired and fired again. Ward felt something hit him a savage blow and his knee buckled under him. He fired from one knee, taking his time and lining the sights as in a shooting contest. Red staggered back and sat down hard, then rolled over and got up.

Ward fired again, then again. Red Lund got up again and, his face bloody, started toward McQueen. There was firing from the stage station porch and firing from behind Gelvin's store, but through the dust and smoke, Ward McQueen saw Red Lund go down again. He forced himself up and turned his head, stiffly, seeking Jim Yount.

The frock-coated gambler was clinging to his saddle-horn with his left hand, still gripping a gun in his right. Rip was down on the steps, crawling toward his own gun which had been knocked from his fingers. Yount, seemingly injured, was trying to get up a gun to kill Rip.

Bracing himself in a teetering, rolling street, Ward McQueen lifted his gun, his eyes intent on Yount. A rifle barked somewhere behind him or off to his right, and he felt a bullet whiff by his face. He blinked his eyes, steadied the gun, and fired.

Yount's gray horse lunged, breaking the bridle that tied it to the hitchrail. There was a thunder of hoofs down the street, and Ward saw a dark, flashing figure crouching low over a flame-red horse come sweeping into the street. He clung low like an Indian, and as he rode his six-gun was blazing from under the horse's neck. He seemed to be shooting at something off to the right.

Yount was down in the dust and trying to get up. Suddenly, Ward saw that the gambler had a knife and was crawling toward the girl who was crouched against the steps where she had dropped to clear the field for Rip. Yount's knife was gripped with the blade up in his right hand, and his face twisted viciously as he edged toward the girl.

McQueen knew he couldn't walk that far. He forced his six-gun up. He pulled the trigger, and it clicked on an empty chamber.

Hazily he lifted his left hand. He lifted it waist high, staring at Yount. He rarely shot a gun with his left hand and was praying as he squeezed off the shot.

Jim Yount contracted himself suddenly in an agonized jerk and his face twisted more. McQueen squeezed the trigger again and Yount rolled over on his back. Both shots had hit him in the left side.

McQueen remembered Abel rushing from the saloon, and then Gelvin from his store. Ruth was running toward him, and for a moment, he blacked out.

When he could see again, Ruth was bending over him, his head cradled in her arms. Kim Sartain was standing by the porch, the red horse behind him.

McQueen tried to sit up. "What—happened?" he gasped.

Kim shrugged. "Clean sweep, looks like." He started building a smoke. "Charlie Quayle got to us, and we headed for the ranch. That Hollier hombre was there, and we smoked him out. He got Charlie. First shot. Then Bud Fox got him. I rode on into town while they were shakin' the place down to see if there was any more there. When I come in, yuh had the job about done, only for Pete Dodson. Gelvin shot at him from behind the store, and that helped keep him busy. He missed one shot at you as I come up, and I rode up on him, got a couple of bullets into this before I rode him down. He's dead."

"Red Lund?"

"Got four bullets in him. Ready for Boot Hill. Yount's alive and cussin', but he won't be long. He got two bullets into Rip, and Rip hit him once. You got him twice in the side, and burned him once. Packer's dead." Kim lighted his smoke. "Ward," he said, "I been thinkin' about the south range. Mebbe we should round up some cows and put 'em north of the creek for a while. Save that south grass."

"Good idea," Ward said. "If I'm still foreman." He looked up at Ruth.

"You always were," she said. "They told me you'd packed up and quit me. Then Yount made me fire Kim and the boys."

Rip hobbled toward them, leaning on Gelvin's shoulder.

"My name's Coker, Ward. I was trailin' Lund. Couldn't figger no way to bust up Yount's show unless I could get the straight of it from Miss Kermitt, so I faked that package to get 'em into town. I didn't figger them to gang up on me like they done."

Baldy Jackson and Bud Fox were loping toward them. When they reined in, Bud glanced at Ruth, then at Ward.

"Yuh know that old mossy horn, Ward? Found him while ridin' in this mornin'! He's got about thirty head wit him, back in the purtiest little valley yuh ever saw! Reckon he's holed up there to stay!"

Ward looked up at Ruth, then grinned at Bud.

"I reckon I am, too!" he said. "I reckon he's like me. So used to this range he wouldn't be noways happy any place else!"

"Why even think of anywhere else?" Ruth asked softly. "I want you to stay, Ward. Always! I think," she added, "you'd better take full charge after this!"

"Of everything?"

"Everything!" she said.

THE TURKEYFEATHER RIDERS

CHAPTER ONE: Trouble on the Range

Jim Sandifer swung down from his buckskin and stood for a long minute staring across the saddle toward the dark bulk of Bearwallow Mountain. His was the grave, careful look of a man accustomed to his own company under the sun and in the face of the wind. For three years he had been riding for the B Bar and for two of those years he had been ranch foreman. What he was about to do would bring an end to that, an end to the job, to the life here, to his chance to win the girl he loved.

Voices sounded inside, the low rumble of Gray Bowen's bass, and the quick, light voice of his daughter, Elaine. The sound of her voice sent a quick spasm of pain across Sandifer's face. Tying the buckskin to the hitchrail, he ducked under it and walked up the steps, his boots sounding loud on the planed boards, his spurs tinkling lightly.

The sound of his steps brought instant stillness to the group inside, and then the quick tatoo of Elaine's feet as she hurried to meet him. It was a sound he would never tire of hearing, a sound that had brought gladness to him such as he had never known before. Yet when her eyes met his at the door her flashing smile faded.

"Jim! What's wrong?" Then she noticed the blood on his shoulder and the tear where the bullet had ripped his shirt, and her face went white to the lips. "You're hurt!"

"No—only a scratch." He put aside her detaining hand. "Wait. I'll talk to your Dad first." His hands dropped to hers and as she looked up, startled at his touch, he said gravely and sincerely, "No matter what happens now, I want you to know that I've loved you since the day we met. I've thought of little else, believe that." He dropped her hands then and stepped past her into the huge room where Gray Bowen waited, his big body relaxed in a homemade chair of cowhide.

Rose Martin was there, too, and her tall, handsome son, Lee. Jim's eyes avoided them for he knew what their faces were like, he knew the quiet serenity of Rose Martin's face, masking a cunning as cold and calculating as her son's flaming temper. It was these two who were destroying the B Bar, these who had brought the big ranch to the verge of a deadly range war by their conniving. A war that could have begun this morning, but for him.

Even as he began to speak he knew his words would put him right where they wanted him, that when he had finished, he would be through here, and Gray Bowen and his daughter would be left unguarded to the machinations of this woman and her son. Yet he could no longer refrain from speaking. The lives of men depended on it.

Bowen's lips thinned when he saw the blood. "You've seen Katrishen? Had a run-in with him?"

"No!" Sandifer's eyes blazed. "There's no harm in Katrishen if he's left alone. No trouble unless we make it. I ask you to recall, Gray, that for two years we've lived at peace with the Katrishens.

We have had no trouble until the last three months." He paused, hoping the idea would soak in that trouble had begun with the coming of the Martins. "He won't give us any trouble if we leave him alone!"

"Leave him alone to steal our range!" Lee Martin flared.

Sandifer's eyes swung. *"Our* range? Are you now a partner in the B Bar?"

Lee smiled, covering his slip. "Naturally, as I am a friend of Mr. Bowen's, I think of his interests as mine."

Bowen waved an impatient hand. "That's no matter! What happened?"

Here it was, then. The end of all his dreaming, his planning, his hoping. "It wasn't Katrishen. It was Klee Mont."

"Who?" Bowen came out of his chair with a lunge, veins swelling. "Mont shot *you?* What for? Why, in Heavens' name?"

"Mont was over there with the Mello boys and Art Dunn. He had gone over to run the Katrishens off their Iron Creek holdings. If they had tried that they would have started a first-class range war with no holds barred. I stopped them."

Rose Martin flopped her knitting in her lap and glanced up at him, smiling smugly. Lee began to roll a smoke, one eyebrow lifted. This was what they had wanted, for he alone had blocked them here. The others they could influence, but not Jim Sandifer.

Bowen's eyes glittered with his anger. He was a choleric man, given to sudden bursts of fury, a man who hated being thwarted and who was impatient of all restraint.

"You stopped them? Did they tell you whose orders took them over there? Did they?"

"They did. I told them to hold off until I could talk with you, but Mont refused to listen. He said his orders had been given him and he would follow them to the letter."

"He did right!" Bowen's voice boomed in the big room. "Exactly right! And you stopped them? *You* countermanded my orders?"

"I did." Sandifer laid it flatly on the line. "I told them there would be no burning or killing while I was foreman. I told them they weren't going to run us into a range war for nothing."

Gray Bowen balled his big hands into fists. "You've got a gall, Jim! You know better than to countermand an order of mine! And you'll leave me to decide what range I need! Katrishen's got no business on Iron Creek an' I told him so! I told him to get off an' get out! As for this range-war talk, that's foolishness! He won't fight!"

"Putting them off would be a very simple matter," Lee Martin interposed quietly. "If you hadn't interfered, Sandifer, they would be off now and the whole matter settled."

"Settled nothin'!" Jim exploded. "Where did you get this idea that Bill Katrishen could be pushed around? The man was an officer in the Army during the war, an' he's fought Indians on the plains."

"You must be a great friend of his," Rose Martin said gently, "you know so much about him."

The suggestion was there and Gray Bowen got it. He stopped in his pacing and his face was like a rock. "You been talkin' with Katrishen? You sidin' that outfit?"

"This is my outfit, I ride for the brand," Sandifer replied. "I know Katrishen, of course. I've talked to him."

"And to his daughter?" Lee suggested, his eyes bright with malice. "With his pretty daughter?"

Out of the tail of his eye Jim saw Elaine's head come up quickly, but he ignored Lee's comment. "Stop and think," he said to Bowen, "when did this trouble start? When Mrs. Martin and her son came here! You got along fine with Katrishen until then! They've been putting you up to this!"

Bowen's eyes narrowed. "That will be enough of that!" He said sharply. He was really furious now, not the flaring, hot fury that Jim knew so well, but a cold, hard anger that nothing could touch. For the first time Jim realized how futile any argument

was going to be. Rose Martin and her son had insinuated themselves too much and too well into the picture of Gray Bowen's
life.

"You wanted my report," Sandifer said quietly. "Mont
wouldn't listen to my arguments for time. He said he had his
orders and would take none from me. I told him then that if
he rode forward it was against my gun. He laughed at me, then
reached for his gun. I shot him."

Gray Bowen's widened eyes expressed his amazement.

"You shot *Mont?* You beat him to the draw?"

"That's right. I didn't want to kill him but I shot the gun out
of his hand and held my gun on him for a minute to let him
know what it meant to be close to death. Then I started them
back here."

Bowen's anger was momentarily swallowed by his astonishment. He recalled suddenly that in the three years Sandifer had
worked for him there had been no occasion for him to draw a
gun in anger. There had been a few brushes with Apaches and
one with rustlers, but all rifle work. Klee Mont was a killer with
seven known killings on his record and had been reputed to be
the fastest gunhand west of the Rio Grande.

"It seems peculiar," Mrs. Martin said composedly, "for you
to turn your gun on men who ride for Mr. Bowen, taking sides
against him. No doubt you meant well, but it does seem strange."

"Not if you know the Katrishens," Jim replied grimly. "Bill
was assured he could settle on that Iron Creek holding before
he moved in. He was told that we made no claim on anything
beyond Willow and Gilita Creeks."

"Who," Lee insinuated, "assured him of that?"

"I did," Jim said coolly. "Since I've been foreman we've never
run any cattle beyond that boundary. Iron Mesa is a block that
cuts us off from the country south of there, and the range to the
east is much better and open for us clear to Beaver Creek and
south to the Middle Fork."

"So you decide what range will be used? I think for a hired hand you take a good deal of authority. Personally, I'm wondering how much your loyalty is divided. Or if it is divided. It seems to me you act more as a friend of the Katrishens—or their daughter."

Sandifer took a step forward. "Martin," he said evenly, "are you aimin' to say that I'd double-cross the boss? If you are, you're a liar!"

Bowen looked up, a chill light in his eyes that Sandifer had never seen there before. "That will be all, Jim. You better go."

Sandifer turned on his heel and strode outside.

CHAPTER TWO: Fight in the Hills

When Sandifer walked into the bunkhouse, the men were already back. The room was silent, but he was aware of the hatred in the cold blue eyes of Mont as he lay sprawled in his bunk. His right hand and wrist were bandaged. The Mello boys snored in their bunks while Art Dunn idly shuffled cards at the table. These were new hands, hired since the coming of the Martins. Only three of the older hands were in, none of them spoke.

"Hello—lucky," Mont rolled up on his elbow. "Lose your job?"

"Not yet," Jim said shortly, aware that his remark brought a fleeting anger to Mont's eyes.

"You will!" Mont assured him. "If you are in the country when this hand gets well, I'll kill you!"

Jim Sandifer laughed shortly. He was aware that the older hands were listening, although none would have guessed it without knowing them.

"You called me lucky, Klee. It was you who were lucky in that I didn't figure on killin' you. That was no miss. I aimed for your gunhand. Furthermore, don't try pullin' a gun on me again. You're too slow!"

"*Slow?*" Mont's face flamed. He reared up in his bunk. "Slow? Why, you two-bit bluffer!"

Sandifer shrugged. "Look at your hand," he said calmly. "If you don't know what happened, I do. That bullet didn't cut your thumb off. It doesn't go up your hand or arm; the wound runs *across* your hand!"

They all knew what he meant. Sandifer's bullet must have hit his hand as he was in the act of drawing and before the gun came level, indicating that Sandifer had beaten Mont to the draw by a safe margin. That Klee Mont realized the implication was plain for his face darkened, then paled around the lips. There was pure hatred in his eyes when he looked up at Sandifer.

"I'll kill you!" he said viciously. "I'll kill you!"

As Sandifer started outside "Rep" Dean followed him. With Grimes and Sparkman he was one of the older hands.

"What's come over this place, Jim? Six months ago there wasn't a better spread in the country!"

Sandifer did not reply, and Dean built a smoke. "It's that woman," he said. "She twists the boss around her little finger. If it wasn't for you, I'd quit, but I'm thinkin' that there's nothin' she wouldn't like better than for all of the old hands to ask for their time."

Sparkman and Grimes had followed them from the bunkhouse. Sparkman was a lean-bodied Texan with some reputation as an Indian fighter.

"You watch your step," Grimes warned. "Next time Mont will backshoot you!"

They talked among themselves and, as they conversed, he ran his thoughts over the developments of the past few months. He had heard enough of Mrs. Martin's sly insinuating remarks to understand how she had worked Bowen up to ordering Katrishen driven off, yet there was no apparent motive. It seemed obvious that the woman had her mind set on marrying Gray Bowen, but for that it was not essential that any move be made against the Katrishens.

Sandifer's limitation of B Bar range had been planned for the best interests of the ranch. The ranch they now had in use was bounded easily by streams and mountain ranges and was rich in grass and water, a range easily controlled with a small number of hands and with little danger of loss from raiding Indians, rustlers or varmints.

His willingness to have the Katrishens move in on Iron Creek was not without the B Bar in mind. He well knew that range lying so much out of the orbit of the ranch could not be long held tenantless, and the Katrishens were stable, honest people who would make good neighbors and good allies. Thinking back, he could remember almost to the day when the first rumors began to spread, and most of them had stemmed from Lee Martin himself. Later, one of the Mello boys had come in with a bullet hole in the crown of his hat and a tale of being fired on from Iron Mesa.

"What I can't figure out," Grimes was saying, "is what that no account Lee Martin would be doin' over on the Turkeyfeather."

Sandifer turned his head. "On the Turkeyfeather? That's beyond Iron Mesa! Why, that's clear over the other side of Katrishens'!"

"Sure enough! I was huntin' that brindle steer who's always leadin' stock off into the canyons when I seen Martin fordin' the Willow. He was ridin' plumb careful, an' he sure wasn't playin' no tenderfoot then! I was right wary of him so I took in behind an' trailed him over to that rough country near Turkeyfeather Pass. Then I lost him."

The door slammed up at the house and they saw Lee Martin come down the steps and start toward them. It was dusk, but still light enough to distinguish faces. Martin walked up to Sandifer.

"Here's your time." He held out an envelope. "You're through!"

"I'll want that from Bowen himself," Sandifer replied stiffly.

"He doesn't want to see you. He sent this note." Martin handed over a sheet of the coarse brown paper on which Bowen kept his accounts. On it, in Bowen's hand, was his dismissal.

I won't have a man who won't obey orders. Leave
tonight.

Sandifer stared at the note which he could barely read in the
dim light. He had worked hard for the B Bar, and this was his
answer.

"All right," he said briefly. "Tell him I'm leaving. It won't take
any great time to saddle up."

Martin laughed. "That won't take time, either. You'll walk
out. No horse leaves this ranch."

Jim turned back, his face white. "You keep out of this,
Martin. That buckskin is my own horse. You get back in your
hole an' stay there!"

Martin stepped closer. "Why, you cheap, big-mouth!"

The blow had been waiting for a long time, but it came
fast now. It was a smashing left that caught Martin on the
chin and spilled him on his back in the dust. With a muttered
curse, Martin came off the ground and rushed, but Sandifer
stepped in, blocking a right and whipping his own right into
Lee's midsection. Martin doubled over and Jim straightened
him with a left uppercut, then knocked him crashing into the
corral fence.

Abruptly, Sandifer turned and threw the saddle on the buckskin. Sparkman swore. "I'm quittin' too!" he said.

"An' me!" Grimes snapped. "I'll be doggoned if I'll work here
now!"

Heavily, Martin got to his feet. His white shirt was bloody
and they could vaguely see a blotch of blood over the lower part
of his face. He limped away, muttering.

"Sparky," Jim said, low voiced, "don't quit. All of you stay on.
I reckon this fight ain't over, an' the boss may need a friend. You
stick here. I'll not be far off!"

Sandifer had no plan, yet it was Lee Martin's ride to the
Turkeyfeather that puzzled him most, and almost of its own

230

volition, his horse took that route. As he rode he turned the problem over and over in his mind, seeking for a solution yet none appeared that was satisfactory. Revenge for some old grudge against the Katrishens was considered and put aside, but he could not but feel that whatever the reason for the plotting of the Martins there had to be profit in it somewhere.

Certainly, there seemed little to prevent Rose Martin from marrying Gray Bowen if she wished. The old man was well aware that Elaine was a lovely, desirable girl. The cowhands and other male visitors who came to call for one excuse or another were evidence of that. She would not be with him long, and if she left, he was faced with the dismal prospect of ending his years alone. Rose Martin was a shrewd woman, and attractive for her years, and she knew how to make Gray comfortable and how to appeal to him. Yet obviously there was something more in her mind than this, and it was that something more in which Sandifer was interested.

Riding due east Jim crossed the Iron near Clayton and turned west by south through the broken country. It was very late and vague moonlight filtered through the yellow pine and fir that guarded the way he rode with their tall columns. Twice he halted briefly, fleeing a strange uneasiness, yet listen as he might he could detect no alien sound, nothing but the faint stirring of the slight breeze through the needles of the pines and the occasional rustle of a blown leaf. He rode on, but now he avoided the bright moonlight and kept more to the deep shadows under the trees.

After skirting the end of the Jerky Mountains, he headed for the Turkeyfeather Pass. Somewhere off to his left, lost against the blackness of the ridge shadow, a faint sound came to him. He drew up, listening. He did not hear it again, yet his senses could not have lied. It was the sound of a dead branch scraping along leather, such a sound as might be made by a horseman riding through brush.

Sliding his Winchester from its scabbard, he rode forward, every sense alert. His attention was drawn to the buckskin whose ears were up, and who, when he stopped, lifted its head and stared off toward the darkness. Sandifer started the horse forward moving easily.

To the left towered the ridge of Turkeyfeather Pass, lifting all of five hundred feet above him, black, towering, ominous in the moonlight. The trees fell away, massing their legions to right and left, but leaving before him an open glade, grassy and still. Off to the right Iron Creek hustled over the stones, whispering wordless messages to the rocks on either bank. Somewhere a quail called mournfully into the night, and the hoofs of the buckskin made light whispering sounds as they moved through the grass at the edge of the glade.

Jim drew up under the trees near the Creek and swung down, warning the buckskin to be still. Taking his rifle he circled the glade under the trees, moving like a prowling wolf. Whoever was over there was stalking him, watching a chance to kill him, or perhaps only following to see where he went. In any case, Jim meant to know who and why.

Suddenly he heard a vague sound before him, a creak of saddle leather. Freezing in place, he listened and heard it again, followed by the crunch of gravel. Then he caught the glint of moonlight on a rifle barrel and moved forward, shifting position to get the unseen man silhouetted against the sky. Sandifer swung his rifle.

"All right," he said calmly, "drop that rifle and lift your hands! I've got you dead to rights!"

As he spoke the man was moving forward and instantly the fellow dived headlong. Sandifer's rifle spat fire and he heard a grunt, followed by a stab of flame. A bullet whipped past his ear. Shifting ground on cat feet, Jim studied the spot carefully.

The man lay in absolute darkness, but listening he could hear the heavy breathing that proved his shot had gone true. He waited, listening for movement, but there was none. After awhile the breathing grew less and he took a chance.

"Better give up!" he said. "No use dyin' there!"

There was silence, then a slight movement of gravel. Then a six-shooter flew through the air to land in the open space between them.

"What about that rifle?" Sandifer demanded cautiously.

"Lost . . . For God's sake, help . . . me!"

There was no mistaking the choking sound. Jim Sandifer got up and holding his rifle on the spot where the voice had sounded, crossed into the shadows. As it was, he almost stumbled over the wounded man before he saw him. It was Dan Mello, and the heavy slug had torn through his body but had not emerged.

Working swiftly, Jim got the wounded man into an easier position and carefully pulled his shirt away from the wound. There was no mistaking the fact that Dan Mello was hit hard. Jim gave the wounded man a drink, then hastily built a fire to work by. His guess that the bullet had not emerged proved true, but moving his hand gently down the wounded man's back he could feel something hard near his spine. When he straightened, Mello's eyes sought his face.

"Don't you move," Sandifer warned. "It's right near your spine. I've got to get a doctor."

He was worried, knowing little of such wounds. The man might be bleeding bad internally.

"No, don't leave me!" Mello pleaded. "Some varmint might come!" The effort of speaking left him panting.

Jim Sandifer swore softly, uncertain as to his proper course. He had little hope that Mello could be saved even if he rode for a doctor. The nearest one was miles away, and movement of the wounded man would be very dangerous. Nor was Mello's fear without cause for there were mountain lions, wolves and coyotes in the area, and the scent of blood was sure to call them.

"Legs—gone," Mello panted. "Can't feel nothing."

"Take it easy," Jim advised. The nearest place was Bill Katrishens, and Bill might be some hand with a wounded man. He said as much to Mello. "Can't be more'n three, four miles," he added. "I'll give you back your gun an' build up the fire."

"You—you'll sure come back?" Mello pleaded.

"What kind of a coyote do you think I am?" Sandifer asked irritably. "I'll get back as soon as ever I can." He looked down at him. "Why were you gunnin' for me? Mont put you up to it?"

Mello shook his head. "Mont, he—he ain't—bad. It's that Martin—you watch. He's a pizen—mean."

CHAPTER THREE: Entombed!

Leaving the fire blazing brightly, Jim returned to his buckskin and crawled into the saddle. The moon was higher now, and the avenues through the trees were like roads, eerily lighted. Touching a spur to the horse, Jim raced through the night, the cool wind fanning his face. Once a deer scurried from in front of him, then bounded off through the trees, and once he thought he saw the lumbering shadow of an old grizzly.

The Katrishen log cabin and pole corrals lay bathed in white moonlight as he raced his horse into the yard. The drum of hooves upon the hard packed earth and his call brought movement from inside: "Who is it? What's up?"

Briefly, he explained, and after a minute the door opened.

"Come in, Jim. Figured I heard a shot awhile back. Dan Mello, you say? He's a bad one."

Hurrying to the corral, Jim harnessed two mustangs and hitched them to the buckboard. A moment later Bill Katrishen, tall and gray-haired came from the cabin, carrying a lantern in one hand and a black bag in the other.

"I'm no medical man," he said, "but I fixed a sight of bullet wounds in my time." He crawled into the buckboard and one of his sons got up beside him. Led by Sandifer they started back over the way he had come.

Mello was still conscious when they stopped beside him. He looked unbelievingly at Katrishen.

"You come?" he said. "You knowed who—who I was?"

"You're hurt, ain't you?" Katrishen asked testily. Carefully, he examined the man, then sat back on his heels. "Mello," he said, "I ain't one for foolin' a man. You're plumb bad off. That bullet seems to have slid off your hip bone an' tore right through you. If we had you down to the house we could work on you a durned sight better, but I don't know whether you'd make it or not."

The wounded man breathed heavily, staring from one to the other. He looked scared, and he was sweating, yet under it his face was pale.

"What you think," he panted, "all right—with me."

"The three of us can put him on them quilts in the back of the buckboard. Jim, you slide your hands under his back."

"Hold up," Mello's eyes wavered, then focused on Jim. "You watch—Martin. He's plumb—bad."

"What's he want, Mello?" Jim said. "What's he after?"

"G—old," Mello panted, and then suddenly he relaxed.

"Fainted," Katrishen said. "Load him up."

All through the remainder of the night they worked over him. It was miles over mountain roads to Silver City and the nearest doctor, and little enough that he could do. Shortly before the sun lifted, Dan Mello died.

Bill Katrishen got up from beside the bed, his face drawn with weariness. He looked across the body of Dan Mello at Sandifer.

"Jim, what's this all about? Why was he gunning for you?"

Hesitating only a moment, Jim Sandifer explained the needling of Gray Bowen by Rose Martin, the undercover machinations of her and her tall son, the hiring of the Mellos at their instigation, and of Art Dunn and Klee Mont. Then he went on to the events preceding his break with the B Bar. Katrishen nodded thoughtfully, but obviously puzzled.

"I never heard of the woman, Jim. I can't figure why she'd have it in for me. What did Mello mean when he said Martin was after gold?"

"You've got me. I know they are money hungry, but the ranch is—" He stopped, and his face lifted, his eyes narrowing. "Bill, did you ever hear of gold around here?"

"Sure, over toward Cooney Canyon. You know, Cooney was a sergeant in the Army, and after his discharge he returned to hunt for gold he located while a soldier. The Apaches finally got him, but he had gold first."

"Maybe that's it. I want a fresh horse, Bill."

"You get some sleep first. The boys an' I'll take care of Dan. Kara will fix breakfast for you."

The sun was high when Jim Sandifer rolled out of his bunk and stumbled sleepily to the door to splash his face in cold water poured from a bucket into the tin basin. Kara heard him moving and came to the door, walking carefully and lifting her hand to catch the door jam.

"Hello, Jim. Are you rested? Dad an' the boys buried Dan Mello over on the knoll."

Jim smiled at her reassuringly.

"I'm rested, but after I eat I'll be ridin', Kara." He looked up at the slender girl with the rusty hair and pale freckles. "You keep the boys in, will you? I don't want them to be where they could be shot at until I can figure a way out of this. I'm going to maintain peace in this country or die tryin'!"

"You're a good man, Jim," the girl said. "This country needs more like you."

Sandifer shook his head somberly. "Not really a good man, Kara, just a man who wants peace and time to build a home. I reckon I've been as bad as most, but this is a country for freedom, and a country for things to be done. We can't do it when we are killin' each other."

The buckskin horse was resting but the iron gray that Katrishen had provided was a good mountain horse. Jim Sandifer pulled his gray hat low over his eyes and squinted against the sun. He liked the smell of pine needles, the pungent smell of sage. He moved carefully, searching the trail for the way Lee Martin's horse had gone the day Grimes followed him.

Twice he lost the trail, then found it again only to lose it finally in the sand of a wash. The area covered by the sand was small, a place where water had spilled down a steep mountain-side eating out a raw wound in the cliff, yet there the trail vanished. Dismounting, a careful search disclosed a brushed over spot near the cliff, and then a chafed place on a small tree. Here Lee Martin had tied his horse, and from here he must have gone on foot.

It was a small rock, only half as big as his fist that was the telltale clue. The rock showed where it had lain in the earth but had been recently rolled aside. Moving close, he could see that the stone had rolled from under a clump of brush, and parting the brush, the clump rolled easily under his hand. Then he saw that although the roots were still in the soil, that at some time part of it had been pulled free, and the clump had been rolled over to cover an opening no more than a couple of feet wide and twice as high. It was a man made tunnel, but one not recently made.

Concealing the gray in the trees some distance off, Sandifer walked back to the hole, stared around uneasily, then ducked his head and entered. Once inside, the tunnel was higher and wider, and then it opened into a fair sized room. Here the ore had been stoped out, and he looked around, holding a match high. The light caught and glinted upon the rock, and moving closer he picked up a small chunk of rose quartz, seamed with gold!

Pocketing the sample he walked further in until he saw a black hole yawning before him, and beside it lay a notched pole such as the Indians had used in Spanish times to climb out of mine shafts. Looking over into the hole he saw a longer pole reaching down into the darkness. He peered over, then straightened. This, then, was what Dan Mello had meant! The Martins wanted gold.

The match flickered out, and standing there in the cool darkness, he thought it over and understood. This place was on land used, and probably claimed, by Bill Katrishen, and could not be worked unless they were driven off. But could he make Gray Bowen believe him? What would Lee do if his scheme was exposed? Why had Mello been so insistent that Martin was dangerous?

He bent over and started into the tunnel exit, then stopped. Kneeling just outside were Lee Martin, Art Dunn, and Jay Mello. Lee had a shotgun pointed at Jim's body. Jim jerked back around the corner of stone even as the shotgun thundered.

"You dirty, murderin' rat!" he yelled. "Let me out in the open and try that!"

Martin laughed. "I wouldn't think of it! You're right where I want you now and you'll stay there!"

Desperately, Jim stared around. Martin was right. He was bottled up now. He drew his gun, wanting to chance a shot at Martin while yet there was time, but when he stole a glance around the corner of the tunnel there was nothing to be seen. Suddenly, he heard a sound of metal striking stone, a rattle of rock, then a thunderous crash and the tunnel was filled with dust, stifling and thick. Lee Martin had closed off the tunnel mouth and he was entombed alive!

Jim Sandifer leaned back against the rock wall of the slope and closed his eyes. He was frightened. He was frightened with a deep, soul-shaking fear, for this was something against which he could not fight, those walls of living rock around him, and the dead debris of the rock-choked tunnel. Had there been time and air a man might work out an escape, but there was so little time, so little air. He was buried alive.

Slowly, the dust settled from the heavy air. Saving his few matches he got down on his knees and crawled into the tunnel, but there was barely room enough. Mentally, he tried to calculate the distance out, and he could see that there was no less than fifteen feet of rock between him and escape—not an impossible task if more rock did not slide down from above. Remembering the mountain, he knew that above the tunnel mouth it was almost one vast slide.

He could hear nothing, and the air was hot and close. On his knees he began to feel his way around, crawling until he reached the tunnel and the notched pole. Here he hesitated, wondering what the darkness below would hold.

Water, perhaps? Or even snakes? He had heard of snakes taking over old mines and once crawling down the ladder into an old shaft had seen an enormous rattler, the biggest he had ever seen, coiled about the ladder just below him. Nevertheless, he began to descend—down, down into the abysmal blackness below him. He seemed to have climbed down an interminable distance when suddenly his boot touched rock.

Standing upright, one hand on the pole, he reached out. His hand found rock on three sides, on the other, only empty space. He turned in that direction and ran smack into the rock wall, knocking sparks from his skull. He drew back, swearing, and found the tunnel. At the same time his hand touched something else, a sort of ledge in the corner of the rock, and on the ledge—his heart gave a leap!

Candles!

Quickly, he got out a match and lit the first one. Then he walked into the tunnel. Here was more of the rose quartz, and it was incredibly seamed with gold. Lee Martin had made a strike. Rather, studying the walls, he had found an old mine, perhaps an old Spanish working, although work had been done down here within the last few weeks. Suddenly Jim saw a pick and he grinned. There might yet be a way out. Yet a few minutes of exploration sufficed to indicate that there was no other opening. If he went out it must be by the way he came.

Taking the candles with him he climbed the notched pole and stuck a lighted candle on a rock. Then, with the pick at his side, he started to work at the debris choking the tunnel. He lifted a rock and moved it aside, then another.

An hour later, soaked with sweat, he was still working away, pausing each minute or so to examine the hanging wall. The tunnel was cramped and the work moved slowly ahead for every stone removed had to be shoved back into the stope behind him. He reached the broken part overhead, and when he moved a rock, more slid down. He worked on, his breath coming in great gasps, sweat dripping from his face and neck to his hands.

A new sound came to him, a faint tapping. He held still, listening, trying to quiet his breathing and the pound of his heart. Then he heard it again, an unmistakable tapping!

Grasping his pick, he tapped three times, then an interval, then three times again. Then he heard somebody pull at the rocks of the tunnel and his heart pounded with exultation. He had help! He had been found!

CHAPTER FOUR: Guns Out

How the following hours passed Sandifer never quite knew, but working feverishly, he fought his way through the border of time that divided him from the outer world and the clean, pine-scented air. Suddenly, a stone was moved and an arrow of light stabbed the darkness, and with it the cool air he wanted. He took a deep breath, filling his lungs with air so liquid it might almost be water, and then he went to work, helping the hands outside to enlarge the opening. When there was room enough, he thrust his head and shoulders through, then pulled himself out and stood up, dusting himself off— and found he was facing, not Bill Katrishen or one of his sons, but Jay Mello!

"You?" he was astonished. "What brought you back?"

Jay wiped his thick hands on his jeans and looked uncomfortable.

"Never figured to bury no man alive," he said. "That was Martin's idee. Anyway, Katrishen told me what you done for Dan."

"Did he tell you I'd killed him? I'm sorry, Jay. It was him or me."

"Sure. I knowed that when he come after you. I didn't like it nohow. What I meant, well—you could've left him lie. You didn't need to go git help for him. I went huntin' Dan, when I found

242

you was alive, an' I figured it was like that, that he was dead. Katrishen give me his clothes, an' I found this—"

It was a note, scrawled painfully, perhaps on a rifle stock, or a flat rock, written, no doubt, while Jim was gone for help.

Jay:

> *Git shet of Marten. Sandfer's all right. He's gone for hulp to Katrisshn. I'm hard hit. Sandfer shore is wite. So long, Jay, good ridin.*

Dan.

"I'm sorry, Jay. He was game."

"Sure." Jay Mello scowled. "It was Martin got us into this, him an' Klee Mont. We never done no killin' before, maybe stole a few hosses or run off a few head of cows."

"What happened? How long was I in there?" Jim glanced at the sun.

"About five, six hours. She'll be dark soon." Mello hesitated, "I reckon I'm goin' to take out—light a shuck for Texas."

Sandifer thrust out his hand. "Good luck, Jay. Maybe we'll meet again."

The outlaw nodded. He stared at the ground, and then he looked up, his tough, unshaven face strangely lonely in the late afternoon sun.

"Sure wish Dan was ridin' with me. We always rode together, him an' me, since we was kids." He rubbed a hard hand over his lips. "What d'you know? That girl back to Katrishen's? She put some flowers on his grave! Sure enough!"

He turned and walked to his horse, swung into the saddle and walked his horse down the trail, a somber figure captured momentarily by the sunlight before he turned away under the pines. Incongruously, Jim noticed that the man's vest was split up the back, and the crown of his hat was torn.

The gray waited patiently by the brush, but Jim Sandifer untied him and swung into the saddle. It was a fast ride he made back to the ranch on Iron Creek. There he swapped saddles, explaining all to Katrishen. "I'm riding," he said, "there's no room in this country for Lee Martin now."

"Want us to come?" Bill asked.

"No, they might think it was war. You stay out of it, for we want no Pleasant Valley War here. Leave it lay. I'll settle this."

He turned from the trail before he reached the B Bar, riding through the cottonwoods and sycamores along the creek. Then he rode up between the buildings and stopped beside the corral. The saddle leather creaked when he swung down, and he saw a slight movement at the corner of the corral.

"Klee? Is that you?" It was Art Dunn. "What's goin' on up at the house?"

Jim Sandifer took a long step forward. "No, Art," he said, swiftly, "it's me!"

Dunn took a quick step back and grabbed for his gun, but Jim was already moving, expecting him, to reach. Sandifer's left hand dropped to Art's wrist and his right smashed up in a wicked uppercut to the solar plexus.

Dunn grunted and his knees sagged. Jim let go of his wrist then, and hooked sharply to the chin, hearing Dunn's teeth click as the blow smashed home. Four times more Jim hit him, rocking his head on his shoulders, then smashed another punch to the wind, and grabbing Dunn's belt buckle, jerked his gun belt open.

The belt slipped down and Dunn staggered and went to his knees. The outlaw pawed wildly, trying to get at Jim, but he was still gasping for the wind that had been knocked out of him.

The bunkhouse door opened and Sparkman stepped into the light. "What's the matter?" he asked. "What goes on?"

Sandifer called softly, and Sparkman grunted and came down off the steps. "Jim! You here? There's the devil to pay up at the house, man! I don't know what came off up there, but there was a shootin'! When we tried to go up, Mont was on the steps with a shot gun to drive us back."

"Take care of this hombre. I'll find out what's wrong fast enough. Where's Grimes an' Rep?"

"Rep Dean rode over to the line cabin on Canyon Creek to round up some boys in case of trouble. Grimes is inside."

"Then take Dunn an' keep your eyes open! I may need help. If I yell, come loaded for bear an' huntin' hair!"

Jim Sandifer turned swiftly and started for the house. He walked rapidly, circling as he went toward the little-used front door, opened only on company occasions. That door, he knew, opened into a large, old-fashioned parlor that was rarely used. It was a show place, stiff and uncomfortable, and mostly gilt and plush. The front door was usually locked, but he remembered that he had occasion to help move some furniture not long before and the door had been left unlocked. There was every chance that it still was, for the room was so little used as to be almost forgotten.

Easing up on the veranda, he tiptoed across to the door and gently turned the knob. The door opened inward, and he stepped swiftly through and closed it behind him. All was dark and silent, but there was light under the intervening door, and a sound of movement. With the thick carpet muffling his footfalls, he worked his way across the room to the door.

"How's the old man?" Martin was asking.

His mother replied. "He's all right. He'll live."

Martin swore. "If that girl hadn't bumped me, I'd have killed him and we'd be better off. We could easy enough fix things so that Sandifer would get blamed for it."

"Don't be in a hurry," Rose Martin intervened. "You're always in such a fret. The girl's here, an' we can use her to help. As long as we have her, the old man will listen, and while he's hurt, she'll do as she's told."

Martin muttered under his breath. "If we'd started by killing Sandifer like I wanted, all would be well," he said irritably. "What he said about the Katrishen trouble startin' with our comin' got the old man to thinkin'. Then I figure Bowen was sorry he fired his foreman."

"No matter!" Rose Martin was brusque. "We've got this place and we can handle the Katrishens ourselves. There's plenty of time now Sandifer's gone."

Steps sounded. "Lee, the old man's comin' out of it. He wants his daughter."

"Tell him to go climb a tree!" Martin replied stiffly. "You watch him."

"Where's Art?" Klee protested. "I don't like it, Lee! He's been gone too long. Somethin's up!"

"Aw, forget it! Quit cryin'! You do more yelpin' than a mangy coyote!"

Sandifer stood very still, thinking. There was no sound of Elaine so she must be a prisoner in her room. Turning, he tiptoed across the room toward the far side. A door there, beyond the old piano, opened into Elaine's room. Carefully, he tried the knob. It held.

At that very instant a door opened abruptly and he saw light under the door before him. He heard a startled gasp from Elaine, and Lee Martin's voice, taunting, familiar.

"What's the matter? Scared?" Martin laughed. "I just came in to see if you was all right. If you'd kept that pretty mouth of yours shut, your Dad would still be all right! You tellin' him Sandifer was correct about the Katrishens, an' that he shouldn't of fired him!"

"He shouldn't have," the girl said quietly. "If he was here now he'd kill you. Get out of my room!"

"Maybe I ain't ready to go?" he taunted. "An' from now on I'm goin' to come an' go as I like."

His steps advanced into the room, and Jim tightened his grip on the knob. He remembered that lock, and it was not set very

246

securely. Suddenly, an idea came to him. Turning, he picked up an old glass lamp, large and ornate. Balancing it momentarily in his hand, he drew it back and hurled it with a long overhand swing, through the window!

Glass crashed on the verandah and the lamp hit, went down a step and lay there. Inside the girl's room there was a startled exclamation, and he heard running footsteps from both the girl's room and the old man's. Somebody yelled, "What's that? What happened?" And he hurled his shoulder against the door.

As he had expected the flimsy lock carried away, and he was catapulted through the door into Elaine's bedroom. Catching himself, he wheeled like a cat and sprang for the door that opened into the living room beyond. He reached it just as Mont jerked the curtain back, but not wanting to endanger the girl, he swung hard with his fist instead of drawing his gun.

The blow came out of a clear sky to smash Mont on the jaw and he staggered back into the room. Jim Sandifer sprang through, legs spread, hands wide.

"You, Martin!" he said sharply. "Draw!"

Lee Martin was a killer, but no gunman. White to the lips, his eyes deadly, he sprang behind his mother and grabbed for the shotgun.

"Shoot, Jim!" Elaine cried. "Shoot!"

He could not. Rose Martin stood between him and his target and Martin had the shotgun now and was swinging it. Jim lunged, shoving the table over and the lamp shattered in a crash. He fired, then fired again. Flame stabbed the darkness at him and he fell back against the wall, switching his gun. Fire laced the darkness into a stabbing crimson crossfire and the room thundered with sound, then died to stillness that was the stillness of death itself.

No sounded remained, only the acrid smell of gunpowder mingled with the smell of coal oil and the faint, sickish sweet smell of blood. His guns ready, Jim crouched in the darkness, alert for movement. Somebody groaned, then sighed deeply, and a spur grated on the floor. From the next room, Gray Bowen called weakly. "Daughter? Daughter, what's happened? What's wrong?"

There was no movement yet, but the darkness grew more familiar. Jim's eyes became more accustomed to it. He could see no one standing. Yet it was Elaine who broke the stillness.

"Jim? Jim, are you all right? Oh, Jim—are you safe?"

Maybe they were waiting for this.

"I'm all right," he said.

"Light your lamp, will you?" Deliberately, he moved, and there was no sound within the room—only, outside, a running of feet on the hard-packed earth. Then a door slammed open and Sparkman stood there, gun in hand.

"It's all right, I think," Sandifer said. "We shot it out."

Elaine entered the room with a light and caught herself with a gasp at the sight before her. Jim reached for the lamp.

"Go to your father," he said swiftly. "We'll take care of this!"

Sparkman looked around, followed into the room by Grimes. "Good grief!" he gasped. "They are all dead! All of them!"

"The woman, too?" Sandifer's face paled. "I hope I didn't—"

"You didn't," Grimes said. "She was shot in the back, by her own son. Shootin' in the dark, blind an' gun crazy."

"Maybe it's better," Sparkman said, "She was an old hellion."

Klee Mont had caught his right at the end of his eyebrow, and a second shot along the ribs. Sandifer walked away from him and stood over Lee Martin. His face twisted in a sneer, the dead man lay sprawled on the floor literally shot to doll rags.

"You didn't miss many," Sparkman said grimly.

"I didn't figure to," Jim said. "I'll see the old man, then, give you a hand."

"Forget it." Grimes looked up, his eyes faintly humorous. "You stay in there. An' don't spend all your time with the old man. We need a new setup on this here spread, an' with a new son-in-law who's a first-rate cattleman, Gray could set back an' relax!"

Sandifer stopped with his hand on the curtain. "Maybe you got something there," he said thoughtfully. "Maybe you have!"

"You can take my word for it," Elaine said, stepping into the door beside Jim. "He has! He surely has!"